THE LAST BALLARD

I0577422

"I'm still haunted by it in the best possible way."
— H. EVEREND, AUTHOR

"Filled with danger, humor, horror, and heart to spare, The Last Ballard is a superb novel, a stunning debut, and quite simply the best book I've yet reviewed in 2025."
— DAMASCUS MINCEMEYER, CRITICAL BLAST

"This book owned me in the best way. Rhea Ballard is one of the most relatable FMCs I've read in a while..."
— HORROMANTASY BOOK MOM, @horromantasybookmom

"This one is for readers who love haunted houses with real ghosts, emotional depth, and a slow unraveling of dark family secrets. Definitely a standout gothic horror read."
— ALISHIA BAKER, @lilbeereadsbooks

"Kay Hanifen's The Last Ballard is a richly layered, slow-burning gothic horror that lingers long after the final page."
— KIMBERLY GERVING, @bookscoffeebrews

"The Last Ballard by Kay Hanifen is a chilling, suspenseful, and heartbreakingly beautiful tale of love, loss, and the ghosts that haunt us"
— ERIN SHERMAN, @bookitwithkali

THE
LAST
BALLARD

THE BALLARD MANOR

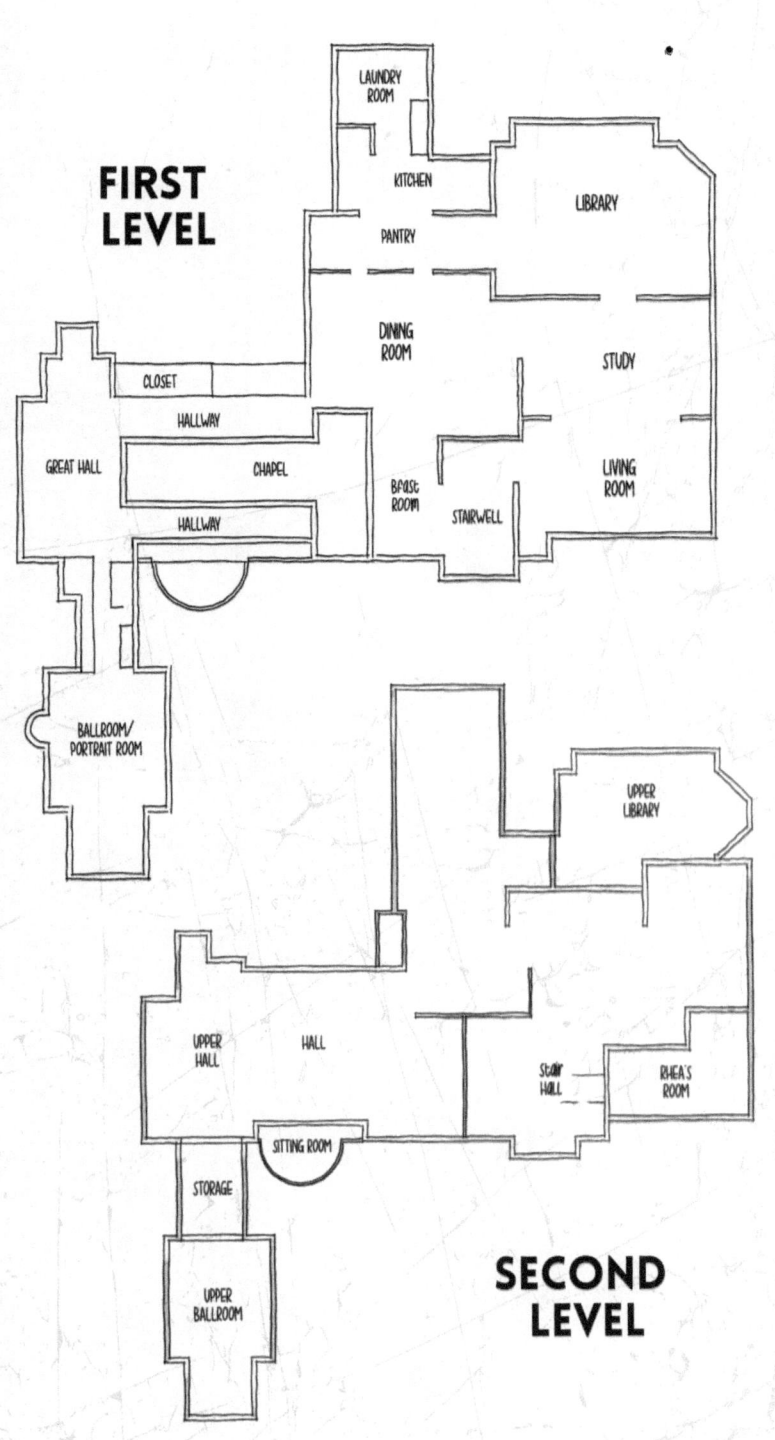

FIRST LEVEL

LAUNDRY ROOM

KITCHEN

LIBRARY

PANTRY

CLOSET

DINING ROOM

STUDY

HALLWAY

GREAT HALL

CHAPEL

BRFST ROOM

LIVING ROOM

HALLWAY

STAIRWELL

BALLROOM/ PORTRAIT ROOM

UPPER LIBRARY

UPPER HALL

HALL

STAIR HALL

RHEA'S ROOM

SITTING ROOM

STORAGE

UPPER BALLROOM

SECOND LEVEL

FOR MY FAMILY.
THANK YOU FOR BEING NOTHING LIKE THE BALLARDS

THE
LAST
BALLARD

KAY HANIFEN

MIRAVALLE
BOOKS

The Last Ballard

Copyright © 2025 by Kay Hanifen.
All Rights Reserved.

Standard Paperback: 979-8-9926549-0-5
eBook: 979-8-9926549-1-2
Audiobook available on Audible and Apple Books

Miravalle Books published books may be purchased in bulk discounted quantities for promotional, educational, and/or business use. Please contact your local bookseller or visit our website to learn more and/or to inquire about placing a bulk order.

Miravalle Books ™ is a trademark of Miravalle Books LLC, a Texas based Limited Liability Company.

Miravalle Books
PO BOX 731
Edinburg, TX 78540

Ballard Manor Sketch and Layout by Rusty (@Rusy31)

Printed in the United States of America

10 9 8 7 6 5 4 3 2 1

"OUR FATHERS SINNED AND ARE NO MORE,
BUT WE BEAR THEIR INQUITIES"

LAMENTATIONS 5:7

CHAPTER ONE

The morning was spitefully pleasant. *It should be raining,* Rhea Ballard thought, her eyes tracing the intricate metal swirls of the wrought iron gate that marked the entrance to her ancestral home, *it always rains for funerals.* Instead, the sky was the deepest blue she had ever seen, and a cool breeze rustled gently through the trees and blooming flowers. A spring day perfect for a picnic or lazing in the sun like a contented cat. The earth itself seemed to rejoice over the deaths of her grandparents, and she almost couldn't blame it.

With a deep breath, she straightened her black dress, the first dress she'd worn since leaving home six years ago. Most days, she favored jeans and button downs thrifted from the men's sections. Astrid would have wanted her to wear the black dress, and she was nothing if not obedient to her grandmother. Not that it would have helped much, had she been alive to see it. Astrid would have been aghast at Rhea's close-cropped dark hair, which, when combined with her clothing, frequently led to her being mistaken for a man.

If she could, she'd spend the whole day pondering the gate and breathing in the spring air. If she could, she'd turn heel and go back to her dingy studio apartment with barely enough room for her to move around in, let alone any guests. If she could, she'd burn the whole place to the ground. But there was no point in putting it off any longer by wishing about what she could do. She pressed the buzzer on the intercom.

"Hello?" From the other end, only static. She tried again. "Hello?"

"Hi, who is this?" asked the person—a woman she thought—on the other end.

"I'm Rhea—" She paused, clearing her throat. Her grandparents always insisted on her full name. Their caregiver likely wouldn't know her by anything else. "Rhiannon Ballard, the granddaughter."

"Oh Rhiannon! Give me a second." With a buzz, the gates opened, and Rhea began her trek up to the long driveway to the mansion. She didn't know what to expect as she approached home for the first time in six years. In that time, it had become warped in her memory, all cracks in faded gilding and judgmental angels lining each of the windows. Approaching it on the beautiful spring day, she supposed it could use a touch-up of paint outside, but it was otherwise not nearly as foreboding as she remembered.

Grandpa Bert called the mansion a mix of Tudor and Rococo style, with its soft blue paint and ornate eggshell angel reliefs that lined the windows combined with half timbering and overlapping gables. The clashing design elements were a result of a dispute between her great-great grandparents, Joshua and Charity Ballard. Joshua liked the Tudor style while Charity was infatuated with Catherine the Great's Winter Palace. This was their compromise, but it was far from the first Ballard house. There had been a Ballard on that property for longer than America had been a nation. The house stood first as a shack that sheltered the first Ballard's in America, then as a farmhouse, then a manor before the first bullets fired at Lexington and Concord, and finally, this Gilded Age monstrosity. Rhea believed it would keep standing long after the last Ballard returned to the Earth.

As she approached, she counted the chimneys like she used to as a kid. Because of the building's unusual z-shape, there were seven visible from the front and three she knew could best be seen from the back. The tower was only visible from the back as well, and she was grateful for it. She wouldn't have been brave enough to take another step closer otherwise.

The massive oak door opened while she stood there gawking, and a short, Filipina woman dressed all in black poked her head out the door. She looked to be Rhea's age, with long raven hair cascading down her shoulders, and puffy, red eyes as though she had been crying recently. Still, the moment she set her sights on Rhea, she sniffled and gave a warm smile.

"Rhiannon?"

Rhea gave a wan smile back as she approached. "Just Rhea, actually."

The woman stepped out the door. "I'm Morgan. Morgan Reyes. I was their live-in caregiver in the last year or so."

"I think we spoke on the phone. Thank you, by the way, helping with the funeral arrangements. I know it's not in the job description, so I'll try to make sure you're compensated for it," she said, holding out a hand. Somehow, anyway. It wasn't like she was seeing a cent of the inheritance, but she'd still talk to her grandparents' lawyer, Mr. Ellis, and whoever Bert and Astrid left the estate to. Hopefully, she'd have enough pull for that, at least.

Morgan glanced down at it and asked, "Can I give you a hug?"

Rhea nodded, barely able to contain her surprise. She let Morgan wrap her arms around her and squeeze, like a mouse in the grips of a python. People hugged at funerals. They hugged the bereaved, and the bereaved took comfort in these tokens of contact. That's how it's supposed to work, right?

After a moment, she realized she hadn't hugged back, so she limply wrapped her arms around Morgan. Eventually, Morgan stepped back and looked her up and down.

"It's nice to finally meet you. They loved to tell me stories about you as a kid."

Her stomach dropped. Which Rhea did they tell her about? Was it the ungrateful granddaughter who ran away? Or the Mensa-level genius version of her that lived only in their heads? Was she rich and accomplished, or did she amount to nothing? Honestly, she wasn't sure if she wanted to know either way. "All about how I was a little monster, I'm sure."

Morgan chuckled. "It depended on the day. Sometimes, yeah. But other times, you were the most darling little girl they'd ever met. But I usually like to reserve my judgement until after I get to know someone."

The part about her being a darling little girl didn't sound like them. Even as a child, no matter what she did, she was wrong in some way. She was too loud, too quiet, too smart, too stupid. Nothing she did pleased them. But who knows? Maybe they softened in their old age. A small part of her dared to hope that they even missed her.

She rolled her eyes. "And then I became a horrible, disrespectful teenager."

"Didn't we all? They made you sound...one of a kind."

"I don't know if I should take that as a compliment."

"With Bert and Astrid, it was impossible to tell them from their insults." Morgan changed her pitch, imitating Grandma Astrid. "Oh, Miss Reyes, you're so pretty *and* you can cook. Why haven't you landed yourself a man?"

Rhea let out a surprised laugh. "You knew them well."

"Living with them for a year will do that."

"Try eleven."

Morgan winced. "Okay, you beat me. They were..."

"What polite society would call 'characters' but anyone else would call cantankerous old farts?"

Morgan chuckled, but then her face fell. *Right, calling the people who raised you 'cantankerous old farts' on the day of their funeral? Class act, Rhea.* She took a deep breath. Best change the subject. "You sound like you were really close to them in the end. Were you the one who...?" She trailed off, unsure if she really wanted to know the answer.

5

Morgan nodded, her smile watery. "Yeah. Astrid was in bed, and I found Bert in the water. I guess he found her and decided that he didn't want to live in a world without her."

"I'm sorry. That must have been upsetting." Rhea felt hollowed out at this. She knew that they loved each other. That or they didn't want the embarrassment of divorce. They were, in a way, like two puzzle pieces that fit together perfectly, but she also remembered the sniping and cold silences that permeated the house. *Just make it through the eulogy*, she thought, *and you never have to see this place again.*

"I can only hope they're at peace." She stepped aside, letting Rhea into the threshold.

"Me too," she said, taking in her old home. All in all, it hadn't changed much. The grand staircase to her left still spiraled towards the heavens, though the floral carpet atop the marble was dingy with age. The paintings of her illustrious ancestors that looked down on her from the wall were slightly faded by sun and dust but hadn't moved or been changed out. The vaulted ceilings towered above her, the frescoes somehow still vibrant. Inspired by *baroque il bel composto*, the paintings of Christ's ascension were best seen in the center of the room. From there, the painting, sculpture and architecture blended together so perfectly that it was impossible to tell where one began and the other ended. She ignored the illusion in favor of the ding still on the right-hand wall from the time she unwisely decided to ride down the stairs in a laundry basket. That time, they thought the head wound was more punishment than they could dole out, so they simply sent her to bed without supper. She was too nauseated to eat that night anyway.

"Can I take your bag?"

She blinked and shook her head clutching her backpack closer. "Thanks, but I'll just put it in my room."

"The guests should arrive in about two hours. I'll be in the kitchen if you need me."

"And my grandparents?"

Morgan gave her a sad smile. "They're in the portrait room. It's where they said they wanted the service to be held. I could take you there first." Ordinarily, service would be held in the small chapel on the opposite end of the house, but the deaths of the patriarch and matriarch of the esteemed Ballard family brought in the whole town. Technically, she was the last in her family line, she supposed, but she never truly felt like one of them, not even when she lived under their thumb. Bert and Astrid were town institutions, so this was more than just a funeral: it was the end of an era.

Rhea glanced down the hall towards what was once the ballroom but now housed the portraits of all the ancestors that lived on the estate. She would be the last of them. "I'll be okay, thank you."

Sensing her dismissal, Morgan nodded and headed off. Rhea tried not to feel too guilty. Morgan seemed kind, but Rhea didn't know what she really thought of the girl who hadn't spoken to the people who raised her for six years. She shook her head. Best not to drive herself crazy wondering what they might have said. She needed to put her baggage away and figure out what she'd say for the eulogy.

She ascended the stairs as she had done so many times before. As a child, she would put on her sparkly princess dresses and dance down the stairs as though she was

Cinderella at the ball. Sometimes, she would flee, leaving behind a slipper for her prince to find. As she got older, she played both parts, the princess locked in the tower and the knight on a quest to slay the dragon and rescue her.

Her bedroom was straight down the hall at the very end of the house. She made her way slowly, noting the buildup of dust and wondering how many people were needed to keep a place like this properly maintained. Surely more than just Morgan and the groundskeeper that the lawyer mentioned. She remembered there being a small revolving door of staff when she was a kid, though she wasn't supposed to talk to "the help." In her prime, Astrid would never have been caught dead with the house this dirty, but she also would have hated for the staff to see her as she and Bert started to decline. Maybe she fired them all for the sake of her pride.

She expected her bedroom to be a time capsule in the same way the rest of the house was. Maybe a little dusty and faded with age, but undoubtably the place she lived in during her tumultuous teenage years.

It *was* a time capsule, but not of that era. In the time since she'd left, they had taken down her band posters and dark curtains and replaced them with the soft pinks and floral patterns of a little girl's room. Her bed was covered with stuffed animals and a wooden rocking horse sat in the corner, the blonde porcelain doll atop it staring up at her with blank glass eyes. The little reading nook overlooking the lake was also covered in dolls of all shapes and sizes. Between it and her bed was a big, pink roofed dollhouse. The furniture was still inside along with the dolls sitting at the table, waiting for a breakfast they'd never receive. The only relic of a post-Victorian era childhood left was the Walkman on her dresser, a CD still inside.

It was clear who they missed after she left.

She threw the backpack onto the bed. The first thing she did was take the grid off the floor vent in search of her mother's perfume bottle, one of the last things Rhea had of her. It, along with everything else she had squirreled away there as a teenager, was gone. She supposed she shouldn't have been surprised. When she left, her grandparents likely tore up the place looking for a clue as to where she had gone. If they found her secret stash of contraband, they likely threw it all away. The thought of losing that final connection to her mother created a lump in her throat.

But then one tawny teddy bear in the center of the pile of plushies caught her eye. It was more worn than the others, slightly misshapen from years of being hugged on cold nights and covered in clumsy stitches from where she'd try to repair the occasional tear.

"Hi there, Otso," she said, picking up the bear and hugging it to her chest. She pressed her nose to his head and inhaled. By some miracle, it still smelled faintly of jasmine and honeysuckle. After her parents died, she swiped a bottle her mother's perfume and sprayed it on the bear whenever the scent grew faint. Otso was the last gift her father gave her, and it smelled of her mother. A little piece of both of them for her to hold as she slept. It felt silly to be a grown woman clutching a stuffed bear. It felt even sillier to admit that she missed him and wished she hadn't left him behind. But as she sat on the bed cuddling the stuffed animal, she couldn't help but feel like she'd been reunited with an old friend. She had no idea how it still smelled of her mother's perfume, but inhaling the scent for the first time in years brought genuine tears to her eyes. Clutching the bear, she stared out at the gentle water and tried to get lost in pleasant memories.

CHAPTER TWO

Once upon a time, the portrait room was the ballroom. Like the grand foyer, it was light and airy, with high vaulted ceilings and frescoes of Dionysus and his maenads surrounded by gilded angels. The portraits lined the wall opposite the lake view. Each generation looked down on the current one as they danced, reminding the young ones not to have too much fun. They had a reputation to uphold, and God help you if you embarrassed the family.

At the very end of the room, there was the portrait of the Ballard heir. The portraits were done on the heir's wedding day, so she didn't have one before she left. Instead, it was her parents smiling beatifically down at her. Ordinarily, half the portrait was covered with a thick, black cloth, the side with her mother, who her grandparents did not like. As a child, she would sneak into the portrait room, uncover her mother, and spend hours talking to them as though they were there in the flesh. Sometimes she would just stare at them, willing them to come to life in their frames.

Her father, Julien Ballard, was gangly and sharp, all angles with very little softness. His eyes were blue and hair a dirty blond. He was an anthropology professor who focused his studies on legends and folklore. Her mother, Faith Dominguez-Ballard, was the opposite. She had rounded cheeks, raven hair, and warm, brown eyes. She was a poet who met him while researching Child Ballads. They complemented each other—head and heart, emotions and analysis.

As a child, she looked more like her mother than her father. Bert once speculated that he wasn't her biological grandfather. Now, at twenty-three, she could have been a carbon copy of her mother. In a rush of defiance against the corpses in their caskets, she pulled the cloth down so that her mother would never again be erased.

The caskets holding her grandparents sat at that end of the room, along with a small podium. They were open, and Rhea's heart picked up as she approached, her pulse pounding in her ears. This would be the first time she saw them in years, and it wasn't really them. A part of her wished that they were closed, so she wouldn't have to look at them, but another part was glad. Seeing them lying there motionless as mannequins let her prove to herself that they were really dead. People like to say that the dead look like they're sleeping, but she didn't think Bert or Astrid looked asleep. They looked inanimate. Empty. Nothing but wrinkled skin powdered heavily with makeup to give the illusion of life. And staring at their frail corpses, she didn't know how to feel about it.

After running away, she often found herself wondering what she would say if she ever saw them again. Sometimes, she imagined herself letting loose and laying out all the ways she'd been messed up. She'd fantasize about them realizing just how monstrous they had been and groveling for her forgiveness. Depending on her mood, she would either grant it or let her spite win and send them away unredeemed. Other times, when she had to choose between heat and groceries, she imagined herself begging for *their* forgiveness and telling them that she'll be good if they let her come home.

Now, though, they were dead, and her daydreams of resolution would never come to pass. Maybe it was for the best. As much as she wanted to love and be loved by them, the ugliest parts of her wanted to tell them to rot.

The mourners filed in slowly, filling up the seats in and leaving people standing in the back.

It was a veritable who's who in the town of Cherub's Cove. There were some people she vaguely recognized as her grandparents' friends, but most, she did not. All acted like they knew her, though, embracing her and offering their condolences. Rhea shook hands with every member of the town council up to and including Mayor Parker, a young man with a smile slick as oil.

"With them, we have the end of an era, Ms. Ballard," he said as he shook her hand, "such a tragedy for them to die on the same day like that. I can't imagine how you must feel."

She flashed what she hoped was a grateful smile. "Thank you."

"You know, Bert and Astrid were very involved this wonderful little town. They supported the police, the school, the library, the historical society. You name it, they helped make it great." Was there anything in the town her grandparents didn't have influence over?

"They could be very generous," she replied, her tone carefully neutral.

"Very. And your family has always been a gift to this town. The Ballard name means something in this town, doesn't it?"

"It does." This time, she let herself be a little short. He meant it in a positive way, but she knew the awful power of her family name better than anyone, and she was glad to be rid of it.

His grin became more forced as panic reached his eyes. He was after something, but Rhea wasn't interested in rising to the bait. He would have to spell out what he wanted from her. "You seem like the kind of person who would carry on that legacy."

Oh. Oh dear. He wanted her to keep funding the town with an inheritance her grandparents most definitely did not bequeath her. At least she now knew the story they told everyone. Rhea the success, not Rhea the disappointment.

"I, uh…" She spotted Morgan standing on the sidelines with an attractive young man. "I don't know what they told you, but, in all honesty, I'm the family disgrace. The only thing they're gonna leave me is intimacy issues, so you'd have better luck talking with their lawyer, David Ellis."

With that, she escaped to Morgan and the mystery man.

"Ms. Ballard," the man said, barely hiding his surprise when she joined them. He looked strong, with rough hands from hard work. The groundskeeper, she presumed.

She held out a hand. "Just call me Rhea."

He smiled, taking it. "It's nice to finally meet you, Rhea. I'm Andy Higgins. I do the upkeep on this old place."

She glanced around. "All by yourself? That's a lot of work."

He flashed a friendly smile. "I do my best."

"How are you holding up?" Morgan asked.

Rhea laughed, running a hand through her short hair. "It's really weird being here after so long. Everyone's acting like I'm the lady of the house or something, but..." She trailed off with a shrug. "We weren't on the best terms when I left. I'd be shocked if they wanted anything to do with me."

Morgan tilted her head, her brow furrowed in confusion. "But they wanted you here. Near the end, they were asking Mr. Ellis to find you."

The ground crumbled beneath her feet. They wanted her with them? That couldn't be right. "I—I didn't—" The priest entered and made eye contact with her, signaling that it was almost time to begin the service. Rhea motioned over to the front rows and the three empty seats she saved. "Oh. It's time."

Morgan shook her head. "We'll just find seats in the back. It's all right."

Rhea sighed letting her smile drop. The muscles of her face ached from forcing it all day. "Unlike me, you were with them 'til the end. You have as much right to be in the front row as I do." With that, she turned heel and took her seat. Seconds later, they both took their seats beside her. She could hear whispers behind her, and sensed glares shot in her direction, but did her best to ignore them, reminding herself that she would never have to see any of these people ever again after the funeral. Morgan, though, sank a little in her seat, her shoulders so tense they were practically up by her ears.

Rhea tuned out most of the funeral. The words and songs washed over her as she tried to put her life with her grandparents to words. None came. Finally, the priest motioned for her to stand. She took a deep breath and walked to the front of the crowd of people who admired and respected her grandparents. She could feel their eyes from the portraits baring down on her as she did in life, a silent threat if she made a mistake. *For God's sake, stand up straight and project your voice,* she could hear Astrid admonish, *make yourself presentable for once.*

"Hi," she said, glancing around the room of black clad mourners. They stared back at her with severe, solemn faces. She swallowed. "You might not remember me. It's been a while. I'm Rhea, their granddaughter. I'd like to say a few words about the people that raised me after the death of my parents."

They are the monsters that still haunt my nightmares, the reason why I need therapy, and the reason I can't afford it. Being here, back in this damned house, I expect them to be just in the other room, ready to barge in and punish me for a sin I didn't know I'd committed. But, against logic, some mad part of me still loves them and mourns the grandparents I should have had. You all stand here, beatifying them in this rotten reliquary where they died, but you don't really care about the old man and woman. You care about what will become of their wealth.

This is what she wanted to say.

What she actually said was this: "Once there was a couple. They were elderly, poor, and very much in love. One day, Zeus and Hermes disguised themselves as humans to see how their subjects treated one another. They found their way to a village, knocking on every door and getting no response until they reached the shack of the elderly couple. The couple let the travelers in, feeding them their best food and giving up their beds for the night. The next morning, the gods revealed themselves, and told the couple they meant no harm. In exchange for their hospitality, the gods would grant them a favor. The couple didn't ask for wealth or a nice home or any worldly possessions. They simply asked to die at the same time, so that one would never be without the other. Years later, at the moment of their passing, the gods turned them into twin willow trees with their trunks entwined so that they will never be parted."

She smiled, her eyes meeting the painted faces of her parents once more as she pretended that she was giving their eulogy instead. "All love stories are tragedies if you step back far enough. Even if the love is perfect and they stay together until they're old and frail and barely recognize each other, one will eventually leave the other behind. My family is blessed, though. Between them, my parents, and my great-grandparents, going out with the one you love seems to be a pattern." And she was always the one left behind. "I can only hope I'll know the kind of love they did."

With that, she took her seat. Others came forward and told stories of their generosity, of Astrid's hostess skills and wit and Bert's hunting prowess and audacity. They washed over her like waves on the surf, clearing away any imperfection in the sand. She should be crying. She sobbed at her parents' funeral, demanded to know why mommy and daddy were sleeping in the coffins and wouldn't they be scared when they woke up in the ground? Now, she was old enough to know there would be no waking up, but though her chest ached with some sadness, it was an empty kind of grief. She just felt hollow. What kind of sociopath doesn't cry for the people who raised her? She should be feeling something more than the numbness in her chest.

She bent over, putting her head in her hands. Probably mistaking the gesture for silent sobs, she felt Morgan's hand on her shoulder, a point of warmth in the winter chill she felt all over.

Before she knew it, the service was over, and the pallbearers carried the caskets to the family plots near the edge of the woods. The family cemetery, like the family home, overlooked the lake at the edge of the property. A lawn large enough for garden parties and grand backyard weddings stood between them.

She passed through the iron gate that caged in the dead and took in the moss-covered angels and headstones with epitaphs worn with age that stood in neat little lines. In the center was a mausoleum lined with Corinthian columns and adorned with reliefs of angels: the graves of Joshua, Charity, and the children that did not make it to adulthood. Surrounding it was the graves of her parents, some cousins, and now the open plots for her grandparents. All told, the little cemetery was serene and picturesque.

As a teenager, this was her favorite spot for solitude on beautiful spring days like today. She would go through and read each headstone until she knew them all by heart or sit underneath the weeping willow just outside the gates that overlooked the water. It was quiet there, as though the dead were truly resting.

She listened to the priest drone, "All are from the dust and to the dust all return" as her grandparents were lowered into the ground and lingered as each mourner grabbed a handful of dirt and dropped it on each casket. With pitying looks, they left her to watch as the gravediggers went to work.

Once she was alone, she opened her mouth to speak, but the words clogged her throat. What is there to say to them? An "I love you" was too strong and a "good riddance, I hope you burn in Hell" was too severe.

On the day of her parents' funeral, it was raining. The world wept with the little girl who stood over her parents' graves, not understanding why she could never see them again and why they left her alone. Her grandmother's hand gripped her smaller one tightly, her black gloves chafing like sandpaper. Her grandfather stood on her other side, his fingers digging into her shoulder whenever her crying got too loud.

Even now, looking at the freshly filled graves, Rhea felt the phantom fingers digging into her shoulder. She plucked two roses from her grandparents' graves and left them on her parents'. It wasn't much to honor them, but it was something.

A splash caught her attention. She turned to look for the source of the noise, expecting a bird or tree branch that the wind had knocked in. Instead, a woman stood in the water underneath the willow tree, her red hair cascading to her waist and face obscured by the branches. No, not in. On top of the water.

That part of the lake was deceptively deep. Right at the edge, there was a small drop off instead of a gradual incline, and the water there was about four feet deep. The way the woman stood, though, it looked as though it couldn't have been more than a couple inches.

Looking at her, Rhea felt an old, strangely familiar ache in her chest, as though she should know this woman, but had no memory of her. She blinked and the woman disappeared.

No. I am not doing this, she thought, shaking the image from her mind. Crazy, unstable Rhea jumping at things that weren't there. That woman was not walking on water. It was an optical illusion brought on by a weird perspective.

Obviously, the woman was just standing beside the tree, and the white flowers that lined the lake obscured her feet.

That was it.

If the woman wanted to pay her respects, she could join the rest of the bereaved.

CHAPTER THREE

The reception was held in the dining room. People milled about holding plates piled high with macarons, cucumber sandwiches, and chicken cordon bleu, as well as bowls of beef bourguignon and lobster bisque. All of Bert and Astrid's favorite dishes were laid out on the table to sample. Her stomach rumbled. When was the last time she ate? She'd skipped breakfast to catch the bus to Cherub Cove and hadn't eaten lunch in her haste to get to the house. It was coming on three o'clock, and she was suddenly very hungry. She grabbed a plate and sampled the lobster bisque. Her eyes widened in surprise and appreciation at the taste.

"So, you like it?" Morgan asked, stepping out of the shadows.

Rhea just barely managed to jump without spilling her soup. "Uh, yeah. It's—it's amazing. Who made it?"

Morgan beamed with pride. "I did. Everything but the macarons. I never could get those right."

She nearly spit out her soup. "You cooked this whole feast by yourself? You didn't have to do that."

"Well, I enlisted some family members to help," Morgan said, waving at a group of Filipina women bringing out plates.

Rhea shook her head. "What—I—why? Thank you, but why not get a caterer? This is a lot of work."

She shrugged. "Now that I'm no longer looking after your grandparents, I hope to start my own restaurant. As morbid as it is, I knew the whole town would be here to try my cooking, and I wasn't sure I would get another chance. Besides, it felt right. They were..." She paused, and Rhea could see the struggle to find a diplomatic way to sum up her grandparents. "Lonely, I think. It's funny, Andy and I spent so much time alone with them in this big, empty house, but as soon as they're gone, it's filled with mourners."

More like scavengers. Vultures descending upon her grandparents' corpses, scrounging for any respectability by association. Now, they can say that they attended the funeral of town royalty, watched the esteemed Bert and Astrid lower into the ground and tossed their handful of grave dirt down those six-foot holes. They wailed their laments and prayed that their grief was loud enough to earn them a sliver of what they left behind. Well, let them fight over it like hyenas tearing apart a lion's kill. Let them loot the Ming vases, pocket the diamond necklaces, and tear the family portraits asunder in their feeding frenzy.

They could tear this house apart by brick and floorboard and foundation for all she cared.

"Would you like to meet my family?" Morgan asked, interrupting her train of thought.

Rhea blinked. "Uh, sure."

She waved over an older looking woman. Though her face was lined with crow's feet and smile lines, she looked just like Morgan. "Nay, this is Rhea. She's the Ballard's granddaughter."

"Nay?" Rhea asked.

"Tagalog for mom," Morgan explained, wrapping an arm around her mother's shoulders in a side hug.

The woman smiled and held out a hand. "Nice to meet you. I'm Mariana." She spoke with a faint, clipped Filipino accent.

"Nice to meet you too. And thank you for helping set all this up." It was strange seeing mother and daughter be so casually close. She wondered if she would have acted like that around her own mother if she had been able to grow up with her.

"Morgan, Tita Annabelle wanted me to give you this, especially if you insist on spending more time here." Mariana pulled a small pendant from her pocket and pressed it into Morgan's hand.

"Mom..." Morgan groaned, her face coloring.

Mariana ignored her, beaming at Rhea. "I can get you one too, Rhea. For protection."

"What is it?" she asked, trying to subtly get a better look at Morgan's pendant.

"It's an *agimat*," Morgan explained as she put it around her neck. "They're charms used to ward off evil. Astrid made me stop wearing mine because it was too pagan for her."

That sounded about right. "I'm sorry she was...well, like that," Rhea said.

"I'll get one for you too," Mariana said. "Annabelle has a bunch lying around. You can never have too much protection in a place like this."

Morgan's mom had no idea. But Rhea didn't like the idea of Mariana going even further out of her way for the family. "Oh, that's okay. I won't be staying here longer than a night."

Mariana's eyebrows shot up, probably surprised that Rhea had no intention of staying any longer than necessary. "Are you sure?"

"It's really kind of you, but you all have done plenty already."

Mariana looked like she was about to argue, but then one of their relatives called her from the kitchen. "Duty calls. It was a pleasure to meet you, Rhea, and if you change your mind, just tell Morgan." With a final squeeze of her daughter's shoulder, she bustled off.

"Sorry about that," Morgan said with a laugh. "My mom can be a bit much, but she means well."

"I don't mind. She was...really nice." Mariana, like Morgan, seemed to be kind for the sake of being kind, without wanting anything from her, which was oddly refreshing.

A man behind her cleared his throat, stepping in front of her and blocking Morgan as though he didn't see her. The face of David Ellis was one she'd grown well acquainted with over the years. The family lawyer had been there when her parents died, ensuring that Bert and Astrid were granted custody. Her strongest memory of him, though, was in the jailhouse, when she was picked up for underage drinking with Eliza one of the few times she snuck out. He said a few words to the sheriff, and before she knew it, she and Eliza were free. And here he was again, his hair white and the same cold calculation in his eyes.

"Miss Ballard," he said primly.

She bristled at the way he stepped between them, as though Morgan was little more than a prop in the little play of his life. "Can I help you?" she asked, her tone equally prim. "I was in the middle of a conversation." She gestured to Morgan, whose eyes were wide in surprise that she was being addressed.

Before he could respond, Morgan said, "I should actually check on my cousins. I'll leave you to it."

Rhea watched her disappear into the crowd before turning back to Mr. Ellis. "Look, I know I'm probably not welcome here, but it's their funeral. I'll be leaving tomorrow, so I don't want any trouble. I just wanted to say goodbye."

He blinked as though taken aback. "Leaving? But you were named the estate's primary caretaker."

It was her turn to be taken aback. "I—I—After I left, I assumed they disowned me."

25

He shook his head. "Miss Ballard, they left everything to you."

She set her soup down on a nearby table so as not to drop it. Suddenly, she felt dizzy.

No, this couldn't be right. She was an embarrassment, a disgrace, the biggest disappointment to the Ballard name since Mad Minerva, who disappeared around the time her great-grandfather got married. It had to be a mistake.

Or, maybe, the secret wish she'd buried so deep into her heart that it had become fossilized came true. In the end, her grandparents regretted the way they treated her and wanted to make it up to her. But no, that wasn't right either. They didn't have the capacity to regret their choices, so it must be a trick or a trap of some kind. Or, perhaps, they cared more about continuing the family name than their own pride. Or—

"Miss Ballard? Rhiannon?" Mr. Ellis said, cutting through the buzzing in her ears, "Are you alright?"

She nodded. "Sorry. I just didn't expect that."

"We can go over the finer details later," he said, "It comes out to three million dollars, but a lot of it will be tied up for a while in probate. In the meantime, the trust your parents left will be released to you."

She blinked. "What trust?"

His eyes widened for a split second, the only indication that he was surprised. "Bert and Astrid never mentioned it to you? Faith and Julian left you most of their savings plus interest to be received on your 25th birthday or in the event of the deaths of your guardians," he said. "It amounts to about a hundred thousand dollars. To be honest, I didn't expect for you to come out of the shadows until your twenty-fifth birthday."

"Oh," she said weakly. "They, um, they didn't talk finances with me much."

He eyed her critically. She wondered what he thought of her, what he knew of her escape. Shame welled up inside her. What must he think of her? The girl who abandoned her grandparents, left them to die without family. A spoiled brat who only came back in the hopes of financial windfall.

No, she was not about to shame spiral now. There was a reason that she left. She counted her breaths, just like she had read about in that beaten up library book when her panic attacks began happening almost daily.

In...two...three...four... *Out*...two...three...four...

Mr. Ellis was still talking. She tuned back in. "—sorry for your loss and will be happy to speak to you when you're ready."

She forced a smile. "Thank you. I'll call you tomorrow." He patted her once awkwardly on the shoulder before leaving to talk to an old hunting buddy of Bert's. She watched Morgan bring out a plate of bacon wrapped dates. Three million, one hundred thousand dollars...she knew the first way would spend it.

She stood apart from the rest of the mourners, shaking their hands and taking their condolences with a smile so forced that her cheeks ached with the effort every time someone approached with their empty condolences.

When she wasn't playing the role of the grieving granddaughter, she sampled the rest of Morgan's cooking.

The beef bourguignon was just as delicious as the lobster bisque and the chicken cordon bleu. The pastries were sweet and flaky without being cloying. After a diet of instant ramen and takeout, this was mana from heaven.

Goodness sake, she could hear Astrid admonish, *you'll never find love if you look like a pig.* The next swallow went down harder, with a sudden awareness of her soft curves and love handles. She set down her plate.

Therapy.

Therapy was the second way she would spend her money.

An old woman dressed all in black came up to greet her. "Rhiannon? I'm sure you remember me, I'm—"

"Mrs. Waters," Rhea said, "You were in my grandmother's book club."

The woman smiled, revealing false, too straight and white dentures. "Astrid always had the most delightful insights in whatever we were reading that week. When we had our last book club, it broke my heart to see how much she was struggling to get through the discussion without freezing or losing focus. She was quite the intellectual in her prime. And so are you, I hear. How was Dartmouth?"

"Dartmouth?"

"I never saw you after you left for college. Astrid and Bert were so proud of you and your achievements! Graduating high school a year early. Top of your class. And I hear you're a rising star at your investment firm. You really must have the Ballard brilliance."

She almost laughed in the old woman's face. She knew that they lied about where she'd been the past six years, but this was pathetic. An Ivy league school and successful career. The perfect, high achieving granddaughter, not the girl who ran away and eked out a living on three minimum wage jobs that helped pay for a roach infested studio apartment.

Overcompensation, thy name is Bert and Astrid.

Instead, she forced a smile and simply said, "Thank you. My one regret is that I wasn't able to come and visit more."

Mrs. Waters nodded. "They understood. I'm looking forward to seeing what you make of yourself."

She sighed, watching the old woman totter off. "Yeah," she said to herself, "me too." The stuffy air made hotter by the throngs of people and wall of noise made her want to hide somewhere cool and quiet like a sick cat.

"—was the best shot in the state—"

"—And I said to Emmet, if you come near my daughter again—"

"—was a bit of a recluse, wasn't she? Barely even knew they had a granddaughter—"

Rhea pricked up her ears. They were talking about her, weren't they? She edged closer, years of practicing being seen and not heard rendering her nearly invisible.

"From what Astrid said, she was a bit of a troubled child. She didn't fit in well with other kids, so she was homeschooled," a woman Rhea recognized as Astrid's friend, Mrs. Hooper, said. "Astrid always claimed that it was because she was too smart for her peers, but I just think they didn't get her the right therapist after her parents died. To lose them both at such a young age, it's bound to affect a child. I wouldn't be surprised if she turned out...a little strange."

Rhea nearly gave herself away with a bitter laugh. Astrid and Bert believed in therapy as much as they believed the world was flat. "It's all pseudoscience and feel-good crap meant to scam weak minded people out of their hard-earned cash," Bert once said. Astrid agreed. They didn't believe in the public school system for similar reasons—"It's a waste of taxpayer money!"—instead opting to homeschool her so she could learn to be a "proper lady." How's that for strange?

Then came a voice, one that she would never forget. One that still haunted her dreams and nightmares. "I knew her, actually, when we were both teenagers," the all-too familiar voice said, "she's not like that at all. She was sweet."

Rhea saw her across the room, and a thousand little moments flickered through her mind like a sputtering candle. A red lipped smile and perfect blonde ringlets. Mischievous eyes and soft lips under the willow tree. Her Sunday best dress the night they met, perfectly styled like a porcelain doll, and the disheveled pajamas and sleep mussed hair the night she closed the door and left Rhea alone. Eliza Young, her first love and her first heartbreak.

Eliza spotted her staring and gave a small wave. Her smile didn't quite reach her blue eyes, but she looked as lovely as Rhea remembered, her dress perfectly fitted to her slim body and her makeup impeccable. She always was too pretty for Rhea. For a moment, Rhea thought she was about to approach her, but then she turned around and spoke to an old man in a suit so ragged it looked as though it had been recently stolen off a corpse.

Air. Rhea needed air. The room was too hot, too loud, too many people packed in close quarters. "Excuse me," she said, pushing her way through the crowd. She needed to get away from people and their judging stares and empty platitudes and be somewhere where she could breathe.

CHAPTER FOUR

All things considered; the family chapel wasn't her best hiding place. She'd simply swapped out the judgement of one hundred of her grandparents' closest friends to that of saints, Jesus on the cross, and the Virgin Mary. But it was quiet and cool, and she could ignore the phantom ache in her knees from when they forced her to kneel before the crucifix for hours and confess all her sins to God and her ancestors.

She sat on a splintery pew—*no sinner should be comfortable under the gaze of the lord, Astrid would say every time she complained about sitting for hours on end*—and put her head between her knees. *Breathe in four. Breathe out seven.* God, all it took was one look at Eliza and she was seventeen again, freezing cold with a twisted ankle and watching the only person who loved her by choice and not obligation close the door on her.

She couldn't muster the tears for the eulogy, but now they threatened to spill over. Jesus glared down at her from the altar. She met it with one of her own. "What are you looking at?" Just like those hours she sat in this room, listening for a voice her grandparents said she should hear, the crucifix stayed silent as stone. She laughed bitterly to herself. "Right, I don't know what I expected."

Sitting alone in the pew, she remembered the first time she saw Eliza. It was at one of her grandmother's famous parties, the kind where she had to be the little China doll in the corner, pretty and silent. Pull her string and she'll say up to five phrases. "School is going well." "My favorite subject is English." "My favorite book is *One Hundred Years of Solitude*." "I'm looking at Harvard and Dartmouth." "I want to study literature." That's all the adults really cared to ask. And then they'd get bored of her and find someone else to talk to.

But that night, Grandma Astrid invited the new family in town, and they brought Eliza, the first girl her age she'd seen in a long time. And she was beautiful. Like a princess in her old storybooks. Eliza scanned the party. When their eyes met, she gave a relieved smile and walked straight up to her.

"I am so glad I'm not the youngest person here," she said as her way of greeting. "I'm Eliza."

Rhea opened and closed her mouth, suddenly tongue tied and shy. This wasn't one of her five phrases. Finally, she smiled and said, "How do you know? I might have just had a lot of work done."

Eliza laughed and it was what Rhea imagined angels sounded like. "Then whatever plastic surgeon you have is a wizard and I will need his number when I'm older." She took Rhea by the hand and nodded away from the party. "How about we go somewhere that doesn't require a senior citizen discount for entry?"

Rhea led her through the house and outside towards the willow. The night was cool, with a gentle breeze rustling through the trees and so many stars that Rhea could make out every constellation she knew. Orion, and Ursa Minor, and the Big Dipper all winked above her. Eliza stopped short.

"A cemetery? If you're going to sacrifice me to Satan, you should at least tell me your name first," she said.

Rhea blushed. Right. Names. It's polite to give your name to new people. "I'm Rhiannon, but my friends call me Rhea. Rhea Ballard." At least, she imagined her friends would, if she had them. Rhea was what her mother and father called her, but her grandparents insisted on Rhiannon. And because they insisted on it, the rest of the staff followed suit. But she kept the nickname close to her heart, hoping that she would someday find someone who would call her by it.

Eliza's eyes widened. "Wait, you live here? This place is amazing. It's like something out of a fairytale."

"Well, I've been locked in enough towers to qualify as a princess," she said ruefully as she headed towards the willow.

Eliza gave a half chuckle as though she wasn't sure if she should laugh or not. "I guess I'll have to leave one of my shoes behind, so you'll know how to find me again," she replied, following her.

"I think leaving behind a phone number would make it easier on me." Rhea sat down underneath the tree, gazing out at the full moon reflecting on the lake and listening to the muffled revelry of the partygoers inside the house.

Eliza sat down beside her. "Sounds good to me. I need both my shoes anyway. They're my only pair of heels." She looked out on the water. Rhea watched her watching the lake, noting the way her golden ringlets reflected in the moon light and the bright blueness of her eyes. "It's beautiful out here," Eliza said.

"Yeah," Rhea replied, not taking her eyes off Eliza, "it is beautiful."

Now twenty-three years old, sitting on that splintery pew at her grandparents' funeral, she fought to keep her breathing deep and even, and tears unshed under the baleful gaze of the saints that lined the wall. *You think you suffered? They seemed to say. That you're a martyr, the patron saint of long suffering and abandoned children? You know nothing of pain. See the way we've bled for our love, but you ran away. The prodigal daughter returned only to reap her family fortune.*

Letting out a stuttering breath, she let herself crumple, curling away from their holy gazes.

"Ms. Ballard?" asked a voice from behind.

She jumped, straightening up and wiping her face free of unshed tears. "Jesus Christ!"

"Nah, but we do share a love of carpentry," Andy Higgins said, taking a seat beside her, "Sorry, did I disturb your raging against the heavens?"

"Not much raging going on. I just needed some quiet," she replied with a chuckle. "And I told you to call me Rhea."

Andy stretched, leaning lazily back against the pew in a way that she knew was uncomfortable, but he managed to look as relaxing as a hammock in summer. "Right, of course. Because the paintings of martyrs with their wounds on display are somehow less judgmental than the people outside." He pointed to a renaissance painting of a flayed man. "Like that dude holding his own skin? Much better company than Mayor Parker."

In spite of herself, her lips quirked into a small smile. "Saint Bartholomew. Yeah, at least he doesn't bring up his hopes that I'll carry on my grandparents' legacy and become a generous benefactor to the town at their own funeral."

Andy rolled his eyes. "He couldn't wait until they were cold in the ground?"

"Apparently not." She shrugged and picked at a splinter in the pew.

"What did you tell him?"

"The truth. I'm the family disgrace and they almost certainly disowned me." She hesitated, gnawing at her already anxiety torn lip. "At least, I thought it was. Turns out all of this is now mine." The laugh she let out verged on hysterical.

"You don't sound very happy about it."

She didn't look at him, instead studying the painting of St. Peter of Verona placidly reading a book with his head cleaved in two. "Well, I think lying in a house of God is a bit of a no-no."

"More like a room of God." He shuddered. "This place creeps me out. I get that they're saints and supposed to be the good guys, but they're still artistic renderings of a dude getting barbecued and shot up with arrows. Yeesh."

"Saint Lawrence and Saint Sebastian," she replied automatically.

Andy arched his eyebrows. "You just know all these saints off the top of your head?"

"Pretty much," Rhea replied with a shrug, "The funny thing is, we're not even Catholic. We didn't believe that these saints would intercede on our behalf if we prayed to them. My great-great-grandparents traveled all over Europe and just loved the aesthetic. My grandparents, though, thought it was vital that I learn the names and stories of all the martyrs. Most kids get Cinderella or Snow White as their bedtime stories. I got how Saint Agatha's breasts were ripped off and Saint Lucy had her eyes gouged out."

"You're kidding."

"I wish. My kingdom for a *Captain Underpants* book."

Andy chuckled, and then fell silent, resting his elbows on his knees and fiddling with his cufflinks. It was obvious that he hadn't had much occasion to wear a suit in his lifetime. The outfit was old and ill fitting. He seemed uncomfortable, fidgeting and adjusting his tie, his collar, his lapels. "So," he said, breaking the silence, "do you, uh, believe?" He gestured to the cross above the altar.

"No," she replied, and the guilt born of hours spent in penance and years of praying to a god she could not hear came crashing down on her like the walls of Jericho. "Yes. I don't know. It's complicated. You?"

Andy shook his head. "Nope. I half expected to spontaneously combust the moment I set foot in here."

"Honestly, me too," Rhea replied with a laugh.

He shifted, turning his body towards Rhea. "Then, if you don't mind my asking, what are you doing in here?"

"Like you said. I was raging against the heavens. What about you? You seem pretty sociable. Why aren't you out with the rest of the guests?"

"Honest answer? Morgan saw you run off and asked me to make sure you were okay."

"Oh," Rhea replied, "That's sweet. She didn't have to do that." A feeling of discomfort wormed its way into her stomach. Who was this woman and why was she being so nice? For all she knew, Rhea had condemned her grandparents to a lonely death with her abandonment of them. Maybe it was because she wanted to keep working there and would have to make a good impression on Rhea so she could stay. She could be out to get the family fortune, not that Rhea cares about it beyond what she could live on. Or, and least likely of them all, Morgan was just *that* nice.

"Yeah, she's a sweetheart," Andy said fondly, "at least, until you get in her way in the kitchen. Then the knives come out. Literally."

"I'll remember that."

He clapped his hands to his knees before getting up and stretching with the groan of a man much older than Andy looked. "Speaking of, I'm gonna have some more bon bons before Mrs. Waters shoves them all into her purse. Ready to go back into the lion's den?"

She was feeling better, she supposed, and the guests would probably be wondering where she ran off to, but the idea of leaving this oasis of cool quiet was almost intolerable. "I'll be out soon."

"Take all the time you need. I'll make sure to save you a hearty sampling of her desserts. You've got to try her cookie brownies. They're the best of both worlds." He shot her finger guns before opening the door.

"You don't have to—" she began, but he was already gone. "Do that."

With Andy gone, the silence that had comforted her before now left the air feeling denser than the grape cough syrup her grandparents force fed her when she was sick.

She took a few moments to just count her breaths before forcing herself to her feet.

Once more unto the breach.

CHAPTER FIVE

"Are you sure you're okay with this?" Morgan asked for perhaps the fiftieth time since broaching the subject of how she'd let her lease lapse while living at the house full time and needed a place to stay until she found a new apartment. "My parents won't mind if I move back home for a bit." True, but would Morgan mind? She seemed close to her family, but Rhea knew better than anyone that looks could be deceiving. If Morgan wanted to stay, she could, no questions asked.

It was night, and all the guests were gone, leaving their detritus behind. Andy had gone home for the evening, leaving Morgan and Rhea to face the disaster zone on their own. Fine China piled high in the sink, the intricate delft floral patterns obscured by the uneaten remnants of Morgan and her family's hard work. She and Rhea decided to leave half over night "to soak." Everything between the dining room and the kitchen was a disaster zone. Between the food and the foot traffic, it would take at least a day to clean it all up. Both took one look at the mess and decided that most of it could wait tomorrow.

Rhea yawned, ready to crash before the day's numbness thawed into an emotional breakdown. "Seriously, you're doing me a favor. If you're here, I won't get charged with arson for burning this eyesore to the ground."

Morgan raised her eyebrows but didn't seem too disturbed by Rhea's expressed desire to destroy a historical landmark. Maybe she had similar thoughts. "Well, when you put it like that..." She turned, heading towards the back staircase.

"Wait, where are you going?"

Morgan stopped, confused. "My bedroom?"

"They seriously made you sleep in the servant's quarters?" Morgan didn't have to answer. The way she stood agape at Rhea's righteous indignation was all the answer she needed. She sighed. "Of course, they did. Why am I even surprised? You're welcome to a guest room if you want. Whatever one you want."

"Oh, okay, thanks," Morgan said, her dark eyes wide.

"It's basic decency. Christ, three people living in this crypt and they still want to play out their fetish for feudalism." Her irritated muttering was cut off by another yawn.

"You should probably get to bed," Morgan said with a chuckle, "I'll be right behind you."

...

As exhausted as Rhea was, sleep refused to come. She laid in her childhood bed, clutching Otso like she did years ago, and staring at the lacy canopy above her. Rooms evolve over time, children's rooms especially.

Disney princesses replaced by boy band posters replaced by artwork and little souvenirs of travel.

Well, replaced was not exactly the right word. The remnants of earlier phases were still there, if she knew where to look. The arrangement of stuffed animals on the bed may change in number and type, but Otso will remain. The boy band posters may be gone, but the cd's are still on the shelf. The average childhood bedroom of an adult is a palimpsest of growing up. But not this room. It wasn't just frozen in the time of Rhea's girlhood; it was frozen in the girlhood of a child from a hundred years ago.

Heavy footsteps passed by her room—Morgan, probably. She yawned, willing herself to rest. The footsteps faded and her eyes drifted shut.

Her door creaked open. She froze, scarcely daring to breathe as the floorboard creaked near her bed and a familiar sense of danger made the hairs on her neck prickle.

"Morgan?" she whispered hopefully. She kept her eyes shut, not wanting to confirm what she already knew. The thing in her room was not Morgan.

There was no reply but wheezing, gurgling breath beside her ear. It smelled of decay, of the rat that died in her apartment walls and the putrefaction of meat that had been left too long in the sun. She gagged and buried her head under the covers.

...

The first night she spent in that room, she was alone. Newly orphaned and prone to nightmares of drowning, she laid awake and curled around Otso, tears silently streaming down her face. There was a shifting at the end of the bed, as though someone had sat down. She opened her eyes, expecting Grandma Astrid to be sitting there. Instead, it was an emaciated woman. Her shoulders jutted out from her threadbare white nightgown so translucent that Rhea could make out her ribs and distended belly. Her blonde hair was long, greasy, and lank and her eyes a jaundiced yellow. With a slow smile revealing rotted teeth and making her sharp cheekbones even starker on her angular face, she raised a knobby finger to her lips. *Shh.*

Rhea couldn't scream if she wanted to. Her heart pounded in her throat, forming a lump that blocked anything but a whimper. She clutched the blankets in her small hands, willing the terrifying woman to just go away.

But she didn't. She sat motionless, the too large smile spread across her face and grimy finger to her lips. It took Rhea a small eternity for her to notice that her fingers weren't covered in dirt but blood where her nails had been ripped off and another small eternity for her to decide that she had to get away from the woman smiling at her. Slowly, Rhea slipped out of bed and backed her way to the door. The woman did nothing except slowly turn her head to watch Rhea as she left. Once the door was behind her, she sprinted to the master bedroom.

Even with the adrenaline coursing through her veins, she hesitated at the knob. She didn't know her grandparents well then, but they were scary, with severe faces that looked down on her childish tears with irritation. But this was important. There was an even scarier lady in her room, and she needed to get her out.

She opened the door and stepped inside. To her, the room was cavernous. There was a sitting area, an ornate vanity, and a king sized four poster bed. She closed her eyes for a moment and listened to their breathing. At least they hadn't left her. As she made her slow approach, a floorboard creaked, and she froze, her heart pounding.

Astrid stirred and sat up, affixing Rhea with an irritated stare. Suddenly, she felt like Gretel facing the witch in her Gingerbread house. "What do you want?"

"There's a lady in my room." She hated how small her voice sounded. If anyone asked, she'd deny being afraid of her grandparents, but they offered no warmth or comfort. They looked at her like she was a burden, something fate had saddled them with in their old age.

Astrid stared down her nose at Rhea, her hair mussed from sleep and her eyes tired, making the wrinkles more pronounced. "You were dreaming," Astrid replied, lying back down and turning away from Rhea.

"I wasn't."

"You're lying, then."

"What's going on?" Bert mumbled, rubbing the sleep from his eyes.

"Rhea had a nightmare," Grandma Astrid replied with a syrupy sweetness as she sat up. In the coming years, Rhea would learn to dread this tone, but in that moment, she let her guard down, daring to hope they'd offer some kind of comfort.

"What do you want us to do about it?" Bert asked.

"Can I sleep in your bed tonight?" Rhea asked. If she was with them, they might protect her from the Smiling Lady.

Bert gave a dark chuckle and asked, "I thought you were too old for a thing like that."

And with it, the hope came crashing down on her like the Hindenburg. "I..."

"I thought so too," Astrid replied, her voice wry as though her grandparents were sharing a private joke that Rhea could not begin to understand, "but apparently she had a bad dream."

Bert turned to Rhea. "You couldn't sleep, so you had to drag everyone else awake at this ungodly hour too?"

Rhea had no idea how to respond to that, so she just stared frozen between them like a mouse cornered by a cat.

Bert stared at her a moment longer, his gaze piercing. Like her grandmother, his exhaustion made his wrinkles more pronounced as he glared at her. With his combover undone, revealing a bald spot and awkwardly long hair, he might have looked comical if it wasn't for the disdain in his eyes. Even at that young age, she could tell that he was not a man who abided by anything he saw as weakness. And in that moment, she knew he saw her as weak. The realization made her feel small, like she wanted to shrink into the floorboards and all the way to the earth's core. Eventually, his lips curled in distaste, and he laid back down, rolling on his side facing away from her.

"How old are you, Rhiannon?" Astrid asked.

"Six," she replied, holding up six fingers.

"Are six-year-olds babies, Rhiannon?"

She shook her head, feeling like she was walking into a trap.

"It's polite to use your words," her grandmother admonished.

"No, six-year-olds are not babies."

Grandma Astrid rested chin on her bony hands. "That's what I thought. What do babies do?"

Suddenly the pattern on the carpet was fascinating. She stared at it, her eyes tracing the intricate vines and florals.

"They cry."

"You're right," she said, her voice full of mock praise. "They cry and wake up the whole house with their demands. Are you a baby Rhea?"

"No." Her voice wavered. Tears prickled behind Rhea's eyes, but she refused to let them fall. She wasn't a baby. *She wasn't.*

"I didn't think so. Next time think twice before waking us up. Are you sick? Are you dying? If not, I trust that you're old enough to take care of it yourself."

Her eyes remained steadily on the floor. "Yes, Grandma."

"Now come give me a kiss goodnight."

Rhea did as she told, mechanically crossing the room, planting a kiss on her grandmother's cheek. Old people skin felt strange. Her cheek was papery and seemed almost covered in dust, like the wings of a butterfly. She also got a whiff of the odor particular to the elderly. She'd never smelled it on anyone else. Just old people.

With her grand-daughterly duty done, she walked back to her room. Without thinking, she flicked on the light as she entered.

The Smiling Lady was gone.

Maybe she'd be able to go to sleep after all.

Relieved, she flicked the switch back off.

The Smiling Lady reappeared, sitting at the edge of the bed and staring unblinking at Rhea.

Once again, she disappeared with the light and reappeared in the darkness.

Rhea slept with the lights on that night, and every night until Bert complained about the electric bill.

CHAPTER SIX

Rhea wasn't sure when she fell asleep, but she woke confused and disoriented. This wasn't the bed she had on the floor of her apartment with the springs that dug into her back and made her feel more tired waking than she had getting ready to sleep. The sheets were soft, and the room smelled of old wood. She held something in her hand that smelled of honeysuckle and jasmine. She was home, and for a moment, the previous six years felt like they'd been only a dream. Astrid would yell at her to get her lazy ass out of bed because if she missed breakfast, she'd have to wait until lunch. Not that she couldn't stand to skip a few meals anyway.

If she was being honest with herself, she wasn't sure if she wanted those years to be a dream or not. Her grandparents were miserable, awful people, but at least she knew when her next meal was coming. Most of the time anyway. But for those six years, she was free. Her apartment and meager furnishings were her own and not something that belonged to a long dead ancestor. Her life was her own and beholden to no one else but her bosses and landlord. Now, she was free even from them. If she wanted to, she could sell everything and live off the money for the rest of her life. Maybe she'd travel the world or settle in another country far away from the Ballard name. She always liked the idea of a little cottage in Ireland where she could live alone, free from the expectations of others. Her stomach grumbled. Right, all that could come later. The first step in this new life of complete freedom? Breakfast.

Morgan was already sitting at the counter sipping a cup of coffee when Rhea plodded into the massive kitchen. She looked tired, with dark bags under her eyes as she stared into the steaming mug. As Rhea came into view, though, she looked up and smiled, the exhaustion seeming to all but disappear from her face. "Morning."

"Morning," Rhea echoed with a yawn. She poured herself a cup of coffee and added copious amounts of cream and sugar. She never cared for the bitter drink, but it helped wake her up when she found herself nodding off as she hopped between shifts at her three jobs. The first shift of a typical day was at the gas station. In the afternoons and evenings, she would alternate nights working as a shelf stocker at the grocery store and busking tables at a restaurant.

Most days, she was rarely without her thermos, which she had decorated with a sharpie in her free time. It was currently sitting in her apartment. She didn't think she would need it for the duration of her visit, but now that she was staying longer, she felt oddly bereft without it.

Sipping her drink, Rhea sat down at the wooden table in the center of the kitchen. Bert said that his great grandfather made it out of the wood from the shack that once housed the Ballard's that first came to America. A reminder of where the family came from.

"You want me to make breakfast?"

Rhea blinked. "Why?" She couldn't remember the last time someone offered to make her breakfast, let alone someone she met only the day before.

Morgan let out the kind of staccato chuckle people make when they're not sure if they should laugh or not. "Because I'm hungry and you're probably hungry too." She stood and stretched. "How do you feel about pancakes?"

Pancakes sounded amazing. If they were anything like the food the day before, they'd be heavenly. But having Morgan act like her personal chef didn't sit right with her. Yes, technically, Rhea was still paying her and already secretly decided that she would until Morgan found a new job, but she'd spent so long doing things on her own that accepting this felt wrong. "You really don't have to—"

"I'm making them for myself, but I always make a bit too much," Morgan said, grabbing flour and sugar from the pantry, "It's what happens when you're used to cooking for others. You'd be doing me a favor. Otherwise, they'll go to Andy, and the man is the living embodiment of if you give a mouse a cookie."

Rhea let out a breathy chuckle. The discomfort was still there, but if Morgan was really just cooking for herself, then... "Yeah, okay. Thanks."

She watched Morgan mix the ingredients and sipped her coffee. She wasn't much of a breakfast person. In the past few years, she usually only had time for a granola bar or a bowl of dry cereal if she was lucky before rushing out the door. She couldn't remember the last time she had a slow morning like this, and she savored it like the smell of pancakes coming from the pan Morgan stood over.

"Chocolate chips?" Morgan asked, holding up a bag of semi-sweets.

Chocolate chip pancakes. She couldn't remember the last time she had them. Just imagining the taste filled her with a childish glee. "Yes, please."

"So, you have a sweet tooth." Morgan said airily as she sprinkled a copious amount of chips on the back side of the pancakes.

You need to cut back on the sweets. You're getting fat, Astrid's voice echoed in her ear. The words made her shudder. For years, she had been fighting her grandmother's voice whispering poison in her head. Astrid wasn't supposed to have power over her anymore. But here, Astrid's words were so loud that Rhea picked up her head, half-expecting to see her standing in the kitchen doorway.

What was Morgan getting at? She wished she could see her face and find that little hint of judgement. With her back turned, her body language gave nothing away. "Yeah."

"Oh, so do I. My mom used to hide my Halloween candy so I wouldn't eat it all in one sitting. Let me know if I made them too sweet." She flipped the pancake, revealing a golden-brown top pockmarked with chocolate chips.

Her lips quirked into the first genuine smile she'd made since returning home. "Too sweet? Never."

"Be careful. I might see that as a challenge." She plated the pancake and set it down with butter in front of Rhea.

"You don't have to..."

"I know," Morgan said, "just take the damn pancakes."

Rhea couldn't help the chuckle when she grabbed a fork and replied, "Thanks."

"Any time." Morgan returned to the pan, adding enough mix for her own breakfast and a fistful of chocolate chips.

"You weren't kidding about the sweet tooth," Rhea said with a laugh.

"I warned you." She opened the refrigerator, and Rhea caught a glimpse of the piles of leftovers from the funeral.

"Your family can take the leftovers, you know."

"You don't like my cooking?" Morgan asked, arching an eyebrow.

"No," Rhea said, "it's really good. It's just that I can't eat all of it, and you and your family worked so hard, and I feel bad taking so much, so you should keep it."

Morgan chuckled, patting Rhea's hand. "Relax, I was just giving you a hard time. We already took what we wanted."

Rhea stared at the Morgan's hand as she retracted it. "Oh." She blinked, looking up. "Damn, how much food did you make?"

"Sacrificed enough chickens and cows to populate at least three small farms," she replied with a chuckle.

Rhea took a bite of her food. "Well, it was not in vain. This is amazing. Where did you learn to cook like this?"

"Culinary school," Morgan replied proudly. "Like I said, I'm hoping to open a restaurant one day."

She winced. How could she have forgotten that? "Right, sorry."

Morgan didn't look offended at Rhea's lapse in manners. "No worries. It was a long day for all of us. I'm sure I've forgotten at least a half dozen things I still need to get done."

"You certainly proved your prowess at catering," Rhea said around a mouthful of pancake. "I'll be the first in line when you open your restaurant."

They fell into a companionable silence.

Rhea chewed her food and drank her coffee, dreading the phone call to Mr. Ellis. A long day of confusing legal matters was ahead of her, including how exactly probate worked. From the books she read and the limited number of movies she watched, she was under the impression that as soon at the will was read, she'd be entitled to everything she inherited, but apparently this wasn't the case.

Her gaze drifted to Morgan, watching her as she ate. She was still in her pajamas, her dark hair still mussed from sleep. She seemed lost in thought as she chewed her pancake and scrolled through her phone like Astrid with the morning paper, but her dark eyes were smiling.

It seemed like she was never without a smile.

She wondered what Morgan thought of her. The spoiled rich girl who didn't have time for her grandparents. Or had they told her more? Did they tell her that about how she, the ungrateful granddaughter, ran away from home at the age of seventeen because being rich and respected was just too much for her?

Morgan, for her part, seemed content to sip her coffee and scroll through her phone without fear of reprimand. Not that Rhea would. She knew how tough the service industry was, and she'd worked enough janitorial positions to know how exhausting and thankless the job cleaning can be. Speaking of...

"I don't expect you to be my personal maid," she said breaking the silence.

Morgan looked up at her, surprised. "What?"

"I know that you took care of both my grandparents and the house. I just need you to give me a hand with maintaining the house. I don't expect you cook or do the dishes or any laundry that isn't your own." She watched Morgan's face, the surprise turning to what? Hurt. She came across too brusque, didn't she? Suddenly, the way the cream swirled in her coffee was fascinating. "It isn't that I don't appreciate you offering to cook. It just—I don't know— doesn't feel right asking that of you."

Morgan's face remained hard to read. She seemed to be watching Rhea as much as Rhea was watching her. If she was in Morgan's place, she'd appreciate the news that she wouldn't have to clean up after a woman her age. Finally, Morgan sighed loudly and dramatically. "Darn," she said in mock disappointment, "I guess I'll have to return that sexy French maid uniform I bought for this job."

Rhea let out a surprised laugh. It was stupid to think she would be mad about having to do less work. "I guess so. Did it come with a feather duster? Because we could use as many of those as possible."

"Of course, you'd want me to keep the least fun part of the outfit."

"Not if you use it the way I use it." Rhea regretted the words as soon as they left her mouth. Morgan sputtered and choked, nearly spilling coffee all over the table. "Sorry, sorry," Rhea exclaimed, rushing over and patting her back.

Her face burned. Why would she say that, especially to someone who technically works for her? She knew firsthand how creepy sexual jokes could be coming from the boss. God, she should have kept her mouth shut.

Morgan's coughs turned to laughter. "Oh man, that burns."

Rhea retracted her hands. "That was inappropriate. I'm sorry."

Morgan held up a hand, shaking her head. "You're fine. I worked for your grandparents. Trust me, I've heard worse. You just caught me off guard."

"But still—" Rhea began.

"Rhea, it's okay. No harm done." Morgan grabbed her and Rhea's plate and brought them to the sink. "And I *like* cooking. Much better than dusting. So, yeah, I won't be your personal maid but making some of the meals and sometimes doing the dishes won't be a burden."

"Okay, deal. But you'll have to let me cook sometimes." She chuckled to herself.

"What?"

"I just realized that I'm a reverse landlord. I pay *you* to basically be my roommate."

Morgan chuckled at that too but then grew serious. "So, what do you think you'll do with this place?"

Rhea shrugged. "My grandparents would have called it my birthright, but honestly, this place can burn for all I care. But since everyone else seems to care about it, I'll probably donate it to the historical society. They can turn it into a museum or something."

Morgan raised her eyebrows. "Makes sense. Would be a shame to burn this place down, though. It's beautiful."

"So is Hemlock. Doesn't stop it from being poison," Rhea muttered.

Morgan gave her an odd look, but Andy walked in before she could say anything. He wore a baseball cap and carried a toolbox. "What are we burning to the ground?"

"The patriarchy," Morgan replied.

"I'm with you, sister. Burn it all to the ground." He plopped down on one of the kitchen seats. "So, I don't know where your priorities are, but I've spent the morning working on restoring the boathouse, and thought I might spend the rest of the day working on it, unless you have something else you want me working on."

Before Rhea could speak, Morgan piped up. "Oh, I'd avoid going there. Bert told me that the water moccasins have made it their home."

As a child, Rhea had been forbidden from visiting the boathouse. She always thought she wasn't allowed there because they'd lost her parents to the lake, but maybe there was a less sentimental reason for keeping her away. But if it was true, why didn't they just tell her that? Finally, she said, "Can you think of any immediate repairs that need to be done on the house?"

Andy scratched his chin thoughtfully. "I need to check for a water leak in the attic. Astrid was complaining of a stain in the ceiling. And I've been meaning to repair the servant's staircase. There are some nails starting to stick up."

"*Yeesh,* remind me to keep my shoes on in the house. I think you should fix the stairs first," Rhea replied as she took a sip of her coffee. "I'd rather you get that done than get bitten by a snake over someplace I'm probably not gonna use any time soon. At least until I can get animal control in and deal with the problem."

Andy saluted her. "Will do." He tipped his hat to Morgan. "Milady."

"Mi'*annoyance*," Morgan replied with a warm smile as Andy collected his things.

She checked the clock. It was after nine. Mr. Ellis would probably be in the office by now. "I'm going to go make a call. I'm guessing you know what to do."

Morgan nodded. "Yup. Go ahead and do your thing."

CHAPTER SEVEN

The call to Mr. Ellis was surprisingly short. He confirmed that she already had access to the trust her parents left her and said that the maintenance of the house was also in a trust, meaning that she could appoint whoever she wanted to help take care of it and use the money in it to pay for their salaries and whatever needs to be done on the home.

What she needed to do was begin inventorying the items of value in the house and go through their old documents for deeds, old bonds, and anything else that the court might want to know about. Because she was the appointed caretaker, she could live in the house during this process.

Her next call was to her landlord, giving them notice of her plans to end her lease within the next two weeks, which luckily was up at the end of the month anyway, and finally, to her bosses, quitting her jobs.

"Seriously, Rhea?" Joe, her manager at the grocery store, said. "You know we're short-staffed already. You can't quit right before your shift."

She thought back to all the times he had called while she was sick, at her other jobs, or on her scant time off. Though she felt a twinge of guilt for putting one of her coworkers in that position, she also felt a deep sense of satisfaction when throwing his words back in his face. "I'm sure you can make it work."

She debated braving the bus trip to get her things. On the one hand, she didn't really need her second and third hand purchased clothes and furniture. Most of her clothes from when she was a teenager still fit, so she could get by on what she had before updating her wardrobe to fit her current style. It was bittersweet trying on the outfits she wore back then. A part of her felt oddly triumphant that her body hadn't changed nearly as much as the Astrid constantly whispering in her ear claimed.

Her grandmother made a point of restricting Rhea's food, claiming that she would eat like a pig if Astrid let her.

Apparently, she was capable of self-control.

The other part of her felt chilled as she stared at herself. She'd always had a round face with baby fat, giving her a youthful appearance. Even as a seventeen-year-old, she could occasionally pass for a tall middle schooler. So, when she looked in the mirror, she didn't see herself as she was now—the Rhea who spent six years dragging herself by her fingernails to stand on her own two feet. She saw herself as she was then—a lonely child with a hunted look that never left her eyes, a rabbit among wolves.

Her phone was the only thing of value, and she brought it with her. On the other hand, unlike the centuries old furniture and clothes she's been forced to wear as a teenager, these items were indisputably hers. She bought them with her own sweat, tears, and blistered feet.

Her favorite item was a thrift store find: a dresser with floral carvings. It was her first non-essential purchase for her apartment, and after dragging it home herself, she had laid out plastic garbage bags and painted the shelf just because she had a rare day off and she could.

When she was seven, she had stuck a sticker on her vanity.

When she lived with her parents, she had a bedroom mirror with stickers in the corner, little flashes of her personality and interests over the years. It made her room at home feel like her own. Astrid and Bert, though, were not at all pleased with this act of rebellion and screamed at her for what felt like hours before sending her to bed without dinner. Seeing the painted dresser was a reminder that she no longer had to live in a museum and could choose to do what she wanted with her life and her things. She would have to find a way get it there.

Maybe hire a moving service.

She kept forgetting she could afford to.

But first, she needed to begin her inventory. She headed to Bert's study, hesitating for a moment outside the great oak doors. When he was alive, he forbade her from going in there. "You'll get your sticky little fingers all over my important papers," he'd say.

She grasped the doorknob and waited for calloused hands to grab her by the wrist and drag her away. When none came, she let out breathy laugh. What was she thinking? He was gone. She pushed open the door and took in the room.

It was clear that no one had been in it for a long time. Dust particles floated lazily through the sunbeams shining through the window. A thin layer covered his desk and various hunting trophies. Ignoring the dead animals around her, she sat down in his leatherback chair and began opening the drawers. Someone with heavy tread was walking above her. Andy, probably searching for the source of the water leak or something.

As she searched through the papers at her desk, she had the distinct sensation of being watched. It was probably just the taxidermized trophies—a dozen in total. Twenty-four glass eyes staring blankly at her from walls and shelves. There were more throughout the house, of course, but a lot of it had been consolidated in his office.

She always hated his hunting hobby. Perhaps she was just too soft hearted to look a creature in the eye to kill it. Or, perhaps, she wondered how far a leap it would be to go from hunting animals to hunting humans. With the cavalier way Bert used to point his guns, she wondered how far he was from reenacting *The Most Dangerous Game.*

He took pride in his kills and meticulously cared for his trophies. The fact that they had gone so far downhill was a testament to how much he had lost in his old age. In particular, the stag's head was in need of care. Its glass eyes were clouded over and fur looked ragged. Seeing it always made her heart break. It wasn't one of his prizes but one of hers.

He took her hunting just once. She was ten and had a few shooting lessons with his rifle, but marksmanship was not her strong suit. She trudged obediently through the woods behind her grandfather. It was cold, the late

November chill carrying the first whispers of winter on its breeze, and her camo jacket was not nearly warm enough to block it out. She bit her lip to keep her teeth from chattering. Her feet hurt from her new hiking boots, her stomach grumbled from skipping breakfast, and her eyelids were heavy from her rude awakening before dawn. But she knew better than to complain.

"Keep up, Rhea," Bert said, apparently ignorant of the fact that one of his strides was equivalent to two of hers. Leaves crunched satisfyingly underfoot. If she had her way, she'd spend the day stepping on them, but he warned, "Walk quieter. Do you want every buck in the forest to hear you?"

She wasn't sure how she could keep the pace without making noise, but there was no point in asking him. He'd probably just tell her to shut up and figure it out. A flicker of movement caught the corner of her eye. She tugged on Bert's sleeve. "Grandpa Bert?"

"What?" His tone was flat and irritated.

A wave of dread crested, but she continued. He'd be happy if he knew, though, so she forced herself to be brave. "I saw something."

He froze so still it was like a lion stalking his prey. "Where?" She pointed just past them to their right. Camouflaged among the trees was a stag. He lifted his head, his dark eyes wary. He reminded her of Santa's Reindeer, and she wondered if killing it would put her on the Naughty List.

Bert handed her the rifle.

"Now's the time, Rhea. Aim and fire."

"Me?" She stared agape at the proffered weapon, already feeling sick at the thought of this beautiful creature bleeding out, his eyes glassy and unseeing.

"Yes, you."

"I—I can't."

He pushed the gun into her hands. "You can and you will."

"No, no, I don't want to." Her cry alerted the stag, who began bounding away.

Bert muttered an obscenity to himself, took aim, and fired without missing a beat. The stag went down with a cry that still haunts Rhea's nightmares. They approached carefully. He struggled weakly to get to his feet, the blood seeping from the bullet wound. "Damn." Grandpa Bert handed her the gun. "Here. You were too weak to shoot it before, now put it out of its misery."

Rhea couldn't help the tears that streamed down her face as she stared at the bloody wound and the terrified eyes of the stag. He looked like he was in so much pain. Pain that Rhea caused. Why did she tell Bert about him? She should have just kept her stupid mouth shut. Now, he was going to die, and he knew, no matter hard he struggled against his fate. "Please, I don't—"

"Rhea, it's your fault that this creature is suffering. If you hadn't hesitated, it wouldn't have felt any pain." He pressed the gun into Rhea's hand. "We won't leave this spot until you put a bullet in its brain." Now, she was sobbing so hard she was practically choking. He smacked her across the face. "Get a grip, kid. It's just a stag. Do it before I shoot you instead."

The idea pierced her heart like an icy blade. He wouldn't actually shoot her, would he? She didn't think so, but she also knew that he sometimes acted without thinking when he was angry. Suddenly, she was acutely aware of how much of a burden she was on her grandparents and how alone they were in the woods. There was no one around for miles, no one to hear if a gunshot went off, no one to see that it wasn't a tragic hunting accident that killed her.

She raised the gun and looked away, the nausea bubbling up her throat from her stomach. Between breaths, she closed her eyes and pulled the trigger.

That head was now mounted on the wall hiding the safe. Rhea shuddered at the memory of dragging the massive thing on her own while her grandfather walked ahead, her muscles straining and the taste of bile in her mouth as she searched the desk for the password sheet. She would save the safe for later. Above her, the footsteps seemed to be growing louder, matching a growing pounding in her head. What was Andy doing up there? By the sound of it, he was testing the strength of the floorboards.

She pulled out another file—what looked to be a passcode list. Bingo. Bank account numbers, the code for the wall safe behind his stag's head and all her parents' finances. It was strange seeing her parents' information. She supposed she should have known they would leave her something, but her grandparents never mentioned it to her, and she had never thought to ask.

Those footsteps were driving her crazy. Though she didn't like to shout at people, she was tempted to yell at him to find something less noisy to do while she was working.

Couldn't he work on the servants' staircase instead? That, at least, would have been on the other side of the house.

"So anyway, I told her, don't take it personally. No one's my type," Andy said. Her breath caught in her throat. His voice was coming from down the hall, not from upstairs.

Morgan. It must have been Morgan up there. Why she was up there and making so much noise, Rhea had no idea, but it had to be her.

But then Morgan's laugh carried through the hallway. "Andy, you're the only person I know who would ever turn down a model."

"Like I said, I don't swing that way for anyone. I'm not even on the swingset."

The footsteps abruptly stopped. Heart racing, Rhea leapt to her feet and grabbed a letter opener, the sharpest thing within reach. She poked her head out of the study. Morgan and Andy were in the hallway. No one was upstairs. When they saw the alarmed look on her face, though, they sobered. She quietly gestured for them to come to her. They exchanged confused glances but did as she asked.

"What's—" Andy began, but Rhea shushed him.

"What's wrong?" Morgan whispered.

"I think someone is in the house," she whispered back, pointing above her. The three froze, listening carefully, but whoever was upstairs stopped walking around. "I heard footsteps." Clutching the letter opener, she slipped out of the room, Andy and Morgan close behind.

"Rhea, wait," Andy said, but he barely registered.

There.

Another creak.

This time Morgan and Andy froze, their eyes wide. But Rhea was already halfway up the stairs, skipping the fifth step that always creaked like she had as a child slipping out of the room for something to eat after being trapped all day without a meal. It was strange how easily the rhythm of it came back to her, walking with her knees bent and barely picking her feet up from the ground, sticking close to heavy furniture because the floor was more settled there. She was quiet as a ghost, listening for the creak of footsteps as she reached the top of the steps.

Another creak, this one closer, and a shadow flitting out of the corner of her eye into her grandparents' bedroom.

She knelt and peered through the keyhole. Something passed by, too quick to see.

Morgan and Andy bounded up the stairs, heedless of the creaking of the floor. Rhea put a finger to her lips and listened. "Someone's in there," she mouthed. The creak of footsteps returned, and Morgan paled. Andy straightened, his muscles tensing as he took the door handle. "If anyone's in here, we have guns, so it's better if you just surrender and get out of here," he called out. "If you haven't stolen anything, we'll just let you go."

Seeming to steel himself, he opened the door a crack and peeked inside. With a relieved laugh, he opened it wide, revealing the empty room. "No one's here."

Rhea stood in the doorway as he walked through, checking for potential hiding places, but she paid him no attention. Instead, she stared at the neatly made canopy bed. An orange bottle of pills was still on the nightstand next to a half-empty water glass, and a sleep apnea machine sat in the corner. The room still looked lived in.

Her grandparents were downstairs. Bert was watching golf or football, and Astrid was sitting in the library reading because television rots the brain. And Rhea was playing Scooby Doo alone, trying to convince herself that the rug held a secret code to a buried treasure, one that the house "ghosts" (who were secretly just her grandparents) were trying to scare her away from finding.

The rug that once held the code in its pattern now held a walker atop it. Between one blink and the next, she was standing next to it, running her hand along the top and feeling the transition from metal to the rubber grips and back to metal.

Whose was it? Bert's or Astrid's? She couldn't imagine either of them that frail. Bert, with his height and strength, still winning arm wrestling matches the last time she saw him. Astrid, who was so upright and severe that she could never imagine her back hunched as she leaned on the walker to get from place to place.

"I don't see anyone," Andy said, snapping Rhea out of her reverie, "and I didn't see anything out of place. Maybe it was pipes or the house settling. These old places make all kinds of weird noises." His expression became sly. "Or maybe it was a *g-g-g-ghost!*"

"I feel like Rhea would know what the pipes sound like," Morgan said from the doorway. She had her arms crossed and her eyes narrowed.

"Well, it makes more sense than ghosts. I'm sure there's a logical explanation for this."

Morgan rolled her eyes, her hand going up to the *agimat* around her neck. "Here we go."

Rhea tried to focus on the conversation. It seemed to be an old argument between them, something that wasn't really for her, but Morgan seemed to have had experiences too. Andy seemed to be stubbornly skeptical, but Morgan could be an ally to Rhea, a reality check to make sure she wasn't going crazy.

But as much as she wanted to listen, her mind was occupied by the pill bottle in her hand.

When had she picked it up? The sight made her breakfast turn to stone in her stomach.

The words on the label swam incomprehensibly, so she focused on the tan circles with the score cut in the center. Were her grandparents that strong or was she just weak for failing to stand up to them? She tried to imagine them walking stiff and slow, their strength ebbing away gradually like the melting of the icecaps. Or did they go downhill fast after the shock of losing their only surviving connection to their son?

She wished she could grieve them, but all she felt was cold and numb, like she had already frozen to death and her shambolic corpse now wandered the earth. She wished she could hate them, because hate was still feeling something for the people that raised her. She wished she knew the right way to feel, the right way to grieve, the right way to do anything.

The chill seemed to spread, running from the top of her head and down her face like getting doused in ice water. Despite the warmth of the room, she shivered, her hands shaking like autumn leaves in a windstorm as her vision tunneled. There was a rattling sound, and it took her a moment to realize it was coming from the pill bottle in her hand.

She hadn't realized that her breath was quickening, or her heart was pounding until Morgan appeared in her field of vision saying something.

What was it?

Copy her breathing. But she couldn't.

Her chest was too tight and the air too thin. But Morgan looked concerned and very few people looked at her like that, so she tried, focusing on the rhythm of her breaths. Morgan didn't do the box method like Rhea had taught herself—more like in for four, hold for seven, out for eight. Repeat until she could focus on Morgan's dark eyes and reassuring words.

"Can I touch you?" Morgan asked once Rhea's breathing began to even out.

Rhea took a shuddering breath, her face now burning with humiliation. She nodded and Morgan gently placed a hand on her shoulder.

Andy pressed a glass of water in Rhea's hand with a smile. "Don't worry, I used a clean glass. No dentures have touched this one. I checked."

That surprised a laugh out of Rhea. She took a sip of water, which quickly turned into guzzling it down. She moved to set it down, but he just took it from her. "Thanks."

Morgan gave her shoulder a squeeze. "How about we take a break, yeah?"

She scrubbed her face. "I'm sorry. I guess I wasn't ready to come in here." She laughed bitterly to herself. Crazy little Rhea, making monsters out of shadows. "You guys must think I'm crazy."

"Hey, no apologies necessary. You put your grandparents in the ground yesterday, and now you live in a huge, old house straight out of a gothic novel. I'd be disappointed if nothing spooky happened if I were you," Andy replied, flashing her his boyish smile.

He didn't know the half of it, but Rhea wasn't about to correct him. He'd probably laugh it off, hopefully in a more good-natured way than her grandparents. "Let's get out of here. Let the dead rest."

"On their comfy mattress made of horsehair and rusted springs," Andy said, heading towards the door, "I have no idea how they slept on that thing. It had to be as old as they were."

"Bert would say that back pain builds character," Morgan said. She'd been oddly quiet since they came into the room, and Rhea noticed a slight tremor in her hands. It made sense. She was the one that found them. Rhea wasn't the only one with painful memories associated with this room anymore.

She let Morgan steer her out, Andy barging ahead and calling dibs on the leftover sweets. Once he was out of earshot, she said, "I think I hear things too sometimes, or see things out of the corner of my eye. This place can get creepy, especially when you're on your own. And sometimes things happen, things I can't explain."

"Yeah," Rhea said, thinking back to the woman who sat at the end of her bed and the rank breath she felt on her neck the night before. *Honestly Rhea, you're too old for a nightlight,* Grandma Astrid told her when she was eight and still afraid of the dark, *it's all in your head. Keep spewing nonsense like that and the men in white coats will take you away.* "I don't think Ballard's ever truly leave this house."

"So, you believe in ghosts?" Morgan asked, looking almost painfully earnest.

This had to be the trap.

Rhea would confess to seeing ghosts in the house and Morgan's sweet façade would vanish and she'd laugh and call Rhea crazy. She gave a noncommittal shrug. "Maybe. There are more things in heaven and earth, Horatio—"

"Than are dreamt of in your philosophy," she finished, her eyes sparkling, "I had three separate high school English classes force me to read it. Made me long for Romeo and Juliet."

"Astrid made sure I read all the classics. I don't think she knew any book written after the 80's. Apparently, with very few exceptions, today's authors are far too obsessed with technology to create good literature. I still feel her glare every time I pick up a trashy detective novel."

"She was such a snob," Morgan said with a musical laugh. Her smile was quite nice. "She once judged me for reading *Game of Thrones* in my free time. Her exact words were, '*If you're so desperate for fantasy pornography, there are certainly more efficient ways to get it.*' And she wouldn't hear me say it was far more complex than that."

"That sounds like her. I had to beg her to let me check out the *Dune* series from the library." They turned the corner, passing by the study. She forced herself not to peek inside to see if Bert still sat at his desk. "So, do you believe in ghosts?"

She touched her *agimat* again.

"Like I said, I've seen some things. Shadows that move wrong, lights flicker on and off, and once the TV turned on by itself. I've also felt presences. People watching, not necessarily malicious, but curious," Morgan replied with an enigmatic smile. "When you've looked after the dying, you have to have a little spirituality."

"So, how did you go from culinary school to caretaking for the elderly," she asked.

They turned the corner into the kitchen. Andy already sat at the table munching on a cookie from the open tin. Morgan grabbed herself a shortbread. "It was actually just your grandparents. They hired me as a cook when no one else did, and then, because most of the staff outside of Andy had been fired, quit, or retired, they asked me to help take care of the house."

Admittedly, Rhea was wondering how two people around her age were hired to look after this tomb. Because her grandparents were nightmares to work with, she remembered that there was a revolving door of staff in her childhood.

Eventually, they would have to run out of potential employees in town. A paranoid part of her wondered if they might have been in it for more than the meager salary they were given, but the part of her that wanted to let it all rot didn't care if they stole a couple things here and there. Until yesterday, she didn't think she was getting any of it anyway.

Morgan continued, "So, when Astrid got sick, it made sense for me to start taking care of them."

Rhea paused in the doorway. "How sick was she?" Her stomach twisted with an odd guilt. She had no obligation to her grandmother. Astrid lost the right to a relationship with her after how she and Bert treated her. And yet, it didn't stop her from fantasizing about spending her grandparents' money on college and vacations and nice clothing. And it certainly didn't stop her from choosing to live in their grand house until she could use her inheritance to buy a nice home of her own. What must they think of her to speak ill of the dead so casually?

"Dementia, I think. I tried to get ahold of you when she went downhill and I first started taking care of them, but—"

"I've been kind of off the grid. Sorry. I don't even know how Mr. Ellis found me," she said, sitting at the kitchen table and staring at the cookies. She had received the call a week ago from an unfamiliar number and like everyone else her age, she ignored it. But, out of curiosity, she listened to the voicemail left behind. She'd expected it to be about her nonexistent car's extended warranty and was shocked to hear the prim voice of Mr. Ellis on the other end of the line, telling her that the last of her family was dead.

Morgan shrugged. "It's okay. I did it on my own time."

Though Morgan didn't mean anything by it, guilt still twisted like a knife in Rhea's guts. On a good day, Bert and Astrid were awful. She couldn't imagine what the kind of nightmares they would have been in their final years. As glad as she was to be free of them, she wouldn't have wished that on anyone, especially not someone as sweet as Morgan.

She continued, "Neither of them wanted me to call you at first, but I thought you'd want to know. Then she started talking to people that weren't there—"

"Yeah, like the lady in the water," Andy said, "I know it was just the disease, but the way she'd sit under that willow and talk for hours? So creepy. You'd think there was someone actually responding to her." He took another cookie and popped them in his mouth. "These are delicious. What are they again?"

"Madeleines," Morgan replied through gritted teeth. She tensed up at the mention of the lady in the water, though only Rhea seemed to notice. Morgan got up and grabbed a mug and the milk jug. "Anyway, all my time was devoted to taking care of them, and I had to give up looking for you. I'm sure you would have come if you'd known."

Rhea nodded, but would she really? They clearly didn't bother to look for her. She assumed they found her mother's perfume bottle while searching for a clue to where she had gone, but maybe they had just decided to clear out her things and be done with her.

And despite everything, she'd built a life for herself on her own. It barely counted as one—just work and a studio apartment with bookshelf and a mattress on the floor, but it was hers. Would the obligation of family have brought her back? It certainly worked for the funeral and everything after. She thought she was done with them and their expectations. She thought she was free. And considering the reason she left, she doubted that hearing from them would incite any emotion other than panic. But here she was, sifting through everything they left behind.

She turned to Andy, not wanting to think about it anymore. "Did you figure out where the noise was coming from?"

Andy shrugged. "No intruders, if that's what you're asking. Or holes in the wall or broken windows. I dunno." He wiggled his fingers at Morgan. "Pretty spooky. Whooeeeoo..."

Morgan rolled her eyes, and, turning to Rhea, said, "He's a staunch nonbeliever. Doesn't even believe in the existence of aliens."

"I never said *that*," he retorted, "I just think that whatever life that's out there probably wouldn't care about our tiny backwoods planet. And there's a huge difference between believing in aliens and believing in ghosts."

"Really," Morgan said in a tone that indicated that this was a well-worn argument as she sat down and dipped her cookie in milk, "and what is that?"

"Well, statistically one is more likely than the other, for start. The only evidence we have of ghosts are anecdotes and pseudoscience," he shot back.

Morgan leaned over and muttered in Rhea's ear, "He read Richard Dawkins at a formative age."

She snickered. That explained it.

Andy rolled his eyes and took a spiteful bite of his cookie. "I sincerely regret telling you about my Internet atheist phase."

Morgan hid a smirk behind a sip of milk. "Instant credibility nuke."

"It's not like your witch phase was much better. What happened again with that love spell you cast over Riley Peterson?"

Morgan's face colored. "We do not speak of the love spell."

"You should have seen her in high school. Everything she wore was straight out of Hot Topic."

"And you were the kind of guy who carried around a samurai sword and complained that nice guys finish last," Morgan retorted, flicking his ear.

"You wound me. It was a broadsword."

Rhea laughed along with them, appreciating the way it seemed to cleanse all the lingering tension in the room. "So, you guys knew each other in high school?"

Morgan nodded. "We were classmates but ran in different circles. Andy was a year ahead. We worked together for what? Two years until we figured out that we had the same gym class?"

"That sounds about right," Andy said, "You look like you're about our age. Did you go to high school with us?"

Rhea ran an embarrassed hand through her short, black hair. "No, I was, uh, homeschooled most of my life. Bert and Astrid didn't really believe in public schools. Called them a waste of taxpayer money."

Andy let out a full-throated laugh. "Yeah, that sounds like them. They were hilarious in an oh-God-these-people-vote kind of way."

"Try living with them," Morgan and Rhea said in unison. Their eyes met and both erupted into giggles.

"Believe me, I'm glad I didn't," Andy said, leaning in conspiratorially. "You know those white flowers by the lake? Apparently, they're like, super dangerous, but Astrid didn't tell me. She had me pick some for a flower arrangement. I wasn't wearing gloves and got sick the rest of the day. Honestly, I'm lucky I didn't die."

"Jesus," Morgan said, "when was this?"

"Before your time," Andy replied with a shrug, "I learned a very valuable lesson. Never accept flowers from Astrid."

The air seemed to rush from the room. Or was it from her chest? There was something that itched in the back of her mind—a fragment of a memory. But holding onto it felt like trying to scoop water through open fingers.

Rhea looked down and realized that her hand was trembling. She put it in her lap and swallowed down the bile rising in her throat. She could feel her heartbeat pounding in her chest and at every pulse point.

Was this a panic attack?

Over what?

She needed air. "Excuse me," Rhea said, getting up and walking out of the room without another look.

CHAPTER EIGHT

The day was beautiful. She sat in her favorite spot under the willow, taking deep breaths and staring out at the placid water shimmering like sapphires in the midday sun. The branches swayed gently back and forth, enveloping her like a mother's hug. This place was always a cocoon, a quiet spot where she could be alone and think. For all their faults, Astrid and Bert seemed to recognize the tree as her sacred space and would only infringe upon it when she was truly in trouble.

She could see the flowers in her peripheral vision and forced herself to look away. Her hands were still shaking. Why were they shaking?

There was a gap in her memory that she prodded like a missing tooth as she stared into the hypnotically rippling water. With the adrenaline leaving her system, her eyelids felt heavy, and she drifted.

Whispered on the gentle breeze was a song, comforting like her mother's gentle fingers running through her hair and wiping away her tears.

> *"Meet me by the willow*
> *Where the elder flowers bloom*
> *And the soft grass is your pillow*
> *And the night will be our tomb."*

Without realizing it, she sang along,

> *"Please, my love, don't tarry.*
> *For in the light of day*
> *My fiancé I must marry*
> *But for tonight we'll stay*
>
> *Underneath the willow.*
> *I beg, my love, be true*
> *For in the light of moon glow,*
> *It's only me and you."*

She blinked, shaking herself out of the trance. Her cheeks were wet and her eyes sore as remnants of the song echoed in her ears. It was the lullaby her mother sang to her before bed each night. Her voice wasn't great, she remembered that. She couldn't carry a tune or hit a high note, but the song was still hers. After she died, Rhea sang it to herself until it was tattooed on her soul. As she got older, she tried to find it elsewhere but couldn't. Her mother was a poet, so she must have made it up. But the whispers didn't sound like her mother's voice. So, how could anyone else have known it?

She got to her feet and poked her head out from the willow branches. No one stood out along the tree line surrounding the lake. A flash of movement by the boathouse caught her attention, and the song again carried on the wind. It was far fainter than before, forcing her to strain to hear it.

"Hello?" Rhea called out. No response. She left the safety of the willow branches and followed the singing along the lake to the boathouse. It had once been as architecturally ornate as the house, with Corinthian columns in each corner and covered in powder blue paint, but now it was falling apart. The paint had been worn away by time and the elements, and dry rot ate away at the walls and door. "I should turn around," she muttered, "Nothing good ever comes of investigating the creepy voice."

She couldn't hear anyone moving inside, and the door was locked with a rusty padlock. The song abruptly cut off. "Hello?" she called out again, and then in an embarrassed almost whisper, "Mom, is that you?"

"Rhea?" came a voice from behind.

She nearly screamed, whipping around to find a concerned looking Morgan. "Jesus! Warn a girl!"

"I thought you heard me coming. Are you okay?"

Her cheeks colored as she brushed herself off, anything to avoid Morgan's eyes. "I'm fine."

"Are you sure? Because you don't seem—"

"I am, okay? And even if I wasn't, it's not your business," she snapped, and then instantly regretted it when she saw Morgan's face fall.

"Okay, I guess I'll go, then." She turned to leave.

Rhea sighed. "Wait, I'm sorry. That was uncalled for. Thank you for checking on me. This place just gets to me, you know?"

Morgan turned back to face Rhea, but she didn't meet her eyes. She was looking past her, towards the lake. "Yeah, believe me. I get it. Do you mind telling me what all that was about?"

Rhea shook her head. "Honestly, I barely know myself. It's like trying to remember the details of a nightmare from years ago. Being back here is dredging up some memories, I think. It's weird, though. I remember the feelings more than the details. Does that make sense?"

Morgan nodded, her eyes not leaving the lake. "Yeah, I know what you mean," she said distractedly. Rhea followed her gaze to the water, but didn't see anything. Morgan's eyes snapped back to Rhea's, and she smiled again. "How about we get inside before Andy finishes all the leftover sweets himself."

Rhea knew that kind of smile. It was the one she'd paint on her face while working as a cashier or in customer service. It was far too friendly, far too bright, and far too fake. Morgan was clearly hiding something. Was she that hurt by Rhea's outburst? Maybe she just thought Rhea was weird and was just trying to escape the conversation as quickly as possible. Then, Morgan turned and headed back to the house, glancing once over her shoulder to see if Rhea was coming. No, she was looking past Rhea—at the lake. It was the only thing directly behind her. She seemed to watch it like a prey animal terrified to turn its back on a predator.

And then the obvious answer hit her. Morgan found Bert in the lake. Of course, she wouldn't be comfortable returning to the place where she found a dead body.

God, she felt like an asshole.

Compounding her assholery, she spent the rest of the day avoiding the people in the house and shut up in Bert's office going through the papers in their filing cabinet. Bert and Astrid were the types of people to save every grocery receipt and tax return they had on paper. They were also the types to throw them into random piles and folders, making it difficult to sort the important papers from the chaff. Even better, she found notes saying that paperwork on their inherited stocks and bonds, as well as the deed to the house, were upstairs in the attic, among other apparently important documents.

She groaned. Of all the places in the house—the chapel where she kneeled until her knees bruised, the guest bedroom that was always freezing no matter how warm the rest of the house was, the library where she had to sit still and silent while Astrid held her book club—she hated the attic the most. The day had been too long for her to even think about going up, so she decided to brave it in the light of the next day.

Dinner was leftovers from the funeral. She served herself some of the lobster bisque, sopping up the soup with some bread. It had gone a little chewy already, but she didn't mind. It tasted as deliciously as it did yesterday. Rhea listened without contributing as Morgan and Andy debated the best Star Trek Captain—Morgan liked Picard and Andy preferred Sisko—and which Bachelorette contestant should get the rose.

"Obviously, it should be Michael," Morgan said, "He actually listens to Caroline and respects her, unlike Joe."

"I'm just saying that Michael looks like a toe," Andy retorted, "Rhea, what do you think?"

Rhea froze, her spoon halfway to her mouth. "I—I don't watch the Bachelorette?"

Andy gasped in mock horror. "Morgan, you will have to rectify that. I need her to agree with me that Michael looks like a toe and Caroline should go for Joe."

"Rhea is a sensible young woman of good taste. Obviously, she'll go for Michael."

"I think I'll reserve judgement until I see it," she said, taking a sip of her water. She was way too gay for the Bachelorette, but it could be fun, depending on how seriously Morgan takes the drama.

"It's fascinating observing the straights in an enclosed habitat," Andy said, "like animals in a zoo."

Rhea choked on her stew.

Did he...know?

It's not like she hid it, with her close-cropped hair and more masculine clothing, but it was still disconcerting.

Morgan smacked his arm. "Andy!"

"Come on, Rhea seems cool. We can finally be open."

We. We can finally be open. She glanced over at Morgan. When their eyes met, Morgan gave a faint nod as though sensing Rhea's unspoken question. She was queer like Rhea and, apparently, Andy. The realization made her heart flutter just a little. Then, the irony hit.

Rhea couldn't help her maniacal laugh. All the hell they put her through over Eliza, and Bert and Astrid accidentally hire an entirely queer workforce. It wasn't a pleasant laugh.

It was heavy, harsh, and hurt her sides so much she doubled over. Tears welled up in the corner of her eyes. She took a gasping, hiccupping breath. When she was finally in control of herself, she took in the confused and concerned faces of Morgan and Andy and felt a hot wave of embarrassment. Jesus, she must look crazy, and that sent her into another giggling fit.

"Rhea?" Morgan asked, "You okay there?"

She wiped her eyes. "Yeah."

"You wanna talk about it?"

"No." She shoveled bisque into her mouth, working to finish it with a renewed vigor. *Look at that. You've gone and made things awkward,* she imagined Astrid saying to her. *No wonder you don't have any friends.* She finished before the other two and leapt to her feet to load the bowl into the dishwasher. "It's pretty empty, so you can just load it, and I'll run it tomorrow."

"Are these dishwasher safe?" Andy asked, lifting the bowl to check underneath.

Rhea shrugged. "Does it matter?"

"I guess one wash couldn't hurt it."

Rhea gave an exaggerated yawn. "Anyway, I'm off to bed. Thank you for your hard work today, and I'll see you tomorrow."

She lingered for just a moment outside the door to get her breathing under control.

"That was...weird, right?" Andy said.

"A bit, yeah. You think she's okay?"

"No," Andy said bluntly.

"I guess I wouldn't be either. God, imagine being raised by them. I hate to speak ill of the dead, but..."

"Are you going to tell her?"

"I don't know," Morgan replied, "But before I do, I have to be absolutely sure."

"She has a right to know."

"Look, can we change the subject?"

"I really think...okay fine. But this isn't over."

Rhea forced herself to walk away, ignoring the guilt over eavesdropping. What did they know that she didn't? At first, she believed they were nice to her out of pity. The poor little orphan with a childhood that made Jane Eyre's look like *Leave it to Beaver*. She was fine, really. In desperate need of therapy but did okay for herself all things considered.

But now, she saw a new potential reason for their niceness. They had a secret, something they didn't want her to know about. She swallowed the lump in her throat. For a moment, she thought they might have actually wanted to be her friend, but no. An ulterior motive made more sense.

She heard the way they sniped at each other like siblings. It was hard to believe that they'd only really known each other a couple years. She supposed that spending a lot of time in a place where there's only one other person your age will bring you closer together. Still, she couldn't help her jealousy watching the familiar way they bantered compared to how they spoke to her. She was a stranger to them, a prodigal daughter they'd known for only a day.

Of course, they don't actually care about you, Astrid's voice said so clearly that it sounded like it was coming from outside of her head. *Why would they?*

All her life, there had been an invisible wall between her and other people. She could see them interacting, watch their close friendships form, but could never reach through it and form her own friendship. Even with Eliza, she was painfully aware of the difference between them. Eliza was popular. She had a lot of friends to confide in and keep their secrets in turn. She had Friday night sleepovers, gossip about who liked who, and a long phone contact list of people she texted every day. Rhea just had Eliza. And when Eliza shut the door, she had no one.

After a while, she simply figured that she was not built for close relationships. She was meant to watch from the outside, viewing the tableau of lovers in the park or college students laughing among themselves in the library with the dull ache of longing in her chest.

A part of her wanted to give them the benefit of the doubt. Maybe it wasn't as bad as she thought. Maybe they did like her.

What's there to like?

CHAPTER NINE

Rhea closed her eyes, counting her breathing as she stared up at the bed's canopy. Heavy footfalls paced above her. And then the sound of a little girl crying. After years of living in this house you'd think she'd get used to the nightly replay of the house's memories. She told herself that they couldn't hurt her, that they were just recordings, but a quiet voice in the back of her mind whispered, *liar*.

Well, she wasn't getting any sleep tonight. She swung her legs out of bed and padded downstairs to the kitchen. Hot cocoa and late-night television might be just what she needed to entice Mr. Sandman to her. Falling into old habits, she kept the light off as she hunted for a mug and Swiss Miss.

She was just getting the milk from the fridge as a familiar voice behind her shouted, "Put your hands up, and don't move."

"Which is it?" she asked, "Put my hands up, or don't move?" Her snark was a gamble, but even if Morgan was hiding something from her, she still probably didn't want to kill her, even if it looked like an accident. More than anything, though, she couldn't let on that she knew they were hiding something.

She had to smile and joke like she didn't know a thing.

"Jesus, Rhea!" Morgan flicked on the light, revealing one of Bert's revolutionary era muskets in her arms. Her eyes were wide and her hands shaking, but Rhea had to suppress a laugh. Perhaps it was the late hour or the lack of sleep, but there was something comical about her choice in weapon. Was Morgan about to join George Washington's army?

Morgan lowered the gun. "I could've shot you."

Rhea arched an eyebrow. "With one of those? I doubt you could even load it. Of all the weapons in his arsenal, you had to pick the least efficient."

"Well, it's not like I actually wanted to shoot someone. Just wanted to scare them off." She leaned the unloaded gun against the wall and sat down at the kitchen table, holding her head in her hands.

"Hot cocoa?" Rhea asked, holding up the jug of milk.

"Sure."

She poured a mug for Morgan and herself, covered them in a paper towel and set them in the microwave. "So, what are you doing up?"

"I could ask you the same thing. Why were you in here with the lights off?"

"Force of habit," she replied with a shrug.

"Scared the hell out of me. I thought someone broke in."

"And your plan was to threaten them with an antique musket?" she asked, grabbing the whipped cream from the fridge. Throwing her head back, she opened her mouth wide and sprayed some in her mouth.

Morgan nodded to the clock. "Best I could come up with at two a.m. And you didn't answer my question."

"Well, you didn't answer mine." The microwave beeped. Rhea took out the mugs and added the cocoa powder. "Whipped cream?"

"Sure."

Rhea added a nice layer to both and sat down across from her, studying her. Morgan was lying to her. She knew that much. But was that why she was up at this ungodly hour? Was she losing sleep over it? Or was it just the house in general keeping her awake? How terrible was this secret?

Morgan cradled the cocoa in her hands, studying the gentle swirl of the whipped cream. "You remember the footsteps you heard earlier today? Tonight, I heard them too. I thought it was you at first, but the tread was too heavy. So, I thought it was an intruder."

"But it wasn't."

She absently rubbed the *agimat* pendant around her neck. "Apparently not. This might sound weird to say, but ever since you came back, the house feels more awake. Like, before, it was mostly quiet, but now, I don't know. It feels off. Does that make sense?"

Rhea took a sip of her hot cocoa. Was this the secret they were keeping from her? She desperately hoped so, because it wasn't nearly as sinister as she first thought. "I guess so. Nothing like fresh blood to wake the whole system up."

"And that doesn't scare you?"

She shrugged, taking another sip of her cocoa. "Is it terrible to say that I'm used to it? As a kid, there was this woman who would sit at the end of my bed. The only way for her to disappear was to sleep with the lights on. So, I did it. For a month. And then Bert got mad at me about the electricity bill and threatened to make me sleep outside if I slept with the lights on again. She sat at the edge of the bed for years. Never touching me. Never speaking. Just smiling down at me like a proud mother."

"That's terrifying."

Rhea shrugged. "Would you believe me if I told you that she wasn't the worst ghost I've had to live with?"

"Like I said, I've seen some things," Morgan replied, sipping her drink. "Nothing as vivid as that. Like, there was this one time I heard Astrid calling my name, but I couldn't find her. I searched everywhere while her shouting just kept getting louder and louder. Eventually, I went into the master bedroom and found her fast asleep. She said she'd never yelled for me."

"You sure she wasn't playing mind games?" Astrid loved her little games. She was usually direct, but when she wanted to, she'd try to convince Rhea that the sky wasn't blue, fossils were a test of faith by God, or that the moon landing was faked. Not because she believed in it, but because she was a spider that enjoyed watching flies get entangled in her web.

When she was ten, she once proudly announced to Astrid's friends that the earth was hollow and full of dinosaurs. Astrid laughed as though she hadn't spent an hour teaching her about the Hollow Earth theory, and, as her friends followed suit in a taunting chorus, she said, "I've been having her read Jules Verne. She's still at an age where she can't quite tell fiction from reality."

"But you said—"

Astrid gave her a sharp look. "That *Journey to the Center of the Earth* would be fantastic as our next book! What do the rest of you say?"

"Sounds wonderful," Mrs. Waters said. The other three old ladies echoed their agreement.

Unshed tears stinging in her eyes, Rhea got to her feet and left.

"Such a strange child," she heard Mrs. Waters say as she left the library, "I don't know how you put up with her."

"I don't think so," Morgan said, bringing Rhea back to the present. "At that point, she was the worst liar. Once I caught her sneaking a candy bar, and she just hid it behind her back like I couldn't see the chocolate on her face."

It was difficult to imagine prim and proper Astrid stooping to sneaking a candy bar and then lying about it like a toddler caught with their hand in the cookie jar. Rhea took contemplative sip of her cocoa, savoring the warmth and sweetness, and yawned wide enough that her jaw cracked. "What did Andy think?"

"That she was lying. Or she forgot why she called me and was too embarrassed to admit it."

"Well, did she lash out at you when you asked her?" Rhea asked.

Morgan shook her head. "Not at all. She just seemed confused that I brought it up."

"You'd know if she was embarrassed. Best case scenario, she's turn it around and verbally eviscerate you, reminding you of your every failing and how this whole thing is your fault, actually, not hers."

Morgan's eyes brightened as she smiled, clearly vindicated. "I love him, but he just doesn't get what it's like here, especially at night. He thinks it can all be explained by the wind or infrasound or a trick of the light. It can't, though, not all of it. And I feel like I can't talk to him about it, and—" Morgan laughed, studying her cup. "Sorry. Probably shouldn't be dumping all this on you."

Rhea raised her glass. "Hey, that what being awake at two a.m. is for. Hot chocolate and oversharing."

"So do you have anything you want to overshare? How are you, really?"

"That's really more of a third date question," she replied with a wink. "Short answer: it's complicated. The long answer is reserved for when I finally get a therapist."

"Fair enough," Morgan said with a chuckle, but then she became serious, "Just do me a favor and stay away from the lake? Keep Andy away too."

"Why?"

"There's something...bad there," she said, studying her mug, "I don't know. Just be careful, okay? I don't want you to add to your future therapist's workload."

"Like ghost bad?"

Morgan shrugged, still not meeting Rhea's eyes. "Honestly, I'm not sure. Whatever it is, it's not like whatever's in the house. I think it's dangerous."

"Noted." She yawned again. "Well, I think I've had enough of ghosts for tonight. You wanna watch bad reality TV with me?"

Morgan drained the last of her mug. "I think the newest episode of The Bachelorette is still on the DVR. You need to be the tie-breaker in the epic battle between Joe and Michael."

"I still reserve my judgement until I've seen all the contestants."

CHAPTER TEN

The television was a massive flat screen that seemed incongruous with the museum-like state of the rest of the house. For most of her childhood, her grandparents had one of those heavy television sets made in the 90's. After lasting nearly fifteen years, it died permanently, and her grandparents replaced it with this monstrosity. After all, Bert was a huge football fan, and, in his words, wanted a TV with a high enough quality that you could see the pimples on the asses of the players.

When Rhea agreed to watch an episode, she didn't realize that they were an hour and a half long. An hour and a half of people going back and forth asking for "clarity" and the bachelorette telling the contestants to "speak from the heart." It was enough to put Rhea to sleep, but Morgan had sat on the couch next to her and drifted off after a few minutes, which wouldn't have been a problem, except that, in her sleep, Morgan had slumped onto Rhea's shoulder.

She sat frozen, unable to focus on the most heterosexual polyamory ever put to screen as the blonde bachelorette went on a date with a guy whose name she couldn't remember while trying not to think about the last time she'd experienced casual affection like this. Instead, she studied Morgan's face—her round cheeks, the soft curve of her nose and lips, the dark hair falling around her like a veil. Small snores occasionally interrupted her gentle breathing, and underneath the panic over this show of trust, Rhea found it all incredibly endearing. Sure, Morgan hugged her, and people shook her hand at the funeral, but that was all impersonal. She was stuck between fleeing the comfort and savoring it while she could.

Her grandparents weren't the touchy-feely type. Hugs were rare enough to be an endangered species. She kept to herself during her time away, hurting too much to accept the rare overtures of friendship her coworkers extended. The only person to have been physically affectionate had been Eliza. Her lips still tingled at the memory of their first kiss.

It was an autumn day, and they were seated on a picnic blanket under the willow nibbling on chips and cookies. Eliza rested her head on Rhea's shoulder as she finished telling a story about a party she'd gone to after homecoming and how she narrowly escaped the cops after a neighbor lodged a noise complaint.

"I wish you could have been there," Eliza said, wiping a mirthful tear from her face.

"Me too." Rhea fished cookie from their bag. "It sounded like fun."

"Maybe you could be my prom date," she said, "I can get special permission for someone outside of school."

Rhea froze, the cookie halfway to her mouth. "I don't know. Grandma Astrid says prom is where all the teenage sluts go to lose their virginity and get pregnant. Maybe if we ask Grandpa Bert first."

"Somehow I doubt the second thing is gonna happen between us," Eliza said, running a finger down Rhea's chest.

She choked on air, her face turning beet red. Eliza patted her on the back. This was a game Rhea had noticed Eliza liked to play. How easily can she get the sheltered girl to blush? The answer was very easily, but she still seemed to like playing it. Rhea's least favorite was when she described various sex acts using terms that sounded like something from Looney Tunes (the Dutch rudder had to be a joke, right?) or used obscure street names for drugs. And then, she laughed when Rhea didn't know what they were. Those smiles had a little more of a condescending edge, like she was laughing at her instead of with her. But this suggestion made Rhea blush for reasons other than embarrassment. "I might find a hot guy to impregnate me," she said with mock indignance.

"Sure, you will," Eliza said soothingly before they both dissolved into a fit of giggles. "Seriously though." She sat up, her face mere inches from Rhea's. "Imagine you and me slow dancing to whatever cheesy pop song they're playing. You in a ballgown, me in a pantsuit—"

"Why do I have to be in the gown?" she asked, not moving closer, but also not pulling away.

Eliza rolled her eyes. "Fine, we'll both be in a pantsuit. Anyway, it gets near the end of the song, and we're dancing real slow. The disco ball glitters like a thousand stars, and we lean in closer and closer, until..." She planted a kiss on Rhea's lips.

Rhea leapt back as though she'd been burned, bumping her head against the tree. Sure, she'd had a crush, a stupid schoolgirl crush, but she didn't expect it to be reciprocated. There was no way this was real. Eliza was the girl who football players and class presidents fawned over. She didn't need Rhea.

Eliza's eyes widened and she recoiled too. "I—I'm sorry. I completely misread things. I should go." She stood to leave, but Rhea caught her wrist.

"Wait. Please." She pulled Eliza down into a kiss, threading her fingers through her blonde hair like she'd fantasized about for the past several months.

It was Eliza that pulled away to ask, "Is this okay?"

Rhea's head spun. Eliza reciprocated her feelings. It wasn't a prank or her imagination. Instead of answering, she pulled her into another kiss.

In the years after, she cherished that memory through cold winters and empty bellies. Her and Eliza carving out a sanctuary underneath the willow by the lake. A willow that Morgan wants her to stay away from for some nebulous reason. Morgan had secrets, that much was obvious. How many of them were Rhea's business was another question entirely. Andy said she had a right to know...something.

Rhea's trust was something closely guarded. Like a skittish animal, it was slowly given and easily lost. A part of her wanted to trust Morgan and Andy. They seemed so nice, and she longed for their easy back and forth, but it was all just too easy.

What, after just over a day, she thought they'd all suddenly become friends? *Ridiculous*. They were obviously hiding something, but what? Her first thought was that they killed her grandparents, but no, as much as she wouldn't blame them for it, she didn't think they were capable of murder. Stealing, then. Honestly, if they had been lifting the occasional valuable, she likely wouldn't have noticed. It wasn't like she had an inventory of every single silver spoon and gold earring. Besides, Morgan said that she needed to be certain of something before she told her. She doubted that Morgan just wanted to know if she was okay with stealing.

Maybe the secret wasn't something that they had done. Maybe it was something her grandparents said.

Abruptly, the television shut off. The sudden silence sucked the air from the room like a vacuum. Rhea stiffened, wondering if one of them sat on the remote, but no, it was sitting right in front of her on the coffee table. Every instinct told her to run, but she instead sat frozen, torn between staying still or fleeing and disturbing Morgan. Then, in the dark reflection of the television set, Rhea saw her. Her hair was still lank and greasy, her cheekbones jutting at sharp angles, and her stomach bulging from her emaciated body. She stood behind the couch, her bony arms braced against it as though it was the only thing holding her up. And that familiar rotten toothed smile was still spread wide in a rictus grin.

Frozen, her heart pounding, Rhea watched as the figure bent down with an aching slowness and with putrid breath and a rasping voice, whispered in her ear, "I missed you, Annie."

Rhea screamed and leapt to her feet, turning around and finding nothing. Morgan was alert in an instant, sitting up and asking, "What's wrong?"

She barely heard her over the buzzing in her own mind. That nickname brought with it the suddenly onslaught of a memory divorced from context. She was young, lying on the floor with her stomach burning, shaking uncontrollably and so very afraid. In the present, she doubled over, falling back on the couch as though the pain was back again.

It took her a moment to realize that Morgan was kneeling in front of her, her eyes wide and terrified. "Rhea, Rhea talk to me," she pleaded, "tell me what's wrong."

She forced a breath in...two three...out...two...three... The phantom pain in her stomach subsided as she focused on the scratchy upholstery of the couch and the warmth of Morgan's hands on her knees. The tactile sensations grounded her, reminded her of what was real and what was...well, she wasn't quite sure. Even if it felt real, it could just as easily have been all in her head.

Finally able to meet Morgan's worried eyes, Rhea chuckled weakly. "You okay there? You look like you've seen a ghost."

Morgan groaned, putting her head in her hands. "Care to share with the class what just happened?"

Rhea forced herself to shrug nonchalantly, certainly not fooling Morgan in the slightest. "I saw another ghost."

"And...?"

She stared at her still trembling hands. "I don't know. I just had this visceral flashback to something I can't remember now."

"Are you...okay?"

"Define okay," she sighed, suddenly exhausted beyond words. What did Morgan want from her? Why did she keep up this act? "I'm alive and in one piece. So, you know, just dandy."

Morgan took her hand and squeezed. "Rhea, seriously."

"Why do you care?"

Morgan looked up at her, confused. "What?"

She reclaimed her hand, pretending she didn't miss the comfort. "I don't know what you want from me. You're being weirdly nice and have this secret that apparently, I have the right to know, and I just don't know what you want."

Morgan stood up. There was an angry glint in her eyes. Good. Now Rhea would get to see the real Morgan. "Is it so hard to believe that I'm worried about the person whose had at least three panic attack right in front of me in the past two days?"

"Yes!" she replied, leaping to her feet.

Morgan stepped back, the simmering anger turning to pity. "Rhea..." Her voice was too soft, too gentle. It was the voice tutors used when she talked about her parents, and Eliza used when Rhea was panicking over something small and stupid like failing a quiz or getting a run in the tights her grandmother forced her to wear.

"It's almost morning, and I haven't slept at all," Rhea said, pushing past her. She didn't look back.

CHAPTER ELEVEN

If her head was under the covers, the Smiling Lady couldn't see her. Seven-year-old Rhea could feel her sitting at the bottom of the bed and waiting patiently for her to poke her head out. But she wouldn't, because the covers were safe and warm, and she had Otso. Grandpa Bert yelled at her that she was wasting their money, but the light was the only thing that kept the lady away. To make sure she'd stopped, he had been patrolling the halls once or twice a night. At least, she thought it was him. She never saw him, but who else could those footsteps belong to? And even if it was something else, Grandpa Bert scared her more than anything walking the halls or the woman who sat at the end of the bed, so she kept them off.

But then, she heard singing. It was muffled by the window, but the tune was unmistakable. *"Meet me by the willow, where the elder flowers bloom"*

The Smiling Lady forgotten, she bolted upright and ran to the window. There, standing on the water amid the white flowers was a woman. It was too dark to see under the cover of the new moon, but she was absolutely certain it was her mother.

As quietly as she could, she snuck down the stairs. One step, the fifth from the bottom, creaked, and she froze, her heart pounding in her ears. When she didn't hear her grandparents stirring, she bolted the rest of the way and out the door. The woman's silhouette stood by the willow tree. With an exclamation of "Mommy!" she sprinted to the tree in her bare feet. The night was cold and cloudy. No matter how close she got, the image of her mother standing at the edge of the lake remained indistinct, like Rhea was viewing it from underwater. With the willow so painfully close, she stumbled. When she righted herself, her mother was gone.

"No, no, no, no, no," she sobbed, falling to the ground in the shelter of the willow tree and curling in on herself, "Mommy, come back, please. I'll be good. I promise I'll be good. Please come back."

"Close your eyes," her mother whispered in her ear, "and keep them closed or I'll have to disappear again."

Her dad liked to tell her stories. Old myths about gods and monsters. She knew them as though they'd been tattooed on her heart. Psyche looked upon Eros and had to do impossible tasks to prove her worthiness. Orpheus doubted and gazed upon Eurydice, sending her back to the underworld. Pandora opened the box and unleashed all of earth's suffering. It was tempting to open her eyes and see the face that was already fading too soon from memory, but if she did, she might never see her mother again. Or worse, she would see her mother as she was in the grave when they buried her—cold and unmoving like a mannequin. "They're closed, mommy."

She felt a slick, cold hand run its pruned fingers through her hair and tried to imagine them warm and dry. Her mother hummed her lullaby as she caressed her.

"I missed you." Her eyelids were heavy as she drifted off.

"I missed you too, serduszko," her mother said as Rhea drifted off to sleep. It was strange, she thought, because that was never a name her mother called her. The next morning, she woke in her own bed, unsure if the night before was just a dream.

Rhea skipped breakfast and holed herself up in her grandfather's office. She would have to face Morgan and Andy eventually but hoped to put it off as long as she could. The look on Morgan's face last night kept popping up in her head. The hurt and the pity. Was she telling Andy about it now? The crazy boss who eavesdropped and then flipped out on her?

She took down the stag she helped murder with a little more force than necessary and punched the combination into the safe—1650, the year the Ballard's first settled the land. Birth certificates—not important. Social security cards—maybe important. Recent stock purchases—definitely important. She set those items aside for Mr. Ellis.

Staring at the tall stack of papers she still needed to sort made her feel as though she had embarked upon one of the twelve labors of Hercules. Honestly, she preferred the idea of fighting the hydra or cleaning out the dung-filled stable belonging to herd of man-eating horses over sorting through all this. While she was debating whether or not Mr. Ellis would want a tax return from three years ago, the paper tower finally lost its battle with gravity and collapsed.

"Damn it." She didn't have the energy to stack everything again, so she just pushed the papers away from the piles of importance she had been building. One envelope had flown further than most, landing in the *very important* pile.

She picked it up off the floor and carefully opened the delicate paper. It was at least a hundred years old, and unfolding the ancient paper revealed a messy scrawl. She squinted, struggling to make out the words.

Dear Mother and Father,

You threaten to cut me off. Remember that I know everything. It would be rather embarrassing if word spread.

-M

A knock at the door. "Rhea?" Morgan called from the other side, "Can I come in?"

Well, best to get it over with. "Yeah, come in."

Morgan lingered in the doorway, staring at the piles of papers strewn about on the floor. "Hey, so about last night..."

Rhea cut her off. "I owe you another apology. So, I'm sorry. I shouldn't have reacted that way." Though this apology was sincere—she shouldn't have snapped like that—she also wanted to demand answers to whatever terrible secret Morgan kept. Sweet, saintly Morgan, who gave up her dreams of owning a restaurant to take care of two old bastards and made all the food for their funeral. Beatific Morgan who was kind and gentle to people she'd just met, going far beyond what's required of her. What dark secret was she hiding?

Unfortunately, the only way to get answers was to stay on her good side.

Morgan was silent, staring at her with wide, sad eyes. Pity, again. Of course. "Would you like to go to the grocery store with me?" she blurted out.

Rhea blinked. "What?"

"It's not healthy to be cooped up in the house all day, especially this house. So, I had the thought that we'd try to get out once a day. Shake off the cobwebs and leave the ghosts to rest. I'm going shopping this afternoon if you want to come with." The words came out in a rush, almost too fast to process.

"I, uh, okay sure. I'll go shopping with you." Rhea sighed, rubbing her already tired eyes. This wasn't where she expected the conversation to go, but at least Morgan wasn't angry at her for her outburst the previous night. Even if she was, the idea of leaving this dust covered tomb was too appealing to pass on.

"And—and for what it's worth, I'm sorry too. I could have reacted better. And I don't think I actually apologized for pointing a gun at you. So, sorry about that too."

Rhea laughed. "Right, because I was definitely in danger of death by antique musket." She returned to the seemingly endless pile of papers she needed to sort. "Let me know when you're heading out."

Cherub's Cove was exactly as she remembered it. It was the kind of idyllic New England seaside town that would attract tourists in the summer for its beaches, seafood, and charm, and bring them in during the fall for the foliage, only to be completely dead come winter. All the buildings had been painted in pastel colors, with gingerbread architecture adding to the postcard-like feel. To top it all off, the town had a motif of angels. There were statues, murals, and reliefs dotted throughout, ostensibly to add to the town's charm. That is, as long as you didn't look too closely at the weathered edges, the spots where paint cracked or had been sun bleached, places where mold gathered along the foundations, or the air of desperation found behind the smile of every souvenir shopkeeper trying to move their wares before business died during the winter months. It wasn't particularly surprising to Rhea that the town was interested in turning the Ballard House into a museum. It would be yet another draw for tourists to come in and spend their money. She shuddered to think what revisionist stories they would tell about how wonderful her family was.

While they shopped, Rhea's mind wandered back to their conversation in the study. It occurred to her as they stood in the produce section that Morgan had successfully deflected answering the question of her dark secret. She watched as Morgan studied the bell peppers, weighing the merits of red, yellow, and green. "So, red bell peppers are just greens that haven't fully ripened. I prefer red to green because they're sweet, but if you don't, let me know. Also, how do you feel about spicy food?"

The question interrupted her musings on Morgan's secret. "I, uh, don't have a pepper preference. And I'm willing to try spicy food if you're making it."

Morgan threw back her head. "Oh, thank god. You know Bert's favorite comfort food? Boiled chicken, no vegetables, no seasoning. I just about died every time I served it to him."

Rhea rolled her eyes. Plain boiled chicken was a meal she'd been subjected to more times than she could count. "Veggies were for hippies and spices for those who don't know how to cook meat. It's a wonder I didn't grow up with scurvy."

"Thank heavens for Astrid's more refined palate." She put a couple red bell peppers in a plastic bag and moved onto the lettuce.

As Rhea followed, the hairs on the back of her neck prickled. It was the all-too familiar sensation of being watched. Between her grandparents and the ghosts, it had been ever-present as a child. After she escaped, it was an early warning sign before creepy customers decided they wanted to get handsy, or on a few memorable occasions, try to follow her home. Needless to say, she'd made a habit of following this particular instinct.

She leaned against the wall and scanned the people milling about. There, behind the apple display, an older woman glared at the two of them. She looked to be in her sixties, with greying hair and a careworn face. Rhea surreptitiously nudged Morgan and leaned in, asking, "Who's that woman over there?"

Morgan turned around and paled, swallowing nervously. "Nobody. I think I have enough produce. Let's get some meats. How do you feel about chicken parmesan tonight?"

Rhea shrugged, not keeping her eyes off the woman. "It sounds good."

In the meat and poultry section, Morgan compared sell by dates of chicken breasts while Rhea studied the lobsters in the tank. As a child, this was her favorite place to visit. She'd watch the lobsters crawl over each other while her mother shopped. On her first shopping trip with her grandmother, she was so excited that Grandma Astrid had bought a couple, thinking they were their new pets. When she came down for dinner and saw one on her plate, boiled alive, she sobbed until they sent her to her room without dinner.

Rhea shook her head, banishing the memory and turning to Morgan. "Hey, so I was wondering...I can't really cook, but I feel bad having you do all the cooking. Do you think you could teach me how to make something more complex than cup ramen?"

Morgan laughed. "For the record, I like cooking. It's why I, you know, went to culinary school? I prefer that to cleaning or sitting on my ass all day. But yeah, I can teach you if you want."

"Right," Rhea replied, studying the turkey bacon as though it was the most interesting thing in the world, "thanks." She felt a hand on her arm and looked up.

"I think it'll be fun," she said. "After all, you're learning from the master."

"You have some nerve," said a voice from behind. Both women whirled around to see the older woman from before standing with her arms crossed.

Morgan deflated. "Hi, Mrs. West."

Mrs. West...she was vaguely familiar. Rhea had seen her at a few of Astrid's book club meetings, sitting in the back and occasionally complaining about the selections. And yet she kept coming back. She was president of the yacht club and the PTA, and loved to brag about her genius, star athlete son Joshua. According to Eliza, who ran in the circles that he did, her son was a shambling pile of relationship red flags. He was a bit of a player but also known to be possessive and jealous. His all-American good looks and charm was mostly what kept him popular and out of trouble.

"Is that all you have to say?" Mrs. West scoffed. "Typical. I'm surprised you didn't skip town after the last of the Ballard's died, God rest their souls. Unless their deaths weren't old age after all."

Rhea stepped in between them and held out her hand. She'd straightened herself to her full, above slightly average height, and looked down her nose like she'd seen Astrid do her whole life. "Hi there, I'm Rhea Ballard, their granddaughter, still alive and kicking, and I'd like to know why you're harassing my frie--employee."

Her eyes widened in surprise. "Rhea? I almost didn't recognize you with the short hair. Not a lot of women can pull it off, but it looks good." She laughed, though there was a tinge of awkwardness to it. "You know, I always wondered what happened to you. Bert and Astrid were always so cagey about where you went."

Rhea shrugged, refusing to soften her glare. "I was a huge disappointment to them. Never made anything of myself. Pretty embarrassing. Anyway, why are you harassing my employee?"

"She killed my son."

Rhea's heart stuttered. *No. No way.*

In her drifting, she'd spent time around convicts and murderers. Her coworker at the gas station had once accidentally killed a man in anger many years ago. He was an older guy, and he had this edge, this underlying rage in him that she recognized in herself. And in those quiet moments eating day old donuts that she'd squirreled away before they could be tossed, he had this haunted look in his eyes. She knew where he really was in those times. Morgan did not have his anger or that haunted look. So, either she was a cold-blooded killer, or she was innocent.

"I didn't! He was—" Morgan took a deep breath and slowly exhaled. "I didn't kill your son. And I was telling the truth about him. I know it must be difficult to think of your child as anything less than innocent, but I didn't lie."

"You should be in prison," Mrs. West spat, jamming a finger in Morgan's face.

"Hey," Rhea snapped, "Mrs. West, right? I don't really know what this is about, but Morgan said she didn't do it, and I would really appreciate it if you let us be."

The scowl didn't leave Mrs. West's face as she stepped closer to Rhea. "Keep your eye on her. She may have the face of an angel, but she's a lying whore."

Rhea matched it with a steely gaze of her own. "I won't ask you again. Stop harassing my employee." Heart racing, Rhea grabbed the chicken, plopped it in the cart, and linked arms with Morgan. "Come on, I'm suddenly craving ice cream from the opposite end of the store." But as she walked off, guilt curdled in her stomach. Rhea may not like this woman, but she was still a grieving mother. Letting out a slow breath, she paused and turned around. "Mrs. West, I am so sorry for your loss, but we really have to go." She didn't wait for Mrs. West to respond.

Once they were out of earshot, Morgan muttered, "Thanks."

She unlinked their arms and squeezed her fists shut to stop them from shaking as the lingering adrenaline left her system. Confrontation like that always terrified her. "To be clear, you didn't actually kill him, did you?"

She stiffly shook her head, hugging her arms close to her chest. "He drowned. They ruled it a suicide. Mrs. West blames me for his death because we'd had issues in the past."

Rhea could tell by her body language that this was far from the whole story, but the way her friend made herself small and her eyes glistened, she couldn't bring herself to push, instead putting a hand on Morgan's shoulder. "I believe you."

The rest of the shopping was uneventful. Rhea retrieved a few items on the side of the store they had to flee while Morgan hunted down some comfort snacks. She was just starting to think that the rest of the trip would go off without another hitch when she heard a new voice in the cereal aisle.

"Miss Ballard?" She turned around to find a tall, black man with greying hair that she did not recognize at first glance.

"Yes?"

He held out a hand. "I'm Michael Harris, president of the historical society."

Oh, she knew where this was going. She shook his hand anyway. "To what do I owe the honor?"

"I'm very sorry for your loss. Your family has left an indelible mark on this town, your grandparents especially. I was wondering if you were interested in partnering with us to see that your family's legacy is preserved."

She did not expect the erupting anger in her chest. "Translation: you want me to donate it so that the house becomes a museum, and/or bed and breakfast."

"If that's how you feel we can best preserve it..."

"No, thanks."

What was she saying? She hated the house. Two days ago, she would have donated it in a heartbeat or have a demolition crew tear it down. This protective rage was new. It felt wrong, like she was a dragon whose hoard had been threatened. Maybe it was just leftover defensiveness from confronting Mrs. West. Yeah, that was probably it.

She shook her head and gave him her best fake smile. "I mean, I'll have to think about it. I'm still trying to get their financials in order for probate and it's kind of hard to think about the future."

Mr. Harris nodded. "Of course. I understand, and if you ever want to talk with me, my door is always open."

"Thanks." She grabbed a box of Count Chocula. "Anyway, it was nice talking to you, but I need to get back."

CHAPTER TWELVE

Rhea hefted the bags onto the counter, sorting what went into the fridge from what went into the pantry. Aside from confronting Mrs. West and Mr. Harris, it had been nice to get out and remind herself that there was a world outside of the Ballard House.

"So, I know this is more of a dinner thing, but how would you like to try your hand at chicken parmesan for lunch?" Morgan asked as she put the milk in the fridge. She had been quiet for most of the trip back, and Rhea didn't push. Seeing Mrs. West clearly rattled her, and no matter what secret she was keeping from Rhea, she didn't deserve to be treated like that. Now that they were away from the prying eyes of the public, though, Morgan seemed to be mostly back to her usual chipper self.

Rhea smiled. "Anything to put off going through even more papers." *And to put off going back into that attic,* though she wouldn't say that out loud. "If I see another tax return older than I am, I might just shove everything into an industrial paper shredder."

"I do not envy you," Morgan replied as she gathered the ingredients: olive oil, flour, breadcrumbs, egg, chicken, cheese, pasta, and tomato sauce. "So, this is a pretty simple recipe. Grab me a pan from beneath the stove?"

"Aye, aye, captain," Rhea said, pulling one from a cabinet and setting it on the stove. "And a pot for the pasta?"

Morgan grinned. "See? You're not hopeless."

"We've only just gotten started." She filled the pot with water and turned on the stove to let it get to a boil. "Plenty of time left for me to set something on fire."

"Luckily, we have an extinguisher for that. Andy was very insistent that I learn to use it." Morgan opened the packet of chicken and set them on a paper towel before rinsing her hands. "So, we got the thin sliced cutlets, making this easier. We don't have to hit them with a mallet. First, you pat them dry and then you dip them in flour. Music?"

"What kind?" Rhea asked as she patted the chicken dry. She had never gotten used to the texture of raw meat. Its sliminess made her skin crawl, especially when she thought about how easy it was to mishandle it and get sick.

"What do you like?" Morgan asked.

Admittedly, she wasn't entirely sure. Bert and Astrid hated any music made before the nineteen forties, so she mostly grew up around classical and hymns. Because she was supposed to grow into a well-rounded young lady, Astrid forced her to learn the piano and the violin. Rhea hated it, though, and purposefully forgot every scale and note she'd learned.

Eliza had introduced her to a couple boybands, and she liked them, but working in retail had killed most of her affection for pop music. Her father's Walkman and the Guns N Roses album inside only conjured mixed feelings of nostalgia and terror. Then, after she left, she never had much time or energy to explore different genres outside of whatever was playing around her. She didn't really know her own taste in music. But Morgan seemed like she would have good taste. "Dealer's choice."

Morgan grinned. "You may regret that. My music taste can be...eclectic."

"All the better to get to know you," she replied, dipping the first of the cutlets in flour.

"My personal playlist it is. I apologize in advance for whatever comes up when I hit shuffle." The first few notes of an electric guitar riffed as an opera singer sang about sirens from the deep emerging to drag sailors to their deaths.

"Who is this?" Rhea asked as she dipped another cutlet in flour.

"Sigrid Thorsdotter. She's a fantasy metal singer I discovered in my witchy goth phase."

"The one where you tried to cast a love spell over a classmate?" Rhea asked, suppressing a smile.

"I'm going to kill Andy for ever bringing that up." With the cutlets floured, Morgan brought over a bowl with an egg and a fork. "You know how to crack an egg, right?"

"Like you said, I'm not completely hopeless," Rhea replied with a smile to soften her tone, taking the egg and cracking it on the side of the bowl. "Now I stir it up?"

"Exactly. Then, we'll do a double coat of egg yolk and bread crumbs." The song ended and was replaced by a rock song from the eighties. It was oddly familiar, and she was hit with a sudden flash of memory. Her father drove as she sat in the back seat, taking her somewhere unimportant in the grand scheme of her memories. When this song came on the radio, he turned it up and they both sang along at the top of their lungs.

"I know this one. My dad liked it."

Morgan's smile turned melancholy. "Mine too. He was a musician and would play it for me on his guitar. Listening to it always makes me think of him."

Morgan had never mentioned her father before. At least, not that Rhea could remember. "Is he still...um...with you?" She winced at the awkwardness of her words, but Morgan didn't seem to care.

"He died in a car accident when I was thirteen," Morgan replied, turning her back to Rhea as she added pasta to the boiling water.

"I'm sorry." Rhea's chest squeezed as she searched for words to say.

Morgan shrugged, the smile becoming more forced. "It's okay. It happened a while ago."

Setting down the stirred eggs, she turned to face Morgan. "Believe me, I know better than most that the hurt doesn't stop. You just grow around it, like a tree absorbing a wire fence. It becomes embedded in you until the only way you can get it out is to destroy yourself. But still, you live, and you grow bigger and stronger than the pain."

The smile never left Morgan's face, but tears glistened in her eyes as she switched it to the next song, an upbeat pop anthem about partying the night away. "Ooh, I love this one!"

As Rhea coated the chicken in the egg and breadcrumbs and laid them out in the pan, the song went from pop to a Broadway musical showtune. "Where's this from?" she asked, and listened as Morgan recounted the plot of *Wicked*, a book that Rhea had been banned from reading as a child.

"Have you ever seen it on stage?" she asked once Morgan was done, and the playlist had moved on to another pop song.

"No, but it's on my bucket list. NYU had pretty good student discounts for Broadway shows, but I never got the chance to go to one."

"Too busy?"

A strange expression crossed Morgan's face, somewhere between uncomfortable and melancholy. "Something like that." Shaking her head as though to dislodge some unpleasant thought, she smiled again. "So, once both sides are a golden brown, we'll transfer them to the pan and add the tomato sauce."

Rhea took the hint and turned her attention to the sizzling chicken. "It feels like I just put them in. How will I know it's cooked the whole way through?"

"It'll bake the rest of the way in the oven. Speaking of..." She set the temperature to 400. "We forgot this step."

Rhea worried her lip. She didn't want to screw up lunch and give them all food poisoning. "Will that be a problem?"

Morgan shook her head. "Nah. It should be warm enough by the time we've set everything up in the pan. Let's also start on the pasta in the meantime. Angel hair doesn't take very long to cook."

Rhea saluted again. "Yes ma'am."

Andy poked his head into the kitchen. "Smell's good! What'cha making?"

"Chicken parmesan," Morgan replied. "Rhea's cooking."

"Cooking lessons from the great Morgan Reyes?" Andy whistled. "You must be special. She refused to teach me anything."

Morgan rolled her eyes. "Because you insisted on learning my lola's secret adobo recipe."

"What's so bad about that?" Apparently deciding it was time for a break, Andy sauntered into the kitchen and sat at the table with a soft *oof*.

"It's a secret. Duh. My lola's most closely guarded secret. She would have rather been tortured than let it fall into the wrong hands. You're lucky I even made it for you."

"I bet you'd teach Rhea," he muttered, pouting like a disappointed child.

With the way that Rhea's own cheeks flushed at that, she almost missed Morgan's cheeks coloring slightly. It had to be her imagination, though. That, or Morgan was embarrassed by the insinuation. "Again. Secret recipe. Not for anyone outside of the family."

Andy sighed, resting his chin in his hand. "It's a shame that I'm not the marrying type then."

"A real shame," Morgan replied, rolling her eyes.

"Many have tried, and many have failed."

"So, are you, um..." Rhea didn't know how to word this part. He and Morgan already confirmed that they were queer like her, but she didn't know what terms they liked to use. "Gay?"

"That would make things a lot less complicated, wouldn't it? I'm nothing, basically. The words are asexual and aromantic, but it basically means that I don't want to be with anyone: male, female, or otherwise inclined." The last part sounded rather rote, like he had an entire speech prepared to justify his existence. Admittedly, Rhea wasn't familiar with the terms, but she was always eager to learn.

"I've never heard of that before. What's it like?" Rhea asked.

Andy looked slightly taken aback. He was probably used to people dismissing his label as not being real. She knew what that was like. "It's a bit like living without a sense of smell. Most of the time, you don't even notice that you don't have it, and you would be fine without it if everyone would stop spraying perfume in your face and telling you that you're missing out."

"Honestly, you're not missing much," Rhea replied, spooning the sauce on the last of the chicken and covering them all with cheese. After Eliza, she hadn't bothered dating anyone else. Why would she when she would inevitably get left behind again?

"Agreed," Morgan said. "It's way overhyped."

"If only everyone else shared your sentiments," Andy replied.

"I guess we'll all have to be anti-romance together then." Rhea shoved the chicken in the oven and set the timer.

"Oh, I don't know about that," Andy said, looking mischievously at Morgan. There was something going on there, but she couldn't parse what it was.

Rhea always hated that. It was like the world was operating by a secret list of rules and she was the only one who was never handed the rulebook.

The first time Rhea snuck out, it had been to meet up with Eliza and her friends. Eliza had drawn a map to her house, which sat on the other side of the state park adjacent to the Ballard House. She waited until she was certain that Bert and Astrid were asleep before sneaking down the steps, always skipping the fifth from the bottom. Then, she slipped out the ballroom door and began her trek, skirting around the lake to get to the woods. As soon as she was no longer in view of the eyes of the Ballard House, a strange sensation overcame her, like she had been sitting at the bottom of the ocean with the pressure crushing every square inch of her, and suddenly, she was now at the surface, free from the oppressive weight.

Eliza was waiting in her backyard, leaning against a tree and checking the time. When she saw Rhea, she grinned and pulled her into a hug. "I was afraid you wouldn't make it."

Rhea grinned back. "Wouldn't miss it for anything."

"Well, then let's go."

Rhea leaned in to kiss her, but Eliza pulled away. Something in her chest squeezed at that. "Sorry."

Her girlfriend shook her head. "No, I'm sorry. But we need to keep things quiet, okay? They don't know we're together like that."

Rhea thought that having friends meant that you could share things like that, but what would she know? Eliza was her first real friend since she was a child. "Just one for the road?"

Eliza smiled and pressed a quick kiss to her lips. "Now come on. We're running late already."

She followed Eliza out of the neighborhood and down to the beach. A group of about ten teenagers gathered around a campfire. The orange light illuminated a small radius of sand, not nearly enough for her to make out anything in the black waters of the ocean, but she could hear the gentle rumbling of the waves.

"Eliza!" a boy called, waving them over. "Thought you weren't gonna show."

"My stupid parents grounded me, so I had to wait 'til they were asleep," Eliza replied. She said it so casually, but Rhea's heart still stuttered. Eliza had been grounded? Was she okay? How did she escape? How dangerous was it for her to be here? Oblivious to Rhea's sudden wave of concern, Eliza nudged her forward. "Besides, I had to wait for Rhiannon Ballard.

And suddenly, all eyes were on her. She felt as though she'd been pushed center stage in the middle of a Broadway play on opening night without learning any of the lines. "Um, hi." She gave them an awkward wave.

"No fucking way," the boy said. "I thought you were lying when you said you knew Rhiannon Ballard." He studied Rhea like she was some kind of specimen in the lab.

"Why the hell would I lie about that, Peter?" Eliza retorted before taking her seat on a free camp chair. Sitting like a queen on a throne, she beckoned Rhea to sit beside her like she was some kind of prized dog.

Peter looked her up and down as though expecting her to reveal herself as a fake somehow. "Because no one knows Rhiannon Ballard."

"Well, now you do," Rhea said, surprising even herself with her ability to speak. "And I prefer Rhea, actually."

"You're really her," a girl piped up. "I was beginning to think you didn't exist."

"Sometimes I wish I didn't," she replied, earning some laughter. The tension inside her began to ease at that sound. She could do this. Just be normal.

"Emmet, Rhea and I are thirsty from our long walk," Eliza said, raising her eyebrows expectantly and fluttering her lashes. "Can you grab us something?"

The boy, Emmet, seemed stunned at first that Eliza was talking to him. Then, he leapt into action, procuring two hard lemonades. "Here you go," he said, looking almost giddy to be talking with her.

Rhea opened her can and took a sip. The alcohol taste was mild and well covered by the lemonade. It was the perfect combination of sweet, tart, and bitter. Way better than the wine Astrid would sometimes let her sip or Bert's hard liquor.

"So, what's it like?" another girl asked.

Rhea blinked. "What?"

"Living in that mansion," she replied. "I always thought it was so pretty and really wished I could see inside, but no one's ever invited us to one of your parties. Is it true there's an orgy?"

Rhea nearly spat out her drink as she tried to picture Bert and Astrid at an orgy. The mental image alone would be enough to scar her for life. "God no. It's mostly just boring, pretentious people acting better than everyone else."

"Sounds like you grandparents," another boy said. He grimaced. "Er, no offense."

Rhea grinned. "None taken."

Despite her assurances, the boy fidgeted uncomfortably.

"It's just that my aunt was one of their maids for a bit. She said they were the worst people she had ever had the displeasure of working with."

Her first urge was what her grandparents had trained her to do: defend the family and their legacy. But that legacy was little more than a bludgeon hammering her into the shape her grandparents wanted. "I know what they're like. It's okay."

"Yeah, they suck," Eliza interjected. "I thought my parents were bad, but they've got nothing on Bert and Astrid."

Once again, Rhea's first instinct was to defend them, just in case they were somehow in earshot, but Eliza was right. It was ungrateful of her, but ninety percent of the time, she hated her grandparents and did everything she could to give them a wide berth. "Yeah, they suck. Like, a lot." It sounded unconvincing even to her ears, but the ten other teenagers were staring at her with rapt attention. Should she elaborate? Or should she wait for another question?

"I knew it," the boy who had insulted them said. "No one believed my aunt. They all acted like *she* was the one who did something wrong."

"So, what do they do?" Peter asked.

Rhea swallowed. She didn't like this. She didn't like the way they stared at her, the way they questioned it. It was like she was just some new toy they all wanted a turn playing with. She shrank in on herself slightly. "I, um, I don't—"

Eliza cut her off, glaring at Peter like a guard dog. "Oh my god, dude, you don't just ask people shit like that. How'd you like everyone to know that your dad still makes you wear pull-ups to bed?"

Peter's face immediately colored. "Right. Sorry, Rhea." He glanced around the crowd. "And for the record, I don't wear pull-ups, Eliza."

She took a long sip of her lemonade as though inviting him to dig himself deeper with another denial. Rhea marveled at the way she seemed to command the party like a queen holding court. It was impressive, but it was also so different from the way she was when it was just the two of them. Eliza was confident, yes, but she shared some of the control with Rhea. This version of Eliza had everyone at the party hanging on her every word. How did she do that?

"So, who wants smores?" a girl asked, breaking the tension by holding up a bag of marshmallows.

In the excitement over burning marshmallows, Rhea's novelty seemed to wear off. She wondered, though, what people said about her. Was she just a tragic orphan? Or did the stories warp until she became a monster, one that had to be locked away and isolated from her peers?

The party thrived around her as she sat, ignored by the others, who didn't seem to know what to do with her. Eliza laughed, snapping Rhea from her reverie. She and Emmet stood at the outskirts of the firelight, silhouetted by the shadows. Eliza doubled over, leaning on him and placing a manicured hand on his shoulder. His hand drifted lower, to her lower back and inching lower still. But she didn't seem to mind. In fact, she seemed kind of into it. Jealousy crested over Rhea like a wave. Was Eliza really flirting with a boy right in front of her?

Bitter tears filling her eyes, she got to her feet and began her trek home. Eliza must have seen this, though, because she ran to join Rhea's side. "Hey, what's going on?" she whispered.

Rhea wasn't sure how to respond to that. It all sounded so stupid. *I have no idea how to act around kids our age. Everyone's looking at me like an escaped zoo animal. You're acting differently and flirting with a boy right in front of me. I think Bert and Astrid might be right and no one will ever really like me.*

Finally, she settled on, "I don't like this."

Eliza's face fell. "Is this about me and Emmet?"

"Yes. No. I don't know." She pressed the heels of her hands against her eyes as though to stave off a headache.

Eliza gave her shoulder a squeeze. "Rhea, you know my parents are just as bad as your grandparents. If they knew about us..." She swallowed. "So, I flirt with boys a little—not enough for them to think of me as a slut but still just enough that everyone gets off my back. You're still my number one."

Rhea sniffled, the lump in her throat loosening. "You mean it?"

Eliza nodded. "I do." She took Rhea's hand. "So come back to the party?"

"Okay." She sighed. "I know I'm being stupid. It's just—"

"Weird. I get it. You don't know any of these people. But I promise they're nice once you do. Just give them a chance, okay?"

Rhea nodded, forcing a smile. "Okay. I'll have another hard lemonade, I guess."

Eliza grinned. "Liquid courage."

The rest of the party wasn't much better. Rhea drank and tried to make conversation with people who had nothing in common with her. Eliza did her best to include her, but Rhea could tell how awkward the rest of her friends felt.

And yet, she was the freest she had ever been. Bert and Astrid's judgmental gazes couldn't reach her on that beach, surrounded by people her own age. As awkward as the party was, she agreed to go to the next one and the one after that. Even if she barely spoke, even if they all ignored her, she was still freed from the house's oppression if only for a little while, like Cinderella at the ball. It made returning to the mansion before the break of dawn all the more miserable.

So, every time Eliza invited her to join the bonfire, she happily accepted. At least, she did until she was arrested for underage drinking and had to call Mr. Ellis to bail her out. It took her a while to convince them to let Eliza back into the house after that.

The kitchen timer dinged. Rhea grabbed the oven mitts and pulled out the chicken parmesan. It looked...like how chicken parmesan was supposed to look, which was a feat considering her attempt to make mac and cheese from scratch ended with her having to temporarily disable the smoke alarm. She set it out on the counter and took a moment to admire her handiwork.

Morgan grinned and patted her shoulder. "It looks great!"

Rhea's heart skipped a few beats. Aside from Morgan, praise was rare for her. Bert and Astrid believed that self-confidence was a tool of the devil and hired tutors who felt the same way, rationing compliments like they would run out. Her bosses and coworkers only seemed to talk to her when she did something wrong. This feeling of pride was rather foreign to her. "I had a great teacher."

"Well, are we going to stand here and admire it or are we going to try it?" Andy asked, handing out plates.

Once her portion was served, she sat at the table and took her first bite. The chicken had the perfect crunch, and the seasoned breadcrumbs mixed well with the tang of the sauce. It came out perfectly. She *did* that. With help, of course, but it turned out way better than expected.

"And you said you were hopeless," Morgan teased as she twirled her pasta.

Andy, who had his mouth too full to speak, simply gave her a thumbs up.

They're just being nice, Astrid's pernicious voice whispered so clearly that it made Rhea flinch. *They secretly hate it, just like they hate you.*

But for the first time, she simply thought back, *shut up,* and continued enjoying the fruits of her labors.

CHAPTER THIRTEEN

After lunch, Rhea lingered at the staircase near Bert's office. She always thought that there were two main approaches to an unpleasant task. Either procrastinate or rip the band-aid off. In general, she preferred the latter, always eating her vegetables before anything else and cleaning the rat traps in her apartment first thing in the morning. She sighed. Best to get the attic out of the way. Then she'd never have to go up there again.

For a moment, she considered asking Morgan or Andy if they would come with her, but no, that was ridiculous. She was being ridiculous. It was just the attic, filled with dusty papers, dusty Christmas decorations, and even dustier furniture. Nothing to be afraid of. Ghosts couldn't hurt her. Memories couldn't hurt her. The only thing that could hurt her was getting tetanus from a rusted antique. Even then, her workplace had mandatory tetanus shots, so her vaccines were up to date.

She forced herself to take the first step, and then the second, fighting against the urge to flee with every step up the main staircase. Just keep breathing and keep climbing. When she reached the top, she flicked on the lightbulb. It cast a weak glow on the dusty space, and she wished she had a mask to filter out the worst of it. She had a vague memory as a child of spending a few days in a hotel by the beach while workers removed asbestos from the house, so at least she wouldn't have to worry about mesothelioma.

From what she understood, the clutter had a sort of organized chaos to it. She was near the old artwork: sculptures, portraits, and paintings commissioned by the Ballard's from the most famous artists at the time. Now, they were gathering dust under white sheets. Directly ahead were the old, important papers hidden in a rusty filing cabinet. Going further in, she'd encounter the Christmas decorations, the tower room, and finally a pile of miscellaneous antiques and odds and ends. Making a beeline for the filing cabinet, she kept her eyes straight ahead, avoiding looking directly at the old oak door like it was a gorgon that would turn her to stone. She pulled at the top drawer, cringing as the sound of metal scraping metal tore through the otherwise silent space.

Her plan was to empty the cabinets and then sort them in his study. It would require several trips with potentially delicate documents, but it wasn't like they weren't already deteriorating in this non-climate-controlled floor of the house.

The first cabinet held very little. Some miscellaneous papers and two old, leather-bound notebooks with the initials, TB and MB, embossed on the front. This cabinet must have belonged to her great-grandfather, Tom. If he was anything like Bert, he would have saved every receipt and tax return. She groaned. It could take her a lifetime to sort it all.

A child's giggle rang out through the silence. She picked up her head, her pulse already quickening as she scanned the furniture. A movement caught her peripheral vision. One of the sheets protecting a sculpture swayed gently as though a breeze had fluttered through the stagnant air of the attic.

Her mouth went dry as she stood, frozen like a prey animal. She needed to get out of there, but she couldn't bring herself to move.

Another giggle. This time, she knew exactly where it came from. The oak door. Slowly, she turned to head to stare at it, as though a sudden movement might entice whatever was with her to attack.

In her nightmares, she often found herself puppeted on strings of fishing line, the hooks digging into her skin and tugging her in the direction of the door and the tower room beyond it. She didn't know what was waiting for her on the other side, but she knew it was something that would consume and digest her.

There were no fishhooks maneuvering her legs as she stood up and approached the door to the tower room, but the tug was still there. The handle rattled, shaking violently as though someone was trying to force their way out. The rattles gave way to echoing bangs as Rhea stood frozen in the face of her nightmares brought to life. Abruptly, all sound stopped, and the door slowly creaked open, revealing an empty room.

It was as spartan as she remembered. A desk. A chair. An old, stained bed. The porthole shaped window overlooking the lake let the light of the sunset in. She knew that if she craned her neck, she would see the meager toilet, and sink. A prison cell for naughty little girls who talked back and failed their math tests. Her breath quickened as her heart thrummed like a hummingbird in her chest. She dropped the papers and bolted, sprinting down the stairs and into her bedroom. Hugging Otso close, she struggled to get her breathing under control.

The first time they sent her to the attic room, it was the day after Bert forbade her from sleeping with the lights on. The Smiling Lady spent the whole night sitting on the edge of her bed staring at her, so she hadn't slept at all. She was tired, missing her parents, and scared of her nightmarish visitor. And then, without asking, Bert took the remote from her and changed the channel from her Saturday morning cartoons to his golf game. The temper tantrum was earth shattering. Eventually, Bert slung her over his shoulders like one of his prize bucks and carried her up two flights of stairs and into the attic.

"Scream and cry all you want," he said. "No one can hear you up here. And if they could, they wouldn't care." With that, he shut the door and locked it.

Rhea screamed herself hoarse and cried until every tear had been wrung out of her like a wet dish towel. Eventually, though, she quieted down. She curled up on the bare mattress and tried not to shiver. Her stomach growled and her throat was parched, but when she had tried the sink, the water came out a rusty brown. Eventually, exhaustion overtook her.

She woke to a girl sitting in the chair by the old, wooden desk. She looked to be a few years older than Rhea, ten maybe, with golden little ringlets illuminated by the moonlight.

"Hi there," she said, waving. Her friendly smile revealed a gap tooth.

Rhea sat up slowly, pinching herself to make sure she was awake. "Who are you?" Her voice was rough, and she sniffled with residual snot.

"Your new best friend."

Her eyes narrowed in suspicion. Grown-ups always told her not to talk to strangers, but if the stranger was a little girl, it was okay, right? "What's your name?"

The girl tilted her head thoughtfully. "You can call me Minnie."

"I'm Rhiannon," she replied. She preferred Rhea, but her grandparents insisted on her full name.

Minnie wrinkled her nose. "That's a mouthful. I'll just call you Annie."

At this point, Minnie could have called her Poopsmell Stinkbrain, and Rhea would have been content if it meant having her as a companion. Before they could be friends, though, she had an important question to ask. "Are you like the Smiling Lady?"

Minnie furrowed her brows, her big brown eyes the picture of innocence. "Who?"

"She sits on my bed when I sleep," she said, pulling her knees in close to her chest and sniffling. "Granma and Grampa say that I'm making her up, but I'm not, and she scares me, and they won't let me do the one thing that keeps her away."

Minnie beamed and sat down next to her. "I'm gonna tell you a secret. You're right. I *am* like the Smiling Lady, and I know how to keep her away. So, let's make a deal. If I can get her to leave you alone, you'll be my best friend."

Rhea already had a best friend, Katie Carlson from Miss Rosie's class, but she hadn't heard from her since her parents died and her grandparents started homeschooling her. Besides, there was nothing in the rules about having two best friends. "Deal."

"Shake on it?" Minnie held out her hand expectantly.

She wasn't sure how shaking hands with a ghost would work, but she thought she'd at least try. Minnie's hands were much bonier than she expected, and unnaturally cold—like stepping outside in a blizzard wearing nothing but a scarf. But she was excited. She had made a friend. The last time she'd even seen a kid her age was at the park her parents took her to a few days before they died. It would be nice to have a friend to play with, even if others couldn't see her.

She yawned, and Minnie patted the top of her head. "You should sleep. They'll come for you in the morning." And even though she was starving and thirsty, Rhea was out as soon as she shut her eyes.

The next night, the Smiling Lady did not sit at the edge of her bed.

In the present, Rhea closed her eyes and inhaled, breathing in the smell of her mother's old perfume. "They're gone," she muttered to herself, "I'm here and they're gone. They can't hurt me anymore." It was a lie, and she knew it, but still she repeated the mantra over and over until her heartbeat slowed down.

"Hey Rhea." Andy knocked on the door and let himself in before she could say anything. "Morgan's about to start dinner, and she wanted to know if you wanted to do another cooking lesson, or—wait, are you okay?"

She sniffled and rubbed her eyes. "I was up in the attic looking for papers and my allergies started acting up."

Andy gave her a skeptical look before replying, "Yeah, I can barely set foot in there before sneezing my brains out. How do you think I got the way I am?"

Rhea chuckled. "I just figured you were raised by television. It rots the brain, according to Astrid."

"Too much Spongebob at a formative age. It's a tragedy, really." He wiped a fake tear from his cheek. "Anyway, in a much less dusty part of the house, Morgan wants to know if you would like to help."

A part of her truly wanted to go down to that kitchen and learn how to make whatever Morgan was planning and then maybe watch some garbage television that would make Astrid turn over in her grave, but a bone deep weariness overcame her. The poor night's sleep combined with the high emotions and the knowledge that Morgan and Andy were hiding something made her just want to curl up in bed and forget the world. She smiled. "Can I ask for a raincheck? I think I'm gonna take a nap. You guys can go ahead and have dinner without me."

"If you feel up for it later, come right on down. Dinner won't be ready for a bit anyway."

"Thanks Andy."

He turned off the light as he left, and she laid down on her side, closing her eyes.

When they opened, she wasn't in her childhood bed. She was on the ancient and lumpy mattress in the tower room. The room was filthy, smelling of excrement and rotten food, and her breath came out in wheezes. Her distended stomach felt like an empty chasm, as though a satisfying meal was a long-forgotten memory. She lacked the strength to sit up and just stared listlessly through the window. She knew that she would die, and no one would notice or care. At least she would no longer be an embarrassment or a problem in need of solving. She heard laughter on the wind and knew that her death would also never bring her peace.

Still, she closed her eyes.

And woke shaking in her childhood bed.

It was just a dream, her brain coming up with a hypothetical future where she had not left home. She wasn't locked in there. She wouldn't starve to death surrounded by her own excrement. She had a future away from this house and that attic and all the bad memories that lurked in her mind like a great beast stalking her, waiting to strike.

With her initial terror abated, she realized that she was starving in the hyperbolic sense rather than the literal as her stomach growled. She made her way downstairs and hoped that Morgan would forgive her for stealing some dinner.

The kitchen clock said that it was around 10:30, and she could hear the television on in the other room. She scooped out some leftover chicken parmesan from lunch out of a Tupperware and inhaled the smell of tomato sauce and garlic before putting it in the microwave.

"Rhea?" Morgan asked from behind.

"Didn't mistake me for an intruder this time. That's progress," she replied, turning around to see a somewhat sleepy looking Morgan.

"Why didn't you have dinner with us?" she asked, pulling out the Tupperware of cookies and taking one.

The microwave beeped, and Rhea took out her late dinner. "Didn't feel up to it. Wasn't your fault or Andy's. Just needed to rest a bit."

"And did you?"

She raised one shoulder in a half-shrug. "About as well as any other soul in this house." She took a bite of the parmesan, noting with pride that it still had a nice crunch. "Thank you again for the cooking lesson. You're a great teacher."

"Thanks." Morgan stared down at the half-eaten cookie. They lapsed into a silence that felt somehow pregnant, like one of them should be filling it, Rhea wasn't sure what she was expected to say, if anything. She shoved chicken and pasta in her mouth. If she was eating, then she wouldn't have to talk first.

Morgan seemed to be thinking the same thing, because she ate her cookie and then grabbed another. Can't have an awkward conversation with your mouth full, apparently. Finally, she spoke again. "Have you ever known a secret about someone else that wasn't yours to tell, but not telling could hurt more in the long run? I don't want to break their trust, but I also don't want to cause them pain."

Rhea hadn't had much opportunity for other people to confide their dark secrets to her, but she understood the principle of snitches get stitches. But she had a pretty good idea of what this was about. Regardless of if she was ready, she had to know. "I would say that the person you're worried about can handle more than you think, and that she has a right to know the truth if it's something that pertains to her."

Morgan's gaze met Rhea's. "Even if I could see that this person is already struggling with everything else going on? Like, if they've had multiple panic attacks since I met them?"

It was easier, she supposed, to speak in hypothetical. It gave everything a comfortable distance. "Even then."

She sighed. "I wanted to spare you a little. You've already had so much to grieve. I didn't want to cause more pain. But since you overheard me and Andy, the cat's outta the bag, I guess. It's better if you hear it from us."

"What is it?"

"You remember how I told you how Astrid had Dementia? Well, she started saying things. Sometimes, she saw Andy and would think he was your dad, and she'd just apologize to him over and over. On really bad days, she thought I was your mom, and she'd yell at me that it's my fault he's dead."

Rhea knew where this was going, but she needed Morgan to say it out loud.

"Rhea, she said she killed your parents."

CHAPTER FOURTEEN

One night, Rhea awoke to the door creaking open and the figure of Grandma Astrid in the doorway, silhouetted by the light behind her. She kept her eyes closed as her grandmother approached on unsteady feet. If she looked like she was asleep, then she wouldn't get into trouble. Astrid leaned in so close that Rhea could smell the wine on her breath and stroked her hair with her gnarled fingers. "The last piece of him I have, and she looks nothing like him," Grandma Astrid slurred.

She felt the bed dip beside her. "Maybe if you resembled him, I could bear looking at you, but I'm stuck the ghost of my worst mistake."

She sounded so sad that Rhea wanted to reach out and comfort her but didn't know how she'd react. Grandma Astrid hated to be seen as anything other than cool, calm, and collected. So, she laid still until her grandmother had enough and tottered back out of the room.

Rhea had mostly forgotten that memory. It was a rare and strange moment of vulnerability borne out of too much to drink, but she hadn't thought much of it beyond that. But if what Morgan said was true...

She was glad that she was already sitting, or her legs likely would have collapsed under her. She knew she was trembling like an earthquake but barely registered it over the buzzing in her ears. Everything was too loud, and yet she couldn't make sense of any sounds. Her flesh itched like maggots crawling under her skin. Hungry, devouring maggots like the ones burrowing into the corpses of her parents. Like the ones eating her grandmother, who was somehow responsible for her parents being in the ground.

And suddenly, there were hands shaking her shoulder and touching her face and someone distantly calling her name and it was all just too much. "Don't touch me!" she snapped, and the hands disappeared. She screwed her eyes shut and forced an inhale and an exhale, counting the lengths of her breaths. *In...two...three...four...out...two...three...four...*

It felt like an eternity, but when her heartbeat and breathing was finally under control, she opened her eyes. Morgan stood a few feet away. "I'm sorry," Rhea said.

"Don't apologize. It's a lot to process, and I'm sorry I didn't tell you sooner. I just didn't know how." She sat down again across from Rhea.

"Honestly, I should have expected as much from her. They hated that he married someone with less money than him, and horror of horrors, Hispanic." She pushed away the chicken parmesan, her appetite killed by nausea at the revelation.

"I don't know if she really did kill them," Morgan said, "or if she just blamed herself for their deaths. I tried to look into it, but all I found was that it was ruled an accident. On days that she thought he was your dad, she told Andy over and over not to eat the carrots. Neither of us knew what she was talking about."

Carrots? What did carrots have to do with Astrid killing her parents? They died in a boating accident. The rowboat they were on capsized in the water. Her mother was knocked unconscious while her father, who never learned how to swim, drowned trying to get help on shore. It was nothing but a tragic, freak accident. All her life, that was the story they told.

A memory pressed at the back of her mind like a butterfly stirring in its cocoon, not yet ready to push itself free. Was the story just another of her grandparents' lies? If it was, how did Astrid kill them? What did it have to do with carrots?

Maybe it had nothing to do with their deaths. Maybe these were all the insane ramblings of an old woman whose brain was in the process of eating itself. But maybe Astrid was finally telling the truth for the first time in her life.

Rhea let out a hysterical laugh which transitioned to a sob so smoothly that even she didn't know where one ended and the other began. "I have to go," she announced, standing on shaking legs.

"Rhea—" Morgan began, reaching out.

She jerked away. "Don't!" Her shoulders sagged at the hurt expression on Morgan's face. "Please. I need some air. I'm not mad at you or kicking you out or anything, but I just...can't right now."

"Okay," Morgan said. As she stormed out of the kitchen, Rhea heard Morgan mumble something so soft that she thought she might have imagined it. "Just be careful, please."

Though the willow was her own private sanctuary, it was not the first place that she went. She went to the cemetery and sat beneath her parents' grave. Both had already put it in their wills that they wanted to be buried together, so her grandparents couldn't completely erase her mother from the family. Their grave was marked by an angel statue now overgrown with moss. Sometimes, when she sat beneath it as a child, she imagined the angel coming to life, stone transforming into flesh and blood like Galatea. The angel would smell like her mother and sound like her father, and it would fly her away to heaven to be with them. It was just a fantasy, but it felt so real that she would sometimes feel the statue for a pulse in case it had already come to life.

On the other end of the plot, there were the freshly dug graves of her grandparents. A cold fury washed over her. Their legacy. Their lie. The king and queen of Cherub's Cove, beloved by all. They could do no wrong.

She got to her feet and crossed the yard to the toolshed near the edge of the woods. Andy kept it pristine, with every tool in its place. She grabbed the first hammer she saw and walked back to the cemetery.

For a moment, she just stood over it and stared at the freshly dug earth. And then, with a yell, she swung it down on Astrid's headstone, hitting it in the epitaph reading "Loved by All." The impact jarred her arm, sending the painful vibrations through her body. It hurt, but was far too satisfying to stop, so she did it again.

Most hammers are made with the expectation that they will hit relatively soft nails. Banging two hammers together can shatter the head, sending steel projectiles flying. As Rhea found out, they can also shatter when hitting four inches of granite. She dropped the broken hammer with a cry and brought her hand up to her cheek. It came away wet and smelling of iron. A piece was embedded in her skin. She was distantly aware of the stinging, of tears mingling with blood, as she pulled it out. She numbly stared at the little projectile, barely half an inch long and only half of that covered in blood.

Just an inch higher and she'd have been blinded in one eye. A few inches lower and it would have embedded itself in her neck, possibly hitting an artery.

"Rhea? Rhea, are you okay?" Morgan called out. She ran into the cemetery barefoot. "I heard you scream." Her eyes drifted down to the broken hammer in the grass, up to the slightly dented gravestone, and finally to Rhea's blank, bloody face. Morgan approached slowly as though one wrong move would send her bolting like a deer and took her hand, examining the sliver of steel.

Rhea curled her fingers around it, her breath hitching. No, she wouldn't cry. She wouldn't give them the satisfaction of crying over their graves.

"Let's get that cleaned up," Morgan said softly, wrapping her fingers around Rhea's wrist and leading her back inside.

She sat Rhea down in the living room and returned with a first aid kit. "You had a tetanus shot?"

Rhea nodded silently. She still hadn't let go of the metal shard.

"We might still have to take you to the doctor," she said, cleaning the wound out with cold water, "Don't want you to get an infection anyway."

A distant part of her screamed to shy away and take care of the wound herself. Morgan didn't want to be cleaning up after Rhea's stupidity. She was too kind, too gentle. Rhea didn't deserve it. Not after the way she snapped and generally made herself unpleasant to be around. Bert liked to call her selfish. She was all take and no give. And she had been doing the exact same thing with Morgan, who's done so much for her. What had she done in return? Nothing.

But she was wrung out, and her hands were shaking too much for her to actually treat her wound, so she let Morgan clean the cut and the rest of her blood covered cheek.

"This might sting," Morgan warned before pressing the alcoholic wipe to the wound.

She hissed as her skin sang with the sudden burning—a flashbang of sensation cutting through the numbness. And then, it faded and she was back to an empty distance from the world around her.

"I'm sorry, I know," Morgan said. She pulled out a large band-aid and pressed it onto Rhea's cheek. "Hopefully, it'll stop bleeding soon. Cheek wounds usually heal quickly, but if it looks bad in the morning, we can go to the doctor."

"Don't have health insurance," she mumbled, her first words since fleeing the kitchen.

Morgan squeezed her shoulder. "I'm sure that inheritance of yours will cover it."

"Right." She felt detached from herself, from the pain in her cheek and Morgan hand on her shoulder. A distinct sense of unreality overcame her, as though she had died in that tower, and this life after was just a vivid and elaborate dream. Morgan was speaking softly to her, but she heard none of it. It all might as well have been happening to someone else.

This happened from time to time. Reality would feel distant and she'd have to go about her day feeling like her life didn't exist. Sometimes, the feeling would pass in a few minutes, but other times, she would have to go to work feeling like an extra in a film. Morgan disappeared, and after a minute wrapped in an eternity, she returned and placed something cold and wet in Rhea's hand.

She looked down at the melting ice cube in the hand not holding the metal shard, blinked, and looked up at Morgan. "Why did you just...?"

"I thought maybe you needed something to ground yourself."

"So, you handed me an ice cube."

"It worked, didn't it?"

Admittedly, it was difficult to feel unreal with such an unexpected concrete and familiar physical sensation. She gently squeezed the shard of the hammer with her other hand, letting it prick her thumb a little to further ground herself. "Yeah...thanks."

"Do you want to talk about it?"

She popped the ice cube in her dry mouth and hugged her knees to her chest. "Not particularly. What's another item added to the list of the ways they've ruined my life?"

The couch dipped slightly as Morgan sat beside her. "I know we haven't known each other long, but I like to think we're friends, right? I want you to feel like you can talk to someone. It doesn't have to be me, but I think you'd feel a lot better if you had someone to talk to, you know?"

A part of her wanted to tell Morgan everything. She was asking, and seemed to genuinely care, but it was all too much to dump on someone she'd just met, even if they're living together. And they both had their secrets. Even with this bombshell, Rhea had a feeling that Morgan still wasn't telling her everything. She crunched the ice cube, letting her tongue go numb from the cold as she debated the next words to come out of her mouth. "I don't know where to start."

"Well, how are you feeling right now?"

"Bad."

Morgan arched an eyebrow, obviously not satisfied with that answer.

"Very bad?"

Morgan did not respond. The expectant silence dragged on.

Rhea rolled her eyes. "Well, I'm sorry if all my repressed trauma makes me bad at recognizing my emotions."

Her friend grinned. "Hey, there we go. You know you've repressed your emotions."

She couldn't help her snort. "Oh, so you're a hospice care worker, professional chef, and now a therapist?"

Morgan smirked. "I'm a woman of many talents."

"You know, it hardly seems fair," Rhea said, stretching out, "I open up to you, but you haven't told me much about yourself." She chewed her lip thoughtfully, the warmth of it jarring against her cold teeth. "Let's play two truths and a lie."

Morgan tucked herself up on the fading couch beside her. "Like a couple of middle schoolers at a sleepover? You wanna paint my toenails while we're at it?"

"You got any polish?"

"Sadly, no. You go first."

"Okay," Rhea said, thinking carefully, "My grandparents used to lock me up in the attic as a punishment. I've tried LSD once but had a bad trip, and I had an emergency go-bag in case I had to run away from home hidden behind the mausoleum."

Morgan scrunched her nose. "I'm going to go with the first one being the lie."

She shook her head. "Nope! It was the second. The hardest stuff I've done is weed."

"Jesus," Morgan said, letting out a breath, "usually, this game isn't as horrifying."

"Hey, you wanted to know more about my trauma," she retorted with a shrug, "This is the easiest way to do it. Your turn."

"Okay, so the ghost of my *Lola,* my grandma, helped teach me how to cook, I was stalked by an ex, and I once beat Bert in a shooting contest," she said, counting the statements off with her fingers.

Rhea laughed. "Oh, that's too easy. Number three is the lie. You wouldn't be here if it was true. He'd fire you to assuage his ego." She paused, her face falling. "I am sorry, though, about getting stalked and your Lola. How did her ghost teach you, if you don't mind me asking?"

"I'm okay now," she said, her smile growing somewhat rueful.

"And it's kind of a weird story. So, she died when I was eleven, and we used to cook together. That was our thing. I was the only one of her grandkids that loved it in the kitchen. She and I would experiment together, and her food was just the best. All her recipes were written down in a book that she kept hidden because she didn't want the church ladies to steal it. But she hid it too well. No one in the family could find it. Then, a month after the funeral, I come home from school and find it just sitting there on my bed. My mom has no idea how it got there, and my relatives are pissed, thinking I took it. But my *Lolo*, grandfather, believed that she sent it to me from beyond, and insisted I keep it. I learned how to cook on my own using that book." She played with the pendant around her neck as she spoke. Seeing the protective charm made something squeeze a little in Rhea.

This was what family was supposed to do, right? They were supposed to take care of each other.

"Wow, you're lucky," Rhea said, wanting to cry again for what she could have had. She blinked the tears away. "Most of the ghosts I run into just want to scare me. Most grandparents too."

"Do you have any nice ghost stories?" Morgan asked.

Her first thought was of Minnie, but no, something went sour there, though she couldn't quite remember what. The Smiling Lady terrified her. And apparently there was something bad in the lake. But the lake wasn't all bad. "I hear my mom, sometimes, usually by the lake. She sings me this lullaby she made up."

Rhea closed her eyes and began to sing:

"Meet me by the willow
Where the elder flowers bloom
And the soft grass is your pillow
And the night will be our tomb.

Please, my love, don't tarry.
For in the light of day
My fiancé I must marry
But for tonight we'll stay

Underneath the willow.
I beg, my love, be true
For in the light of moon glow,
It's only me and you."

"That was beautiful," Morgan said. "You have a lovely voice."

"Oh, uh, thanks," she replied, heat spreading across her face. "My mom didn't have a good singing voice." She looked down, picking a loose thread on the couch. "Is that weird to say? I remember that she used to say she couldn't carry a tune in a bucket. But it was beautiful to me. Given the choice between front row tickets for any concert and hearing her voice again, I'd pick her voice every time."

Morgan shook her head. "I get that. Given the choice between a meal at a five-star restaurant and having Lola's Kare-Kare, I would pick her Kare-Kare every time."

She could imagine a young Morgan bustling around the kitchen with her grandmother, laughing and working together in a way she and Astrid never would. Instead of feeling jealous, though, she was oddly comforted by the image. Morgan deserved happiness, and Rhea refused to drag her friend down.

"Your turn," Morgan said, smiling mischievously.

Rhea blinked. "Hm?"

"Hit me with two more truths and a lie. I need to even the score."

"Right. Um..." To be honest, her mind had drifted so far that she had forgotten the game that started the conversation. She really needed to lighten things up, though. The last one had been a bit too heavy. "I've read every book in Astrid's library. I used to have a mullet. I hate carrot cake."

A look of consternation crossed Morgan's face. "Please tell me it's the mullet."

Laughing, Rhea shook her head. "Nope! It was the library. Some of Astrid's books were painfully dry. I just couldn't do it."

"But why would you have a mullet?" Morgan asked, burying her face in her hands in mock pain.

"I had just escaped them, so I wanted to assert my freedom with a hairstyle that I knew for sure that Astrid would hate. And I also didn't know the first thing about cutting my own hair, so it was that or a bowl cut." She remembered the intoxicating feeling of lightness that overcame her when she made the first few snips, chopping away the matted tresses. When she looked in the mirror after, she felt like she was seeing herself for the first time. As time went on, she cut her hair shorter and shorter, eventually just buying a razor and shaving most of it off.

"As much as I hate mullets on principle, I can respect that." She glanced up at Rhea's current style and then looked away. "For what it's worth, I like your hair now. It suits you. Makes you very handsome."

Rhea wondered if her face had caught fire. It burned with delight at the compliment. She wasn't used to being called pretty and hated being called sexy, but the word "handsome" felt right. It fit her better than pretty ever did and felt oddly affirming in a way she didn't know she needed. "Thank you. I, um, I like your hair too. It's very pretty."

Morgan smiled. "So, my turn?"

They played a few more rounds, both choosing lighter truths and lies after the initial heavy ones. Rhea supposed it defeated the purpose of her talking about her trauma, but it felt good to just laugh with Morgan and share stories for the sake of sharing stories. Their conversation flowed naturally to town gossip, books, and what television she needed to catch up on.

Somewhere, a clock chimed three in the morning. Rhea hadn't even realized how late it had gotten. Talking with Morgan seemed to make the time slip through her fingers like water. She yawned. "I think that's enough heart to hearts and emotional trauma for one night. See you in the morning."

"Sleep well," Morgan called after her.

That night, she dreamt of Bert and Astrid, their heads crushed in by hammers. It was oddly cathartic.

CHAPTER FIFTEEN

"So, how does the whole ghost thing work?" seven-year-old Rhea asked. Anything to distract her from the mandatory reading from the book of Job.

Minnie tapped her fingers on the desk thoughtfully. She had become an inseparable companion in the past few months. Everywhere Rhea went, Minnie followed. And the best part was that her grandparents couldn't get rid of her. "Imagine you're in a box made of two-way mirrors. You can see everything that's going on, but no one can see you. They can't hear you either. Sometimes, you bang on the glass loud enough from a passer-by to hear, and maybe even find a hole large enough for you to stick your hand out and affect the rest of the world. If you're really lucky, someone will see your strange box, and out of curiosity, peer into the glass and just barely make you out."

"That sounds awful," Rhea said.

Minnie shrugged. "Better that than to move on and cease to exist. Or worse, find out that Hell is real, and you're on a first-class trip."

She looked down at the Bible in her lap. "I don't think I'd make it into heaven either. I'm a bad kid. Grandma and Grandpa won't say it, but I can tell every time I laugh too loud or run through the house. They wish they weren't stuck with me."

"And what do you wish?"

Rhea sniffled. "I just want my mom and dad."

The little ghost girl sat down beside Rhea. "Maybe I can help."

"How?"

Minnie threw a cold arm around Rhea's shoulder and pulled her in close. "I teach you how to make a magic whistle. All you'll have to do is blow it and keep blowing until you see them."

"Is that it? Then why haven't Grandma and Grandpa done it."

"It's a rare sort of magic. Only the pure of heart and the innocent can do it. Your grandparents are many things, but they are far from innocent. What do you say?"

She stared down at the Bible for a moment before lifting her head and saying, "I'll do it."

"Would you like me to go with you?" Morgan asked when she caught Rhea at the bottom of the stairs working up the courage to go into the attic.

"What?"

"You said they would lock you up there as a punishment. I wouldn't want to be alone up there if I were you."

Rhea played with her dust mask. A part of her wanted to push Morgan away, to go it alone and reject her kindness because it surely had to be some kind of trick. But the other part was so tired of being alone, and Morgan, whatever her motives, offered her something she hadn't had in a very long time, if ever. Someone to be there for her.

But no, she shouldn't. She was her boss. Morgan was probably so nice to her because she needed Rhea's paycheck. It wasn't right for her to rely so heavily on an employee to deal with her emotions. "I should be okay." She started up the stairs, but stopped in the middle, turning back. "Hey, so, I'm sorry about last night. And if things get to be too much here, I can put you up in a hotel or something." Why she wasn't booking one for herself, she wasn't sure.

Her smile grew sad. "You apologize too much." She looked as though she was about to say something but reconsidered, opening her mouth, closing it, and chewing her lip. Rhea waited patiently with one foot on the next step. Finally, Morgan said, "Andy's going home early, so you wanna go out to dinner tonight? Just, you know, to get out?"

Rhea smiled. "I'd love to."

The first thing she noticed when she reached the attic was that the cabinet drawers were all open, and the papers strewn about on the floor. She groaned. "Really?" she said to whatever lurked in there. Without bothering to sort, she gathered the first pile into a stack and carried it downstairs. It took a few trips to take everything down, but eventually, everything on the floor was picked up and she was checking the open drawers for anything she might have missed.

A creak behind her broke the silence of the attic. She froze. Another creak and the opening of a door. Slowly, she turned around.

Written in the dust on the floor was: *M lies—A.*

M...Was that supposed to be Morgan? Rhea knew her friend wasn't telling the whole truth about what she's experienced, but seeing a ghost try to use Rhea's paranoia to drive a wedge between them made her want to get even closer out of spite.

"Astrid?" she asked the air. No response. She rolled her eyes. "If you're trying to turn me against Morgan, it won't work. So, move on to whatever afterlife you've earned and leave me the hell alone."

Something fell in the tower room. "Okay, I'm out," she announced, heading towards the stairs. Before she could take the first step, a forced pushed her down, sending her sprawling. She screamed as frozen hands grabbed her by the ankle and dragged her into the room. The door shut behind her and locked with a click.

Suddenly, she was six and getting dragged in there by Bert over hitting her breaking point and having a tantrum. She was eleven and sent there for three days for cutting off her waist length hair. She was thirteen and kept in there without food or water every Sunday for six months because she refused to wear a dress to church.

She was seventeen, trapped in there for four months after she was outed.

On the day they were caught, Rhea and Eliza had cuddled together in bed, listening to cheesy love songs. Rhea let out a contented sigh.

"What?" Eliza said, propping herself on her elbows.

"I just realized something. I'm happy with you."

"You didn't know before?" Eliza asked, cocking her head.

Rhea rolled her eyes. "Of course, I did. But living here is like being an antelope among lions. With you, I feel safe."

Eliza pressed a kiss to her temple. "I feel the most like myself with you. Mom and Dad all expect me to be one thing, and my friends want me to be another. You just let me be. When I'm with you, I feel like we're gonna be together forever."

"We won't," Rhea said, closing her eyes, "Every love story is a tragedy if you wait long enough. One will eventually leave the other to mourn."

Eliza flicked her nose. "You're getting emo again."

Rhea laughed at that and pressed a kiss to Eliza's lips. "Yeah. Okay. We're gonna last until the heat death of the universe."

"Damn right, baby," she said, deepening the kiss.

Suddenly, the door flew open, and her grandparents appeared, their faces alight with rage. The girls jolted apart. "Just as I suspected," Grandma Astrid sneered, "I always thought there was something unnatural between the two of you."

Grandpa Bert pointed to Eliza. "Get out." Eliza stayed frozen in place. He gritted his teeth. "Get out now, and I won't grab my gun." His voice was low and cold.

Rhea absolutely believed he would hunt Eliza down like an animal. She had visions of him chasing her through the woods on the property. He would take aim slowly and then shoot. A starburst of red would appear on Eliza's back, and she would fall to the ground, dead. Then a coverup with the sheriff's office, and it would be like she never existed. She squeezed her girlfriend's hand and whispered. "Go. I'll be okay."

Eliza looked back at her, tears in her eyes. "But—"

She tucked a stray blonde lock behind Eliza's ear. "Just do it. I love you."

Eliza nodded shakily and skittered like a mouse past her grandparents and out the door.

"As for you, young lady," Bert growled, stalking over and grabbing Rhea's wrist hard enough to bruise. Despite his age, he was incredibly strong and though Rhea fought against him, she could get no purchase as he dragged her upstairs and threw her into the attic's tower room.

"Read your Bible and repent your sin," Grandma Astrid said, "May God have mercy on your soul." She slammed the door behind her.

Rhea heard the lock click, and she was alone. She curled in on herself and sobbed into her pillow.

In the present, Rhea screamed and banged on the attic door, throwing herself into it, and doing nothing but kicking up dust. Why couldn't they hear her? Why couldn't they let her out? She needed to get out of there. She couldn't breathe, her chest tightening as her rapid breaths yielded no air. Was this what dying felt like? This all-consuming fear that she would be trapped forever in this tower, dying of starvation and dehydration, her spirit slowly going mad from the isolation.

Darkness curled at the edge of her tunneling vision, as she drowned, surrounded by air. Soon, the shadows swallowed her whole.

When she came to, she was on the floor by the door. Sitting on the desk were the two journals she'd practically forgotten about from yesterday. She had left them in the office with the rest of the paperwork in need of sorting, but now, here they were. Waiting for her. "I take it you want me to read these," she said shakily and sat down at the desk. Whatever was in the attic didn't deign to reply. She opened her great-grandfather Tom's journal first.

05/10/20

I met AD in the chapel today. She didn't like the idea of doing anything to offend God in a place of worship, so we only conversed. I admit that I struggled to pay attention to her talk of the old country. I want to kiss her rose petal lips and run my fingers through her fiery hair, but she's resistant to the call of the carnal. Perhaps we can one day sneak away and consummate our passions, but for now, I can be patient.

We came dangerously close to getting caught. Another maid came in to dust, just as we were about to kiss. Damn! Usually, no one ever goes in there. Ingrid had to pick today of all days to dust! That is all for now.

She skimmed through a few entries. Tom Ballard really seemed to love talking about his romantic and sexual exploits. It came as no surprise that AD was just one of many. That poor girl likely got her heart broken.

05/15/20

Today, we hid away in the woods. She told me of Poland's legends—Smok the dragon that stalked the Wawel Hill, Baba Yaga the witch, and the wronged Rusalka, a beautiful woman that died at the hands of men's cruelty and returned to exact her vengeance. I told her some stories of my own, of Paul Bunyan, Pecos Bill, and the terrifying Jersey Devil. Eventually, we ran out of stories and found other ways to occupy ourselves.

After that, the pages were all blank. She flipped to the end.

11/3/20

I have committed a great sin and will be punished for it. Not in this life, perhaps, but certainly the next. God have mercy.

She searched through the previous entries, looking for any indication as to what this sin might be. Nothing. Whatever he did, it was too terrible to write about. She turned to the second book labelled MB. His sister Minerva's journal, perhaps. It was far less salacious than her brother's, mostly just drawings of local flora and notes.

Willow (Salix, Species Unsure)
Bark has pain relieving properties
Wild Onion (Allium Canadense)
Tastes good. No additional properties.

She flipped to the page with the white flowers by the lake, and the world tilted on its axis.

Water Hemlock (Cicuta Douglasii)
Highly poisonous. Fed to rats.
They died unpleasantly.

CHAPTER SIXTEEN

"Are you sure this will work?" Rhea asked, rocking back and forth on her heels. The lake was placid, and the day sunny.

Minnie sat by the willow putting the finishing touches on the whistle made from the hollow stem of one of the white flowers that lined the lake. "There's a way to make extra sure," she said and handed Rhea a piece of the root. "Have a bite. It tastes good."

She wrinkled her nose. "But it's dirty."

Minnie rolled her eyes. "Rinse it in the water. Do you want to see your parents or not?"

"I do," she exclaimed and dipped it into the lake, scrubbing as best she could, though it still had mud in its crevices. Oh well. This was good enough. She popped the root in her mouth. Once she got past the dirt, it wasn't bad. It tasted a bit like a sweet carrot.

"Now blow on this until you see them," Minnie said, handing her the whistle.

Rhea did as she was told. Though the whistle made no sound, she blew into it and stared into the water, willing her parents to rise from the depths. Her stomach burned and her mouth was on fire, but still she stared.

And then she saw them. Her parents floated just below the surface, and her heart soared. Minnie was telling the truth. They were here. They had come for her.

She glanced over at Minnie, who was smiling proudly. "Keep going, Annie! It's working!"

Then, they looked up.

The bloated, agonized faces of her mother and father mouthed a word through rotted lips. At least, that's what it looked like between all the bubbles. Their heads broke the surface, unleashing the putrid odor of decay. "Run," her father moaned.

Her mother, though, glanced between the flowers and the whistle. Her mouth dropped open and kept going, the rotting tendons in her jaw fraying as they stretched beyond human capability. And then she let out a wail, one full of grief and agony unlike anything Rhea had ever heard.

She spat out the whistle and ran on trembling legs to the back door. Her nausea threatened to erupt into vomit, and she knew that if she fell, she wouldn't get back up.

She found Astrid reading in the library. Her grandmother looked up with the kind of vicious scowl that would ordinarily cow her granddaughter, but Rhea must have looked terrible, because her eyes widened in alarm.

"Rhiannon, what's—"

"I ate something bad," she got out, before doubling over and retching. Once her stomach was emptied of everything but bile, she looked up.

Minnie stood behind Grandma Astrid with a smirk on her face. She grew taller and thinner, her blonde ringlets becoming dirty and lank, her stomach distending past her visible ribs. The Smiling Lady waved at Rhea and blew a kiss.

Then the seizures hit.

...

Rhea came back to herself gasping and crying so hard she was nearly retching. She slammed the book shut and staggered away from it. How could she have forgotten the terror, the knowledge that she was going to die as a little girl and be trapped with the Smiling Lady for all eternity? She'd had vague memories of a hospital from a long time ago, but she assumed she'd just gotten very sick. God, not a ghost almost tricking her into suicide at the age of seven.

She trembled all over, her breath shaky and too fast.

The door handle jiggled, and she froze. What now?

"Rhea," Andy called from the other side.

"In here," she said and realized that her voice was practically gone. The lock clicked and the door opened, revealing Andy in all his paint splattered glory. He had his arms wide, reminding her of the paintings of martyred saints in the chapel. She couldn't help herself. She ran into his open arms.

Andy tensed in surprise, awkwardly patting her on the shoulder. "Okay, so we're hugging now. Cool. Cool."

Rhea stepped back out of reach as though she'd been stung. "I'm sorry, I shouldn't have—"

"No, you're fine. I'd hug the first person I saw if I was trapped in this place too. You know, I lost count of how many times I got stuck in here. The door locks automatically when you shut it, and it's damn near impossible to open from the inside. I thought I fixed the stupid thing, though." He glanced around, his brows furrowing in confusion. "What was this place even used for?"

Rhea took a stuttering breath. "Punishment, mostly. It was where they would lock away the family disappointments whenever they wanted to avoid a scandal."

"Jesus. That's—that's awful."

She swallowed dryly. "Yeah, tell me about it."

He swallowed and glanced at the oak door. "I-I guess that explains the scratches I had to buff out. Christ."

Her fingers twitched at the phantom pain of splinters under her fingernails. "I really hate being in here."

"I do too." He slung an arm around her shoulder. "Come on. Morgan made lunch."

"One second," she said, grabbing the books and following Andy as far away from the attic as she could go. She'd known that her family had always been terrible, but it seemed that these books might reveal the extent of the sins of the father.

"What'cha got there?" he asked.

"Some old notebooks. One belonged to my great-grandfather, but half of it's empty." It was a safe enough half-truth. No need to tell Andy the whole story and have him think she was crazy.

"Can I see?"

She wordlessly passed it over to him, watching as he flipped to a blank page in the middle of the blank pages and ran his fingers across the old paper. "It's weird," he said, "I don't see any writing, but I feel indentations as though there had been at one point."

"Like pages were torn out?"

"No, like maybe entries were written in invisible ink or something. My cousins and I used to pretend we were spies and send secret messages to each other in invisible ink. But we haven't done that since I was twelve." He passed it back to her with a shrug. "Weird. Wonder what kind of dark family secrets are written there."

"Knowing my family, it could be anything. Maybe he did a good deed and didn't want the shame that would entail."

Andy snorted but then grew serious. "Seriously, though, are you okay? You look like you've seen a ghost."

"Not seen," she said, rubbing a rapidly forming bruise on her forearm from when the spirit yanked her to the ground, "but there's more than one way to be haunted."

He gave her a piercing look, as though she was a half-finished puzzle he needed to solve. "You didn't answer my question."

She shrugged. "Okay is relative. But I'm out of there, which makes things way better than it was five minutes ago."

He seemed skeptical but didn't push. She liked that about him.

They reached the bottom of the staircase on the ground floor, and she stopped. After that memory, the thought of food made her queasy. "Hey, can you let Morgan know that you two can go ahead and eat? I just need some air."

"You sure? You might feel better if—"

She cut him off, trying to soften her words as much as possible with a gentle tone. "Andy, I know you mean well, but I *am* a grown woman. I know my body, and I know that I don't feel up to eating right now."

"Right," Andy replied, rubbing the back of his neck as though embarrassed, "Sorry. I guess I'm still in caregiver mode. I'll let her know."

"Thanks," she said before heading out the back door.

The day was warm but not unbearable, a mere whispered threat of summer carried on the pleasant breeze. Rhea inhaled slowly through her nose and out through the mouth, relishing the blooming life in the air before heading to the willow. It might not have been the safest place to go, but she needed the peace she felt beneath those gently swaying branches.

From the willow, she could not see the house or the tower whose shadow stretched farther than what it left on the grass in late afternoons.

The first week Rhea spent in that room was boring, but not terrifying. She marked the days by folding the pages in her Bible and entertained herself by staring out the window. A week's grounding was normal. Every morning, her grandmother brought a plain breakfast of toast, butter, an apple, a hunk of cheese, and a glass of water. The cheese always made her gag, but she forced it down anyway because she wouldn't be eating anything else until the evening. The days passed in a maddening monotony. She read her bible, skipping the scant passages on homosexuality in favor of Jesus's teachings of kindness and his disdain for the wealthy.

In past imprisonments, she'd read it cover to cover several times. For all their piety, she doubted her grandparents actually had read it like she had. Considering all their disdain for people they considered below them, they seemed to ignore most of Jesus's teachings.

When she wasn't reading, she'd stare out the window at the world outside, watching the groundskeepers go about their work. She wondered if the staff taking care of the manor even noticed she was gone. She used to try to interact with them, but her grandparents discouraged it. If she got along with someone, they would find a reason to fire them. Probably so she wouldn't get close enough to confide in someone and sully the family's name with what Bert and Astrid Ballard were really like. In retrospect, it was shocking that the ones who stuck around never seemed to notice. Then again, maybe they did, and they just didn't care. Between the two, she wasn't sure which was worse: ignorance or apathy. Frankly, it was a small miracle that her relationship with Eliza lasted as long as it had.

Sometimes, she sang to herself. Her voice wasn't much to write home about, but she had a knack for memorizing lyrics, so she'd sing the love songs she listened to with Eliza or her mother's lullaby.

But singing was risky. If she was too loud, her grandparents would notice and make sure she shut up before the staff could hear her. Not that they would do anything to help her, anyway. They were too scared of her grandparents to step even a toe out of line. The first time she sang too loudly, Bert threw open the door, tied a gag in her mouth, and told her that if she tried to remove it before dinner, he would force her to eat the rag. That was the day she learned to be quiet in the tower. So, she saved her voice for when she knew Bert was out hunting and Astrid was walking the grounds. When she thought they might hear her singing, she chose instead to tell stories to herself. Some were stories that she'd read, but just as many were made up. She'd tell herself that, one night, Eliza would sneak in and free her. They would run away and never look back. Sometimes, that story felt so real she could almost hear Eliza on the other side of the door. When she had the energy to be angry, she imagined that she died and become one of the ghosts that haunt the house, driving her grandparents insane with her tormented rage or that she managed to escape and burn the house down with them in it like Bertha in *Jane Eyre*. A part of her hated herself for these fantasies, but they persisted the longer they kept her trapped.

She became worried after the second week when Grandma Astrid brought schoolwork and a pencil with breakfast. Usually, these punishments were a reprieve from homework, but if they expected her to do it, then they were planning to keep her there for a long time. "I expect you to have completed this when I bring dinner tonight," Grandma Astrid said coldly. It was the first thing she'd said since they locked Rhea up.

She swallowed the lump in her throat. "Yes, ma'am." Steeling herself, she asked, "How long will I be up here?"

Grandma Astrid looked her up and down, wrinkling her nose in disgust. Rhea hadn't bathed in weeks, which, combined with the backed-up toilet, gave the room a putrid odor. "You can leave when we both feel that you have truly repented."

"Can I at least take a shower?"

"We'll see," her grandmother said, turning heel and leaving.

That evening, Grandpa Bert brought up a soapy water basin and towel with Astrid and the meal. Rhea reveled the feeling of being somewhat clean.

A month passed with her stuck up there, and she began to drift in and out of awareness. The fantasies became hallucinations, and she fought to stay awake because the pain of waking up in the same place was unbearable. She would exercise just for something to do—sit-ups, pushups, jumping jacks, squats—anything to prevent the atrophy of her muscles.

In the sixth week of her imprisonment, she gave up on the prospect of them ever letting her out. As much as she hated her grandparents for this, she counted the minutes between seeing them, because they at least acknowledged their existence, even if they rarely spoke. Not even Minnie appeared to her. She would even take her in the nightmarish form of the Smiling Lady. Abandoned, even by ghosts. She remembered reading somewhere about Blanche Monnier, a woman who had been trapped in her mother's attic for twenty-six years for the crime of wanting to marry someone her mother didn't approve of. When she was found, she was emaciated, covered in bugs, feces, and rotting fruit, and suffered from anorexia, schizophrenia, exhibitionism, and coprophilia.

Rhea saw a similar future laid out for her. No one but Eliza would miss her, and even she would just assume Rhea had been sent to boarding school or something. She had no friends, no outside family, no one. It was that understanding that truly made her despair. She'd probably languish in that room until her grandparents died. Then, maybe someone settling the estate would find her before it was too late.

Before she died of starvation or dehydration in that damn attic. If not, they'd find a mummified corpse, and she'd be a curiosity. The tragic story of the girl locked in the attic and forgotten by everyone.

...

In the present, Rhea didn't realize she was crying until she felt a cold hand wipe the tears from her face. A red-haired woman stood on top of the water in front of her. Her face looked almost exactly like Rhea's, give or take ten years. Same eyes, though the woman's were a warmer brown, same cupid's bow on her full lips, same button nose. Her mother's face on another woman's body. The effect was as unsettling as it was comforting. The woman pressed a cold kiss to her forehead and gravity seemed to turn back on as she plunged back below the water. Moments later, the woman returned with an old, musty checkerboard blanket.

"Who—" she began but the lady in the lake shushed her.

"Just rest," she said. Her voice had a slight accent, but Rhea couldn't place where it was from. Was this her mother? She could hardly remember her voice, so maybe she had an accent like that when she was alive.

The woman began to hum, stroking Rhea's hair and gently nudging her to lie down. Her eyes began to slip closed, and before sleep completely took her, she heard the woman say, "Sleep well, my little angel."

CHAPTER SEVENTEEN

A rough hand jerked her awake. In her haze between dreaming and waking, she was several places at once—Bert dragging her out of bed, the tunnel where homeless teens flocked together for the night where she slept with a pocketknife in hand, the group home with Sister Elizabeth waking her bright and early to do her chores and go to work—and she lashed out, striking someone in the chest. "Jesus, Rhea," a familiar voice exclaimed.

She blinked and Morgan came into focus clutching her chest. Her eyes widened when she realized what she'd done. "Oh my god, I am so sorry, I—"

"Just get away from the water," Morgan said with a forced calm. That tight, controlled voice—the same that Bert and Astrid used when they were displeased but unable to lay into her that moment—sent a bolt of fear into Rhea's chest almost worse than the ghosts.

She wordlessly followed Morgan as she led her into the house and sat her down in the kitchen. The silence between them was thick and heavy like a humid summer afternoon right before a thunderstorm. She wanted to break the silence, to apologize again for hitting her, going where she said not to go, and anything else she could think of, but no words would come. Morgan set a plate of warm spaghetti and meatballs in front of her and sat down on the other side of the table with a sigh.

"I'm sorry," Morgan said, "I shouldn't have snapped."

Rhea was stunned. She opened her mouth, made the beginning of a sound, and then closed it. What did Morgan have to apologize for? Rhea was the one that hurt her. "No, I'm sorry." Morgan deserved an explanation. Hopefully, she would see it like that, instead of an excuse. "I—uh—I think you've noticed by now that I tend to startle easily. Historically, I'd only get shaken awake when I was in trouble. But that's a me problem. You have nothing to apologize for."

Morgan reached across the table and took her hand. "If I don't, then you don't either." This time, when the silence fell between them, it was far less oppressive. Morgan was the one who broke it. "Andy told me a little of what happened. That you got trapped in that room in the attic. I went to go check on you, to make sure you were okay. I searched all over the house and the grounds, and I got so scared."

Rhea stared down at the spaghetti as though it might have the perfect response spelled out in the noodles. "Sorry, I just needed some air."

"You apologize too much."

"Sorry—uh, I mean, okay."

Morgan gave her such a kind look, her brown eyes soft and warm and a small smile playing on her lips. She and

Andy both looked at her in a way she hadn't felt before. It was something like pity, but not because they felt superior to her. Compassion, maybe? If she really wanted to be generous to herself, she'd say it was affection, but that didn't make sense. They hadn't known her for long, so how could they feel much more for her than pity?

"Would you like to talk about what happened?"

She shook her head. "Maybe later. I need to get myself together a little more first."

"Then maybe after lunch we can head into town and do some shopping. I wanted to stop by the bookstore. Astrid's library is nice and all, but I'd like to read a book written this century by someone who isn't white, you know?"

Despite her nap, she felt drained and exhausted, but she thought she might scream if she had to spend one more moment at the house. "Sounds nice."

...

Rhea walked side by side with Morgan down Main Street in Cherub's Cove, taking in the postcard perfect shops. "They really haven't changed," she said and pointed to Tommy's Toys. The pastel green building sat on the corner. An angel had been painted in the window. The sun-faded figure smiled as it held a teddy bear in one arm and a toy plane in the other. "That used to be my favorite shop. I could spend hours searching the shelves." Her grandfather rarely gave her hours, though. They preferred the mansion and only came down when they needed food or new clothes. Grandma Astrid was practically an agoraphobe, so it was up to Grandpa Bert to run errands in town. He often brought her along, so she'd have a change of scenery. During those times, he'd often drop her off at the bookstore while he got what they needed and would pick her up when he was finished.

Her favorite time, though, was when he'd get her up a little earlier and they'd pick out new clothes for her. Grandma Astrid insisted that young ladies wore dresses, but Grandpa Bert was more practical. He let her buy jeans and even t-shirts as long as they were pink enough. Still, she stared longingly at the boy's Dinosaur shirts and little suits. She wanted nothing more than to try on something that wasn't frilly or covered in unicorns.

But still, she treasured those outings. She loved sashaying out of the dressing room and hearing her grandfather exclaim, "You look so pretty, princess!" And, afterwards, he would take her to the ice cream shop or the bakery for something sweet to eat. Because Grandma Astrid kept them on a strict diet, this was a little secret shared between them. It was one of the few truly happy times she had with him, and it lasted well into her teenage years, though with less hyperbolic praise as she got older. Their last outing was for her sixteenth birthday, where they bought her a dress for one of Astrid's parties and ate ice cream by the pier.

Though her feelings towards her grandparents would forever be complicated, she smiled at the unexpected fond memory and took a deep breath, relishing the salty air of the nearby sea and the bustle of people going about their daily lives. It was strange, looking back on it. Every time he left, he seemed to walk differently, smiling more easily as he greeted the people around him. On the rare occasion that

Astrid went out, there was something lighter about her too. Maybe they felt the oppressive nature of the house the same way that she did but had grown acclimated to it, feeling like a deep-sea diver surfacing too quickly and getting the bends every time they left their fortress.

Though it was warm at the Ballard House, the ocean breeze in town still carried the last dregs of winter—not cold enough to make her shiver, but just chilly enough that the dead heat of summer felt far away. She and Morgan walked down the pastel Main Street, dodging shoppers and kids running past. It was still early in the season for tourists, but the town was starting to come alive.

Page Turners sat at the end of Main Street and was almost exactly as she remembered it. Sure, there were new titles, and new posters lined the walls, but it had the same chipped blue paint façade and squeaky old floorboards. The moment she stepped in, she closed her eyes and inhaled the comforting smell of old paper. Another thing that hadn't changed was Gus, the owner of the store, who was old even when Rhea was young. His wrinkles were a bit deeper, and his shoulders more slumped, but he still held that mischievous twinkle in his eye.

"Hello there, Miss Morgan and Miss?" he greeted from behind the counter.

She couldn't help her smile when she said, "Hi Gus, it's been a while."

He blinked, and his lips curled into a smile wide enough to show off his gold tooth. "Well, if it isn't little Miss *I'm going to read Les Mis from cover to cover*. Tell me, did you actually finish it?"

"I did," she said with more pride than accomplishment perhaps warranted. It's easy to read a book longer than the Bible when you're locked in a room with nothing else to do for a week or two. "And I didn't even skip the chapters on the Napoleonic wars or Paris's sewer system."

He chuckled. "I'm impressed. Those parts put me to sleep. It's been a while since I've seen you, Miss Ballard. How have you been?"

Well, wasn't that a loaded question. Keeping her smile, she replied, "Well, I've been managing. And you?"

He smiled. "Oh, you know. Same old, same old."

The new book display was calling her name as she skimmed the titles. "So, what do you recommend?"

He gestured to the new arrivals display. "Take your pick."

"Do you have any nonfiction books on the supernatural?" Morgan asked.

Rhea raised an eyebrow as she picked up a fantasy novel that promised humor, adventure, and escapism. If Morgan had wanted to do research, Astrid's personal library held all her father's books. No offense to Gus, but it would probably be a better place to start than a paltry section of a small-town bookstore. Maybe Morgan didn't know that, though.

"You getting into witchcraft again, Reyes?" Gus asked.

Morgan scrunched up her face in disgust. "No, my *The Craft* phase is thankfully long dead. I wanted to know a little more about ghosts."

He pointed to a dark corner of the small bookstore. "It's right over there."

"You know," Rhea said softly as they took in the small section, "my dad studied folklore. He wrote a couple books that Astrid kept in her library."

Once, in a fit of boredom, she snuck into Astrid's library. Before that afternoon, her grandmother had forbidden her from entering, fearing that she would "get her grubby hands all over the first editions" but to forbid a child from doing something is to guarantee that they will eventually try it. And that day, Rhea's curiosity got the better of her and, after checking to see if Grandma Astrid was around, she slowly opened the door so it would not creak and slipped inside.

She stared at the books lining the shelves, not sure of what she was looking for. At the time, the most advanced book she'd read was *Nancy Drew and the Secret of the Old Clock*. These books were all much older and longer. Some of them looked so heavy she wouldn't be able to lift them. One author name, though, caught her eye. Julien Ballard. Her father. She took the book off the shelf and stared at the photo of him on the back of the dust jacket. His blond hair was artfully tussled and he gave a winning smile at the camera, his green eyes sparkling.

She smiled back, wondering if they looked alike. They both had that dimple in their left cheek, and the eye shape was similar. But really, she'd taken after her mother, with her dark hair, brown eyes, and full lips. At least, she assumed that she did. Her grandparents refused to speak of her mother and, aside from the portrait, the only pictures of her were in the wedding album and of her holding Rhea for the first time in the delivery room. There were none of her alone, only ever her with Rhea's father. It was obvious that they only kept them because they couldn't bear to part with any memories of Julien Ballard. Rhea once asked about her mother, and they shut it down quickly, saying that she and her father were not a good match. He was too good for "that gold digger." After those cruel words, Rhea never asked again.

But they were proud of their son. Her father walked on water. He was "a brilliant man" whose intellect surpassed everyone at the college he taught at. And apparently, they bought every book he'd published, no matter how dryly academic. She pulled out *The Evolution of The Fair Folk Around the World*. She liked stories of fairies, especially the dark ones where they were dangerous tricksters instead of pretty girls who wore dresses made of flower petals and flitted through the forest on butterfly wings. She climbed onto the couch and began to read, sounding out the many unfamiliar words. Eventually, she grabbed a dictionary and set it beside her so she could look up anything she couldn't understand through context clues.

Rhea wasn't sure how long it was before Grandma Astrid opened the door. It could have been a few minutes or a few hours. When she saw her, though, they both froze, staring wide eyed like cornered rabbits.

"Is that your father's book?" Grandma Astrid asked softly.

She swallowed the lump in her throat and said, "I'm sorry." Rhea braced for the worst: Grandma Astrid yelling at her, ripping the books from her hand and dragging her to the attic room. But she did no such thing. Instead, her grandmother sat down next to her, craning her wrinkled neck to look at the text.

"What do you think of it?"

Rhea shrugged, unable to process this turn of events. "I don't understand most of it."

Grandma Astrid chuckled warmly. "I'd be surprised if you could. That's a college textbook." She shifted closer, wrapping a wrinkled arm around Rhea's shoulder. "If you read it out loud, I can explain it to you."

"Okay," Rhea said, and began to read.

They spent that afternoon together with her reading and her grandmother explaining what her father meant. Eventually, it devolved into her just telling stories of her father. Rhea hadn't felt truly safe since before the accident, when her parents would comfort her on stormy nights and hold her when she woke from bad dreams, but in that moment, she felt secure with her grandmother beside her, bonded by a mutual grief. A daughter without a father and a mother without a son.

"I think I've seen them," Morgan said, snapping Rhea out of the memory, "Astrid let me read every book in the library but those. They were for family and family only. Probably wouldn't have read them anyway. Academic texts aren't exactly pleasure reading."

"I read them cover to cover several times," Rhea replied running her finger down a leather-bound collection of "true" paranormal encounters of the Northeast. "It made me feel closer to him, even if it was too dense for me to understand."

The store lapsed into a comfortable silence, with Rhea and Morgan scanning titles while Gus worked behind the counter. The bell at the front door hailed the arrival of a new customer, shattering that peace.

"Hey Gus," Eliza said.

Rhea stood frozen in place feeling like a rabbit cornered by a fox. It was too late for her to slip out or hide behind a bookshelf. Eliza had already locked eyes with Rhea and was approaching her with a wide smile as though they were little more than old acquaintances.

"Rhea," she exclaimed, holding her arms out wide for a hug, "I'm sorry we didn't get the chance to talk at the funeral. How are you holding up?"

She stiffened as Eliza wrapped her arms around her. For years, she imagined what it would be like to speak to her again, whether she would let her festering resentment over that night burst like a pustule or if she would fall into Eliza's arms as though she'd never left. It turned out she did neither, the conflicting swirls of happiness and hurt leaving her mute.

Eventually, Eliza stepped back and looked her up and down with a warm smile. "You look good."

"You too," she managed to croak out, her eyes drawn to the wedding ring on Eliza's left hand. In her mind's eye, Eliza had been frozen at seventeen, but they were both adults now. Eliza had married and moved on with her life. What did she expect? The two of them running away together and going to junior prom? Stupid. Rhea was little more than a footnote in the lives of Eliza and everyone else around her.

"I've thought about you every day, you know," Eliza said, "We should catch up. Are you free tomorrow?"

"I—uh—yeah. Just give me the time and place."

"Let me see your phone. I'll put in my contact info." Rhea fished out her old iPhone 4 that she bought second hand after years of saving money and Eliza added herself to the contact list.

Morgan, who had been crowded out of the corner by Eliza, cleared her throat. "Hi, I'm Morg—"

"Morgan Reyes," Eliza said, her voice suddenly growing cold, "I think you were a grade above me. You and Josh."

Morgan's smile tightened at the edges. "Yeah, I remember seeing your around. How have you been?"

Eliza shrugged. "It's tax season, which, for an accountant is like the North Pole in December. Right now, I'm *drowning* in work."

"Except instead of making toys for good girls and boys, you just tell us what we owe the government," Rhea said, trying to defuse the tension she felt building like the beginning of a thunderstorm.

Eliza flashed her one of her beauty pageant smiles. "That's not fair. Sometimes I tell you what the government owes you."

Rhea smiled back, though the hairs on the back of her neck prickled as though she was in danger. "Sorry, toys are still more fun." The tension between the two was palpable, and Rhea hated it. Intellectually, she knew she'd done nothing wrong, but history had taught her that she'd still be struck by lightning even if she tried to avoid the storm.

"Can I talk to you in private?" Eliza said, tugging her away from Morgan. Once they were out of earshot, she whispered, "Didn't you hear what she did?"

"Arrange a lovely funeral for my not-so-lovely grandparents?" She tugged herself free from Eliza's digging grip and met Eliza's disappointed look with defiance.

Eliza deflated. "Josh West was my friend. We hung out in same circles and kept in touch after he graduated. He always talked about this dream girl that he met in high school. One who was an amazing cook but playing hard to get. Then, one day, he's floating face down in the lake next to where she works."

She rubbed at the headache slowly forming behind her eyes. "Look, I don't know the full story, but Morgan's been nothing but kind to me."

"And you'll just attach yourself to anyone that throws you a scrap of kindness?"

That cut deep, probably far deeper than Eliza intended it. Because Eliza got to grow up, get married, go to college, and probably never had to work three jobs just to survive or to choose between rent and her next meal. The world had been kind to Eliza, so she never felt the push and pull of other people's kindness, never feared it while also craving it like a starving man before a feast. "Blame it on the childhood emotional abuse," Rhea replied, failing to keep the acid from her tone.

Eliza flinched, sending a small thrill of satisfaction through Rhea. "Just be careful. Please. I don't want you to get hurt."

"I'll keep it in mind," she said through gritted teeth. Who was Eliza to barge back into her life and dictate who Rhea should fraternize with? She'd made it clear six years ago that Rhea wasn't wanted in her own. Eliza always had friends, had people to fawn over her. Until Morgan and Andy, Rhea had no one.

"I guess that's all I can ask. I did miss you, you know, and I never stopped wondering where you were, if you were okay, or... I guess I want some closure, and I think you might too. And maybe we could start over as friends?"

Rhea sighed, ignoring the ragged edges of the wound Eliza had inflicted with the request to just be friends. She should find an excuse not to, but she could never say no to those blue eyes. "That might be nice," she said, her gaze drawn to the thin, gold band around Eliza's ring finger. For years, she'd daydream about this moment, this second chance for them, but it wasn't one, not really. It was like she'd wished to see Eliza again on a monkey's paw.

And here was the thing: Rhea understood. She understood why Eliza stayed behind, why she turned Rhea away. Eliza wasn't in an easy position, and a part of Rhea always felt guilty for putting her there in the first place. But, she also couldn't help the resentment that burned now that Eliza was in front of her, embracing her like an old friend as though nothing had ever happened, as though the shared horror of their history was nothing. And now she wanted closure, whatever that meant. Did she really want to get to know Rhea again after all these years? Or did she just feel guilty about what happened and want Rhea to absolve her of it?

"How about Margot's Café at noon tomorrow?"

"Okay." A strange numbness spread over her. She was doing this. A lunch not-date with an old girlfriend. It was a bad idea. A terrible idea. And yet...and yet she needed the closure too. Maybe the distant hope curling in her chest at the thought of their reunion could bear fruit, whatever fruit that may be.

Eliza pulled her into a hug she only stiffly returned. "Great! I can't wait."

CHAPTER EIGHTEEN

Morgan was uncharacteristically quiet as they waited for a server to return with their drinks. The restaurant, Captain Cook's, was a typical Cape Cod tourist trap, with dark wood paneling and decorated with boats and fishing nets. The waiter gave them a window seat overlooking the calm water and handed them their menus.

The quiet unnerved Rhea. If Morgan was mad, she wished she'd just yell at her to get it over with. This kind of cold silence was like a bomb she had to defuse. Pick the wrong wire and the night would blow up in her face.

"Everything okay?" she asked.

"Yeah, fine," Morgan said, staring at the menu without reading it.

Great, a guessing game. She always hated those. When her grandparents or Eliza were quietly angry, she'd spend hours shuffling through her mental rolodex of sins and infractions, but she never could quite figure out which ones set them off. "Are you mad at me?"

Morgan looked up; her brows knitted in confusion. "What? No, not you."

"But you're upset about something."

"I'm just tired. Everyone in town treats me like some kind of pariah. The girl who killed the town's golden boy. Everyone but you and Andy, because he believes me and you…"

"Don't know your side of the story," Rhea finished. "I know a thing or two about the fickle public."

"I'll give it to you eventually. I promise. Because we need to talk about what happened today, and I think I owe you an explanation about why I don't like the lake." She sighed, rubbing her forehead. "I'm sorry. It's just—it's a lot, and I don't know how to begin."

Rhea nodded. "Believe me. I get it." The silence that lapsed between them wasn't as uncomfortable as before. "So, what's good here?" she asked, hoping to regain some of the easy conversation they'd had earlier.

"It depends on what you're in the mood for. If you want something comforting, the clam chowder is amazing. The fish and chips are the perfect hangover cure." Her face colored. "I've only had it once, as a birthday gift to myself, but the lobster roll is amazing."

"Are you in the mood for one now?"

Morgan shook her head. "Oh, no, I couldn't—"

Without thinking, Rhea took her hand. "It's my treat. Besides, you've been such a good—" She cut herself off as a wave of fear crested over her. She was about to say friend. Did she consider Morgan a friend? Absolutely. After knowing her for a few days, she'd told Morgan more than she'd told anyone else in her life. But did Morgan *really* consider her a friend? Or was she just a particularly emotionally unstable boss? "Friend," she said, and looking at their entwined hands, snatched hers away with an embarrassed chuckle. Morgan's face was difficult to read, but she almost looked disappointed. "So, two lobster rolls?"

"You don't wanna try something else?" Morgan's eyes sparkled with humor. "How about the raw oysters?"

Rhea gagged. "Been there, done that. Grandma Astrid made me eat them at the parties she hosted and I'm never having a salty loogie like that again as long as I live." She closed the menu and set it on the table. "Besides, if it's Morgan approved, then it has to be good."

Morgan chuckled. "If you say so."

As if to illustrate Morgan's earlier point, the waiter was cold and unfriendly as he took their orders. They both agreed to tip twenty percent anyway. They weren't monsters. The two settled into a comfortable silence as they snacked on the rolls he brought out. It was Rhea who broke it.

"So, Morgan, you know so much about me and my Jane Eyre upbringing. Can you tell me more about you?"

Morgan took a sip of her lemonade. "What do you wanna know?"

Rhea shrugged. "Favorite color...favorite movie... favorite book...stuff that friends know about each other." She braced herself for awkwardness, searching Morgan's face for any signs of discomfort.

Instead, though, her eyes lit up. "Okay, so my favorite color is lavender, my favorite movie is *A Nightmare on Elm Street*, and my favorite book series is *Discworld*."

Rhea couldn't help her surprised snort. "Wait, go back. What was that again?"

"What?" Morgan asked in mock offense, "My favorite color is lavender, my favorite book series is *Discworld*—"

"And your favorite movie is *A Nightmare on Elm Street*?" She laughed. "I'm sorry. I just never pegged you for a horror buff."

"You think I don't have a dark side?" She had an odd expression on her face, and Rhea struggled to read it. It was the kind of carefully blank look that had clearly been practiced to hide an ocean's depth of pain. She knew that look better than anyone. It was the mask she learned to wear around her grandparents. She hardly knew how to take it off anymore.

So, like the master of poor coping measures she was, she decided to deflect with a joke. "Well, when you put it like that, should I be worried? You're not poisoning dinner, are you?" A flash of hurt crossed Morgan's face at the accusation and she winced. Wrong choice. God, she was really putting her foot in it. Without thinking, Rhea took her hand. "Shit, I shouldn't have—I-I mean, that was stupid. Sorry. But I don't believe what they say. I swear."

Morgan looked down at their entwined fingers and then up, her smile growing mischievous. "Notice the taste of bitter almonds in your breakfast?"

"No?"

"Good. My attempts to cover it up are working."

Rhea breathed a laugh. "Bacon and eggs with a side of cyanide. Nothing better to wake you up in the morning." The waiter chose that moment to bring them their sandwiches. He shot Morgan a glare before asking if they wanted anything else. When he disappeared, they dissolved into giggles.

Rhea picked up a fry and popped it into her mouth. Salty greasy perfection. The sandwich, which she had ordered cold with mayonnaise and celery, was the cream of Cape Cod's crop. "You were right. This is great."

"What can I say? I know my food."

Rhea ate another French fry. It was strange how light she felt. It was as though she was truly breathing for the first time in a long time or taking off a winter coat in the middle of summer. She could have blamed it on the oppressive nature of the house, the weight of unpleasant memories bearing down on her, but it was more than that. Was this what it was like to be relaxed around another person? It had been so long that she had truly forgotten the feeling. But something about Morgan put her at ease. Her warm smile, sense of humor, and the way she seemed to genuinely care about others. For all the time Rhea had spent on her guard, Morgan slipped past her defenses like water. She could see herself drawing close and pressing a kiss to her looking soft lips.

She startled at the thought. No, no she would not kiss her employee, especially not when Morgan relied on her for paychecks and housing. What the hell was wrong with her? Eliza was right. She really did fall for anyone who gave her a scrap of positive attention. Morgan was kind and seemed to care about Rhea's wellbeing—the first person to do that in a very long time. They could be friends, and when Morgan finds an apartment and a new job, then maybe... Until then, she would enjoy her company and the warm feelings that came with being with her.

And if some of those feelings towards her were crush-like, then she simply wouldn't act on them. Rhea knew better than anyone the discomfort of being stuck in a place where the person in charge takes a special interest. The manager at the grocery store shamelessly made advances towards her, but she couldn't stand up for herself because she'd then be fired and there went food for that month. So no, she would not be acting on any romantic feelings. But friendship was okay, she supposed. More than okay. Morgan was a good friend, and Rhea was happy just to have met her.

So, she forced herself to relax and enjoy her meal. One thing at a time.

CHAPTER NINETEEN

After dinner, she and Morgan wandered the town, buying ice cream from the old shop her grandfather would take her to and eating it as they watched the sun set over the sea. Rhea suspected that Morgan was procrastinating, looking for excuses to stay out to avoid telling her story, but she was having such a nice time that she didn't care. She went to bed feeling more content than she had in a long time.

The Smiling Lady had stopped visiting after the incident with the Water Hemlock. Rhea barely remembered the weeks she was in the hospital, first to treat the poisoning and then because apparently, she had babbled about Minnie, The Smiling Lady, and wanting to join her parents. That put her on both lithium and suicide watch. Grandma and Grandpa were terribly embarrassed by the whole thing. When they released her from the mental hospital, the doctors having decided that she wasn't a danger to herself or others, her grandparents had locked her in the attic room until she promised she'd stop talking about ghosts. But just because she stopped talking about ghosts didn't mean she'd stopped seeing them.

Case in point: the night after her eighth birthday. She laid in bed clutching Otso and listening to the footsteps pace back and forth above her. The ghost's pace wasn't steady. Sometimes it walked. Sometimes it ran. Sometimes, she swore it was jumping right above her head. Eventually, her exhaustion outweighed her fear, and she leapt out of bed, sprinted to the Walkman in the reading nook, and then sprinted back, praying that the ghost hadn't noticed. She put in her headphones and pressed play without caring what was in the player. The opening notes to "Sweet Child of Mine" filled her ears, blocking out the footsteps. It was her Dad's album. He'd play it for her on car rides and belt out his best Axel Rose impression. If she closed her eyes, she could pretend that she was in their car on a road trip singing along to Guns 'N Roses. By the end of the song, she had drifted off to sleep.

It became routine that every night she would play the Walkman as she drifted off. It got to a point that on the nights when she was locked in the attic, she struggled to fall asleep without her music. The habit lasted long into her teenage years, but those four months at the end kicked her of the habit. Still it was a comfort to have on her nightstand. Evern after all these years, Rhea still touched it reverently as she got ready for bed.

She should have realized that the house was angry when the temperature dropped. It was still early enough in the year for cold snaps, so she didn't think much of it, only piling on extra blankets until she realized that she could see her breath by the light of the moon. And then all hell broke loose. The door rattled, the rocking horse shook, footsteps paced back and forth above her and ran down the hall. Something shattered. She clutched the Walkman hard enough for her knuckles to turn white. It would be so easy to ignore it, to just put her music on and forget everything. But Morgan was out there, and she should check on her, make sure that the house isn't angry at her too.

A movement caught the corner of her eye. She turned to the vanity and her eyes went wide as she fought the urge to scream. Astrid glared back at her. The old woman's thinning, grey hair, usually in a neat bun, hung lank around her wrinkled face. She mouthed something that Rhea couldn't parse, and then pursed her lips in frustration the way she used to when Rhea was doing something she didn't approve of.

Feeling like a child, she snatched Otso and dove under the covers, inhaling her mother's perfume and ignoring the way the bed shook and the feeling of her grandmother's disapproval.

Something had made the entities in the house angry, and just like old habits, she went through her mental rolodex of sins. Low on the list was her encounter with Eliza. They hated her in the end, but that had been years ago. Then, there was her realization about her feelings for Morgan. How dare she keep living the homosexual lifestyle? What will the town think? Most likely was her discovery of the diaries. There was something in them that they didn't want her to see, and they were angry for daring to read the books someone clearly wanted her to read. Regardless, the noise was so loud that the music had no hope of blocking it out. She wondered if it wasn't related to ghosts at all and was instead a perfectly natural earthquake threatening to send this nightmare castle to the ground.

Alas, no luck. All the activity stopped just as quickly as it started. The air returned to its normal temperature, and the silence that befell the house was just as terrifying as the noise. It was as though the house was holding its breath, waiting to see if it would vomit more terrors upon them.

Her bedroom door burst open, and Rhea screamed at the sudden noise and movement. The light flicked on, revealing an ashen Morgan. "Are you okay?" she asked.

Rhea put a hand over her still speeding heart. "I'm fine. What's a little heart attack between friends?"

"What the hell was that?" Morgan's wide eyes scanned the room as though looking for the cause of the earthquake. Under normal circumstances, Rhea would have thought the tousled hair and disheveled cat pajamas made Morgan look rather cute, but now was not the time to think about that.

Rhea chewed her lip. "I guess we somehow pissed off the life deprived members of this household. I think the show's over for tonight, though."

"Oh," she replied, still looking shaken. She glanced at the hallway before stepping in and shutting the door behind her. "I—um—I don't think I can be alone just yet."

Rhea pulled back the covers and swung her legs off the bed, beckoning her to come closer. She offered her the Walkman. Morgan sat on the side of the bed and took it skeptically. "It's how I ignored the ghosts at night for years. Unless something like tonight happens again, this should block it out."

"Your grandparents didn't believe you?" Morgan sat with her back to her, so she couldn't see her face, but she could hear the edge of anger at her voice.

It wasn't directed at her. She knew it was for Bert and Astrid's cruelty and neglect but try telling that to the balled lightning in her chest. Rhea scoffed. "Not really. A good, Christian household like ours haunted? Impossible. I just had a big imagination."

Morgan's grip on the Walkman became white knuckled. "They were so cruel," she said softly.

Rhea pulled her knees up to her chest. Morgan didn't know the half of it, but she didn't want to get into *that* just yet. "Well, at least they're paying for my therapy from beyond the grave."

Morgan's slowly raised her head to meet Rhea's eyes with a smile like a sputtering candle. "Well, I guess there's that. It would have been better if they didn't put you in therapy in the first place."

"But think of how rich I'm gonna make my psychiatrist! I'll probably fund at least one trip to Cancun on therapy bills alone. In the end, they did make me a productive member of society."

Morgan snickered before becoming serious again. "Thank you for this. It's very kind of you to let me borrow it."

She shrugged. "Hey, these ghosts are my problem. Sorry you're getting caught in the crossfire."

"I wish they were just your problem," she muttered.

"What do you mean?"

"Let's just say that some spirits are more dangerous than others." She got to her feet and stretched. "Anyway, I'm sorry I kept you us this long. We should both be headed to bed."

For one absurd moment, Rhea was tempted to offer to share a bed after the night's terrifying events but thought better of it. Still, Morgan lingered at the door as though still reluctant to leave even with a handheld coping mechanism. Before she could think better of it, Rhea said, "Actually, I think I might go downstairs and watch some bad late-night TV. Wanna come?"

The tension left Morgan's shoulders in an instant. "As long as it's not a horror movie."

Rhea chuckled. "I thought you liked horror."

"Not tonight, thank you." Morgan rolled her eyes good naturedly. "I've had enough scares to last me a lifetime."

To minimize the risk of falling asleep on her shoulder or vice versa, Rhea sat at the opposite end of the couch. Morgan looked confused but didn't comment as she put on bad reality television. They sat through two reruns of America's Next Top Model in total silence. Morgan was so quiet that Rhea thought she'd fallen asleep until she spoke up. "That tower room you were trapped in today—it was where your grandparents locked you up, right?"

Rhea curled in on herself, wrapping her arms around her knees. "Yeah, yeah it was. I guess locking me in that room when I misbehaved kept me out of further trouble, and if I decided to throw myself out the window...then I guess that was one less burden for them do deal with." The silence was deafening but she forced herself to continue. "It was the last straw actually. They caught me with a girl and locked me in there for months. When I realized they weren't ever letting me out, I made a rope out of my bedsheets and escaped like a fairytale princess." Picking up her head, her eyes met Morgan's and she gave a small smile. "I think you're the first person I've ever told that story."

Morgan stared at her in wide eyes horror. She braced herself for disbelief, for pity. What she didn't expect was for her to ask, "Can I give you a hug?"

"A hug?" she repeated.

Morgan shifted closer, still leaving enough of a gap for her to pull away if she wanted. "It sounds like you could really use one."

Rhea nodded, not moving from her balled up position as Morgan wrapped her arms around her shoulders and squeezed. It was nice, not as claustrophobia inducing as the hug she gave before the funeral. Morgan seemed to be giving her enough space to get free if she wanted to. She didn't, though. A small part of her always wondered if she was exaggerating what her grandparents put her through, and worried that, if she told anyone else her history, they would validate that fear. It wasn't like they ever hit her beyond a slap or sexually assaulted her. All they did was send her to her room...and their disappointment's room.

As though reading her mind, Morgan rested a cheek on her shoulder and said, "I'm so sorry you went through all that. What they did was horrible, and I'm sorry for every nice thing I've ever said about them."

She let out a stuttering breath. Between revelations about Astrid killing her mother, her assisted suicide attempt at age seven, the possibility that Morgan might have killed a man, constant ghost attacks, and her planned lunch with Eliza, her head felt full to bursting. She wanted to close her eyes and rest.

One day without stunning and painful discoveries about the past. That was all she wanted.

This hug was going on for far too long. Professionalism had been flung out the window like litter from a car on the highway a while ago, but she still didn't want this comfort to end, and Morgan made no moves to end it first.

"The woman in the lake killed Josh West," Morgan said softly.

She pulled back. "What?"

Morgan took it as a cue to shift away. She rested her elbows on her knees and buried her face in her hand, her raven hair falling forward so that Rhea couldn't see her face. "We dated in high school, and it got...intense the way that first loves do. Teenage hormones making every high like Romeo and Juliet and the lows like, well, the end of Romeo and Juliet. It wasn't healthy, and I used going away to culinary school in New York as an excuse to break up." Her voice cracked. "But he didn't want us to be over. In the spring semester, he transferred to NYU so we could be together. When that didn't happen, he got...weird, and I started seeing him more than normal for a city with a population of eight million people." She straightened up, still not looking at Rhea. Instead, her glassy gaze went upwards in the way that girls often did when they were trying not to cry and ruin their mascara. Morgan, of course, wasn't wearing any in the moment, but the habit probably stuck.

"First, I could brush it off. We took the same subway to school, so we'd see each other on our commutes. My favorite coffeeshop? Also not too weird. It had good reviews online and was a popular spot for students. But everywhere I went,

I had this prickling sensation like someone was watching me." She paused, her breath coming out in a stutter. "It got bad when I started dating someone. Things were going fine until one day I got a text from her saying that we're breaking up and she never wants to see me again. Obviously, I'm hurt and confused, so I go to her apartment. She tells me that a guy showed up when she got out of class the other day and told her that he was my boyfriend, and I was cheating on him with her. She didn't believe him, but didn't want to risk angering him, so she decided to end it. I tried filing a police report, but technically he hadn't done anything illegal." Morgan laughed bitterly, a tear streaking down her cheek. Rhea resisted the urge to wipe it away.

"They didn't do jack shit when he *did* cross that line. He broke into my dorm room, and that was the final straw. I transferred to a school halfway across the country and didn't return home until I graduated and couldn't find a job. When the position of cook for Cherub Cove royalty opened up, it was heaven sent. The West family might be powerful, but the Ballard's are gods. When Josh showed up, Bert chased him away with a shotgun, and the police sided with him. For a while, I thought it was the end. As long as I was with your grandparents, I was safe."

There was a sinking feeling in Rhea's stomach. Reaching over, she rested a hand on Morgan's shoulder, half expecting her to flinch away. Instead, Morgan simply rested her hand on Rhea's.

"But then, in the middle of the night, I wake up to a hand over my mouth, and he's there. I'll never forget the way he looked, how the full moon reflected off his white face until it was like a corpse staring over me. I tried to scream, but he held firm, whispering that he just wanted to talk outside." Another pause, another stuttering breath.

"It's okay," Rhea said. "I think I can guess what happened from here."

Morgan shook her head, glaring and pulling back from Rhea's touch. "No, you fucking can't, Rhea! Because if you did, you wouldn't go near that fucking lake," she snapped.

Rhea flinched back, a bolt of fear briefly coursing through her. She had never heard Morgan raise her voice before, not even to the people constantly accusing her of murder. Had she gone too far? It was a familiar terror, one that Morgan would now want nothing to do with her after putting her foot in her mouth again. She resisted the urge to grovel, because then Morgan, as kind as she was, would just comfort her, and she'd been doing enough of that for the past few days. It was her turn to be comforted. "Sorry. Keep going."

Morgan shook her head, the tears flowing freely now. "No, I'm sorry. I didn't mean—"

She crossed the distance between them again and took Morgan's hand, intertwining their fingers and squeezing gently. "I know. It's okay. Please tell me what happened."

Morgan nodded stiffly, still sniffling. "I thought to myself, *This is it. He's going to kill me.* He had prepared a picnic beneath the willow by the lake, with champagne and roses. He really thought, after all these years of terror, he'd win me back by practically kidnapping me. It was so funny to me that I started laughing and just couldn't stop. The harder I laughed, the angrier he got, and eventually, he slapped me. That shut me up. He tried giving me a non-apology about how I made him do it, and I just had enough.

I pushed him away with more force that I expected, and he went stumbling backwards, and he fell in the water. Then, I saw her."

Morgan huffed a weak laugh. "She was wearing my face. I still don't know how, but she was wearing my face. I don't know how long we spent staring, his eyes ping ponging between us. I mean, how do you react to that? Then, I guess some kind of primal instinct kicked in or something, because he tried to pull himself out of the water. But she had him by the foot and every time he scrabbled to get out, she would just yank him back in like a cat toying with a mouse. He begged me for my help. I was about to, but God forgive me, I realized that if this monster took him, then I wouldn't have to live in fear anymore. And in that brief moment, he was gone, and I was relieved. God, I was so relieved, and I hate myself for how glad I still am that he's gone." She turned to Rhea slowly, her eyes puffy from tears. "Because it's the Ballards and they're pillars of the community, the police covered it up and ruled his death a suicide."

Rhea clenched her free hand into a fist, her short nails biting into her palms. She was glad Josh was dead, because if he wasn't, she would have wanted to kill him herself for all the pain he put Morgan through. It was all just so unfair. If someone, *anyone*, had seen the true danger she was in, none of this would have happened, and Josh still would've been alive. And, well, Rhea could relate to that feeling of helplessness, that knowledge that no one cared enough to protect her.

She didn't blame Morgan for her hesitation or for Josh's death. In her position, Rhea would hesitate too. Hell, if she knew about the evil ghost that drowned people, she might have pushed her grandparents into the lake. It was a terrible thought to have, but no less true.

Rhea knew she had to say something. Something to help with the guilt and provide the same comfort she had just received. Comforting people was not a skill that her grandparents had imbued in her. *It wasn't your fault? He had it coming? Don't feel bad because you're relieved someone who hurt you is gone?* Instead, she patted her awkwardly on the knee. "That's terrible. Would you...would you like a hug too?" Nailed it.

Morgan looked at Rhea's hand on her knee and chuckled, leaning against her. "You're sweet."

People rarely called Rhea sweet. Cold. Closed off. Painfully awkward. Never sweet. And compared to Morgan's sugar crusted personality, hers was more like the castor oil her grandmother would sometimes make her drink as punishment. As a rule, Rhea wasn't much for physical contact, so she awkwardly released Morgan's hand and wrapped an arm around her shoulder. Her grandparents were allergic to physical comfort. Their hugs were few and far between. Eliza could be affectionate, but they had to be careful with their touches. And after she ran away, she never let herself get close enough to anyone for physical affection beyond a handshake. Morgan, though, seemed to be more casually affectionate with people, so while she relaxed against her, Rhea tensed, somehow both thrilled and terrified.

Was this appropriate? She'd asked and Morgan was the one who initiated the contact. But she was her boss, and the power dynamics were all wrong. She shouldn't be snuggling with someone who depends on her for her paycheck. That wasn't fair to either of them. Morgan, because she shouldn't feel obligated to cuddle with her employer and Rhea because it got her hopes up that Morgan might actually care about her beyond their professional relationship. Best not to lose sight of that fact. And yet, she didn't pull away, choosing instead to stew in a pot of anxiety and guilt.

Morgan didn't pull away either. Her breathing slowly evened as her grip loosened. Rhea knew that she should extricate herself, give Morgan a blanket, and let her rest, but her own eyelids were growing heavy, and the idea of getting up felt more and more daunting. Resting her eyes for a few minutes wouldn't hurt.

At some point, she must have fallen asleep. When her eyes opened, she was standing in the chapel. In all her time at the Ballard House, she had never sleepwalked. As a child, her nights were full of terror, but she always woke in the same place where she fell asleep. Was this a ghost's doing or was it her own mind finally breaking? Before she could fully get her bearings, someone or something pressed her to the ground, forcing her to kneel on the hard floor before the altar. She struggled to get to her feet, but whatever force held her in a parody of a prayer for repentance had her pinned. Phantom hands forced her own together, and there was no fighting it. The cold pressure became unbearable until she was truly praying—just not repenting for her homosexual ways that Astrid probably wanted. She prayed that it would end soon, that her limbs were once again free to move, and she could get out, escape the chapel, and run to the willow where her mother sang her lullaby. But the willow wasn't safe anymore, and whatever sang the lullaby was not her mother.

"Please, please, please, I'm sorry. Please forgive me. I'm so sorry," she mumbled over and over again.

"No, you're not," Astrid whispered in her ear. "But you will be."

And then she was free. With a gasp, Rhea stumbled to her feet, staggering out of the chapel and up to her room. Clutching Otso, she curled under her covers and wept.

CHAPTER TWENTY

Eliza was ten minutes late. Rhea checked and rechecked the time and address on her phone. It was the right place, and she hadn't texted to let Rhea know she was running late. Well, ten minutes was reasonably late, but worry wormed still its way into the back of her head. Was she hurt? Did she change her mind? Did she secretly hate Rhea all along?

She ran her thumb up and down the pitted ceramic mug. It looked as though a child made it. Hell, one probably did. They advertised how they purchased all their dishes from the pottery place across the street as a cute little bit of cross promotion. She sipped the cooling coffee and stared at the menu. The waitress had been by twice to ask for her order, and each time left with a pitying look in her eyes. She was about to give up when she heard a familiar exclamation of "Rhea!"

Eliza smiled as she approached. It didn't quite meet her blue eyes, but she looked as perfect as Rhea remembered, her dress fitted to her slim body and her blonde hair falling in elegant if windblown ringlets. She was always out of Rhea's league.

The memories of these stolen kisses under the willow or in the privacy of her bedroom sustained Rhea in some of her darkest moments in the fallout of getting outed. She didn't like to think about the day she was caught, how she left, or how Eliza shut the door in her face when she needed her most.

Now, Eliza sat down across from her, hair mussed and slightly out of breath. "Hey, sorry I'm late. My husband lost his car keys, and we just spent an hour turning the house upside down looking for them. You know where they were? My purse. I had completely forgotten that I borrowed his car yesterday because mine had a flat tire."

She laughed, and Rhea joined her just a second too late. It was strange hearing the family sit-com existence when hers seemed to be one misery piled on top of another. It was made all the stranger by the fact that this Eliza was completely different from the one she remembered. She only ever pictured Eliza at seventeen, full of angst and rebellion and willing to take on the world. Then again, Rhea supposed that she had changed too. The years had been much kinder to Eliza, though.

After giving the waitress their orders—a coffee refill and chicken salad sandwich for Rhea and burger with a caramel latte for Eliza—they lapsed into a cold war of silence where each seemed to dare the other to go first. Rhea stirred the sugar and cream in her coffee for far longer than necessary while Eliza turned her wedding ring. It seemed uncomfortable on her finger, forcing her to readjust it every few seconds.

Finally, Eliza sighed and said, "I'm sorry for the way things ended. You have to know that I did what I could."

Rhea knew, but it didn't stop the ache in her heart like a long healed broken bone in winter. It was four months after they'd been caught kissing in her bedroom. Four months of punishment with no sign of her grandparents letting up before she escaped out the third story window, grabbed her emergency go-bag, and limped her way barefoot, soaking wet, and shivering to Eliza's house. She found her bedroom window and tossed pebbles at it until Eliza appeared, gazing blearily outside. When she spotted Rhea, her eyes widened, and she jerked her head towards the front door. Rhea limped her way around just in time to see her open the door a crack.

"Rhea, it's the middle of the night," Eliza said, stifling a yawn, "I can't talk. My parents might hear us."

"I don't know where else to go," she said, leaning to one side to take the weight off her twisted ankle, "I can't go back, and you're the only person I know who would believe me."

Eliza ran a nervous hand through her sleep mussed curls. "My parents were talking about sending me to 'counseling' over what happened. If they catch us..."

Rhea bit back tears of betrayal. Weren't they supposed to be in love, the rest of the world be damned? Wasn't she supposed to be by Rhea's side, no matter what? She thought she didn't have to beg for Eliza's affection, her love. But here she was, and she was never too proud to beg. "Eliza, please."

Eliza worried her lip before saying, "I know where my parents keep the extra cash. I'll give you that plus my babysitting money. That's all I can do." She disappeared behind the door before Rhea could formulate a response.

She reappeared moments later with the cash, change of clothes, a coat, and a pair of shoes. "There should be about five hundred dollars in here. Take these too."

"Thank you," Rhea said, numbly slipping on the shoes and coat. She shoved the cash in her pocket. The change of clothes would happen later because Eliza didn't seem to want to let her into her house. Even with the new coat, Rhea couldn't stop shivering.

Eliza looked at her like she wanted to say something, but the words were stuck in her throat. Finally, she just said, "Be safe" and closed the door, leaving Rhea alone in the dark.

Now both adults, Eliza looked at her as though Rhea could provide absolution for an old sin. She reached out, her hand hovering as though she was unsure if she should touch her or not. "Rhea, can you say something?"

"You turned your back on me." Rhea finally looked up at her. "I was hurt, scared, and alone, and you left me."

"Well, what did you expect me to do?" she asked. Her eyes went glassy as her breath hitched. "Just run away with you? Hide you in the basement? My parents were mad enough that I got caught with a girl, let alone the heir of the most influential family in town, and I was told that if I ever saw you again, they'd send me to therapy for my 'affliction.' You have to know that's not fair to ask of me. I was just a kid."

"I was too." She returned to studying the mug and swirl of coffee before looking up again. Her gut seemed to twist in the same way, anger and hurt warring with guilt. Because as much as she wanted to feel betrayed, Eliza had a point. Rhea had put her in a difficult position. "You're right. It wasn't fair of me to ask that of you." She swallowed the half-decade of hurt that had festered in her soul. "But you were all I had."

Eliza's eyes brimmed with tears. "And a day doesn't go by where it doesn't haunt me. I'm sorry. I did what I thought I could, but obviously it wasn't enough." She gave a weak smile. "It looks like you turned out okay though."

Over the years, Rhea had become adept at forgiveness. Or, at least, ignoring the ways a person had hurt her to maintain the relationship. After everything her grandparents put her through, she still found a way to mourn them. Eliza was not nearly as bad as the people she fled from all those years ago. As a kid, Rhea never told her everything that went on at the Ballard House and Eliza did everything she thought she could to help. She huffed. "I guess it could have been worse."

"If you need anything, I'm here." Eliza took her hand. Rhea froze, staring at the wedding ring. She knew it was there, but it still gutted her, leaving her feeling like the deer that her grandfather would strip down for parts. The part of her that loved Eliza lingered the same way it does for everyone's first love and seeing this broke her heart all over again, washing her soul in bitterness. Sure, Eliza would be there for her, the same way she was there for Rhea all those years ago. Eliza seemed to follow her gaze because she pulled away and covered her left hand with her right.

"Are you happy?" Rhea asked, her voice barely above a rasp.

Eliza smiled tightly. "Yeah. He's the love of my life." Her words were rote and emotionless, as though she'd been repeating them for years in the hope that she would eventually believe them herself.

Rhea swallowed back the bitter lump in her throat and forced a smile. "I'm—I'm glad that you're happy. How did you meet?"

"It's a funny story, actually," she replied, studying her latte. "We were in the same English class, and he wrote this cute poem on a poster to ask me out to prom. Something like, *Roses are red, violets are blue, I'd like to go to prom with you.* You were...not going to make it, so I said yes, and next thing I know, we're crowned prom king and queen."

Each word threatened to disembowel Rhea. *She* was supposed to go with her to prom, to hold her hand and dance the night away like in a fairytale. Her fists clenched hard enough to bite into the skin of her palms. While Eliza was drinking spiked punch and dancing with the prom king, Rhea was sleeping on borrowed time in a girl's group home that would kick her out the moment she turned eighteen. It felt childish to think, but it just wasn't fair. Still, she kept her poker face. "Sounds like a special night."

"It was," she replied with a touch of melancholy behind the smile. "We spent the summer together, went to the same college, and he proposed to me on the day of our graduation."

The waitress brought out their food. Eliza picked up a fry and played with it, swirling it in the ketchup. She was holding back. Even after all these years, she had the same tells. Whenever she was lying or having a difficult conversation, she would play with whatever was in front of her as though that would distract her from the discomfort. But Rhea wasn't sure if she wanted to know whatever it was that Eliza had to say. "What about you? What have you been up to?"

The growing lump in Rhea's throat made talking difficult. She took a bite of her sandwich without tasting it and washed it down with coffee just to buy herself time. "Honestly? I've mostly been trying to survive. I don't want to bring down the mood, so I probably shouldn't get into it." She knew her smile was more of a grimace, but it was the best she could do. "That period of my life is between me and my therapist for now. I mean, hey, I can actually afford one with my inheritance, so I guess Bert and Astrid were good for something."

Judging by the pitying look Eliza gave her, the joke didn't land. "You know, my life isn't perfect," she replied. "Emmet, my husband, wants kids. I mean, really wants them, but we can't have them. It's a combination of my defective uterus and his shooting blanks, but we're never going to conceive."

Rhea nodded sympathetically, though she had no idea why Eliza was telling her this. They hadn't seen each other in years. So, why was she confiding in Rhea like they were still close? "I'm sorry to hear that."

My how things change, she thought. Truthfully, Rhea was never good with children, even as a child herself. Her grandparents raised her so isolated from other kids that she had no idea how to interact with any she came across. Most weren't interested in her analysis of *The Grapes of Wrath* parroted from Astrid, and she had no idea what a Pokémon was. Although Bert and Astrid loved to talk about her carrying on the family bloodline, she didn't like the idea of being responsible for another human and the reproductive actions required to create one. She and Eliza commiserated over their mutual dislike of children. When she was seventeen, Eliza claimed that she had no interest in carrying a parasite for nine months and then pushing it out of her vagina. Now, though, she apparently wanted a baby to complete the white picket image she'd created.

No, that wasn't fair. Some people just change their minds. And Eliza was apparently a popular babysitter, so she probably did like kids more than she'd let on.

"It's been hard," she replied, "but we're looking into surrogates, and if that doesn't work, adoption."

She hummed and took a sip of her coffee just so she wouldn't have to respond just yet. "I have to admit I'm kinda surprised. You always told me you didn't want kids."

"I didn't," Eliza said, her body tense and back ramrod straight. "But people change. Emmet convinced me that we should be growing our family. And I thought..." She trailed off, her gaze returning to her plate.

"You thought what?" Rhea leaned in closer, her brows furrowing as she anticipated what Eliza might say.

Her ex took in a stuttering breath and then let it out. "I thought it wouldn't be so bad if it was yours."

The world dropped out from under Rhea. Eliza wanted her to be a surrogate, to complete the carefully cultivated image she had created by bearing the family a child. "Eliza, what the fuck?"

"Sorry," she said, staring into her the foam of her latte, "it was a stupid question."

What did this mean? Did Eliza still love her? Or was she just using her to curate that picture-perfect life by adding a child it? Was it all she really wanted from her? To be the human incubator for the sake of the life she never got the chance to live?

"Why would you ask me that?" Rhea pressed, the anger burning sudden and all consuming.

"I don't know, okay?" Eliza's eyes grew glassy. "I'm sorry. I don't know why I thought—can we pretend that never happened?"

A part of Rhea wanted to reach out and comfort her first love, but the once buried bitterness in her soul stayed her hand. Eliza *should* be sorry. She got to live a charmed life with a man she said she loves, and she has the *nerve* to ask the girl she'd left in the cold to carry her child for nine months and then give it up so that her picture-perfect suburban life could be complete? How dare she? Rhea realized the hand holding her mug was shaking and set it down. *Deep breaths...count to ten...exhale...*

"Now who's asking too much from someone?" she replied coldly. This was a mistake. What did she expect? That they would just fall back into old habits and jokes like nothing had happened? That they would somehow rekindle the flame she'd carried inside her from the moment she met her at a party? They had nothing in common now, that much was obvious. *Stupid.*

And even if Eliza did still have feelings for her, even if she secretly didn't love her husband at all, she had a life she'd created for herself, one that had no room for Rhea. She had made her choice years ago, taking refuge in the closet and choosing to live the life of the white picket fence and the two and a half kids.

The thought opened up a surprising well of pity. At least Rhea had been able to live as herself. Sure, she was exhausted and barely keeping her head above water, but she didn't have to pretend anymore. She could be who she was.

She went to her first pride parade at eighteen and decorated her apartment with the free flags they gave out. Her work bag, still in her apartment, was adorned with the rainbow buttons she'd collected. She could cut her hair and experience euphoria when people called her sir by mistake. Rhea didn't begrudge Eliza for choosing the safer option when she had the choice, but if her ex still harbored feelings, she also had no interest in being someone's dirty little secret. Never again. And she wouldn't let Eliza use her to complete her perfect image of a perfect life.

Eliza's hand shot out, taking Rhea's. "I see that look in your eye. You're about to run. Please, wait. Let me try this again."

The lump in her throat was too large for her to speak, so she just nodded. She wanted to yell, to scream at her every conflicting feeling in this hurricane of emotion, but it would do no good.

Eliza sighed and relaxed back into her chair. "You know, I was kinda scared to come. I thought you might hate me."

She didn't meet her eyes. "I don't. You, or honestly, even my grandparents." She laughed bitterly. "It would be so much easier if I did. But I understand the position you were in. I do, and I'm happy you did well for yourself." Suddenly exhausted, she sighed and rubbed her eyes. "I think, though, that my wounds are still too raw to have any real relationship with you. Sorry." Pulling out her wallet, she paid for her meal and the tip.

Eliza grabbed her by the hand before she could make her escape, her eyes flashing angrily. "Did Morgan Reyes say something about me? You know she's a liar, right? She killed my friend."

"No, she didn't." Rhea jerked her arm out of Eliza's grip. After last night and the nightmare Morgan went through, it felt especially galling for Eliza to pass judgement on her. "And unlike you, she's a real friend, and one of the kindest people I've ever met."

"Rhea, you're making a mistake. She's dangerous."

"I can handle myself. I have been for the past six years." She couldn't help her bitter laugh. "And believe it or not, I am capable of detaching myself from someone who showed me a scrap of kindness. Goodbye Eliza, I wish you well."

CHAPTER TWENTY-ONE

She walked home, her festering anger spreading with each step she took back to that damned house. Between the rage on her face and the tears streaming down her cheeks, she supposed the townies' whispers were deserved. A part of her ached to turn back, to beg for Eliza's forgiveness and that she'd take her back in whatever capacity she wanted, but the rage fueled her gait.

It took her a moment to realize that she'd reached Bert's study. It seemed as though she had gone from main street to this room between blinks. She spied a framed picture of herself at age ten standing between her two grandparents looking solemn as an old photograph of a corpse. Her grandparents and prison wardens. The people who deprived her of a normal life, of parents, of Eliza. She couldn't stand to look at their smug faces, their eyes so cold they gave her hypothermia of the soul. Her rage overcame her, and she threw the photo against the wall, the glass shattering and falling to the floor. Her desire to express her anger with destruction hadn't faded, so she took the stag's head from the wall hiding the safe and chucked it to the floor. She felt more guilt for that than destroying the picture. The poor stag didn't ask to be mounted on the wall.

But now she was on a roll. She grabbed a lighter from Bert's Cuban cigar drawer and the nearest book—some pretentious philosopher who used Bible verses to justify some atrocity or another—and set it aflame, letting it fall burning into the trashcan.

A knock at the door. Rhea tore her eyes from the fire and looked up, blinking and coming out of her trance.

Morgan and Andy poked their heads in. "Everything okay?" Andy asked. He spotted the flaming trashcan. "Jesus!" Disappearing for a moment, he returned with a fire extinguisher from the hall closet nearby. With so many valuables in a rickety wooden house, Bert and Astrid made a point of stocking up on fire extinguishers—one in every closet.

Tearing open the window, he threw the whole flaming package to the ground below before spraying it with white foam,

"I'm sorry," she muttered, hating herself for leaving them to clean up the mess she made with her little temper tantrum. And because of what? Eliza had grown up and moved on? She already knew that. Her grandparents were shitty human beings that isolated and abused her? She knew that too.

"Rhea? What happened?" Morgan asked tremulously, her eyes wide as she took in the destruction.

Andy rejoined her side, his brows also furrowed with worry. She took a step towards Rhea, but he held her back.

She shook her head, not trusting herself to speak after all that. Compared to ghosts and murderous ladies of the lake, bitter exes was low on her list of crises, but she knew she was coming undone at the seams like Otso after years of love. Closing her eyes, she took a shuddering breath and without bothering to open them, sensed another presence at her side. The floorboards creaked as Andy stood next to her, keeping his distance but not too far away if she decided to go crazy again.

"I've been on bad lunch dates before, but—" he whistled "—never destruction of property bad."

She wiped her eyes with a weak laugh. "You mean to tell me that you've never wanted to break something after catching up with an ex?"

He shrugged. "Honestly, relationships never got that far. Dating has never been my thing. Lucky me I guess."

She took a shuddering breath, collecting herself. The office, with its reminders of the people who ruined her, was not her safe place. That would be the willow, but apparently whatever lurked in the lake made it unsafe. Who or what was she? She didn't behave like any ghosts in the house. Ghosts couldn't kill. After all, if they did, Minnie would have just poisoned Rhea instead of tricking her into killing herself. So, what was it that allowed the lady in the lake to drown Joshua West?

Astrid collected a wide variety of books, including her father's, who was an expert on the topic. Maybe she'd find something there. Even if she didn't, it was an escape from the awkward situation she'd created with her freakout. She got to her feet. "I'm heading to the library."

She didn't think she had the mental energy to talk about her tantrum or her disastrous lunch with Eliza.

"I don't know if you should be alone right now," Andy said.

Rhea massaged the growing headache behind her burning eyes. "It's fine. My tantrum is done, so you don't have to worry about me."

His eyebrows shot up. "Tantrum? Rhea, that was more than a tantrum."

"Well, it's done, and I don't want to talk about it," she snapped.

Morgan crossed her arms. "No offense, but you nearly burned down Bert's office. You clearly can't be trusted not to set any more fires. I'll come with you."

"Whatever you want," Rhea said, and pushed past them.

The library was nearly as grand as the ballroom. It was two levels separated by a spiral staircase and lined with books covering subjects from the classics to the sciences to philosophy and even century old pornography that she'd stumbled upon by accident at the age of twelve. The ceiling was painted with a baroque style fresco of the temptation of Eve at the Tree of Knowledge. She never quite understood why her ancestors chose something that seemed so anti-intellectual. Perhaps it was a warning. You may taste the fruit, but it will leave you forever changed.

Her father's books were on display near the entrance so that any visitor might see his accomplishments. She fondly ran her finger along the spines.

She didn't have many memories of either parent, but she did remember their nighttime routine. Her mother would tuck her in and lie in bed beside her while her father sat at the edge and told her a different story every night. As a child, he seemed like an endless font of knowledge, telling her not only the classic Greek and Norse myths but of Susanoo-no Mikoto in Japan and the Monkey King in China and Mwindo in Congo. Her favorites, though, were the ones related to her namesakes: her full name, Rhiannon and her nickname, Rhea.

"Tell me about Rhiannon," she would say.

"Would you like the story of how she and Pwyll met when she was riding a magic horse or how she was accused of killing and eating her son in her sleep?"

"I think the magic horse might be more appropriate," her mother would reply, running her fingers through Rhea's hair.

"I want the baby eating!" she'd exclaim and both parents would laugh.

"A woman after my own heart," her father would reply, pressing a kiss to Rhea's forehead before telling his story.

The memory was something she hadn't thought of in a long time. It was comforting, though, like a warm blanket on a cold winter's day. She pulled the books off the shelf and stacked any that mentioned water, spirits, or drowning. Once through, she settled into the wingback chair and got to reading.

Morgan was skulking about. She'd followed Rhea, and now was keeping her distance, hovering on the other side of the library, just out of sight. But Rhea could still hear her occasional footsteps. At first, she was annoyed, but as she calmed down, she found it was oddly comforting to know Morgan was nearby even after she had tried to push her away. She still owed Morgan an apology, but that could wait until after her research.

Her father's style was almost painfully dense. She'd read as many books as she could get her hands on at the local library near her apartment but struggled through the language almost as much as she did when she was young. His poor students.

Maybe he had inherited some of her grandparents' pretentiousness after all. She'd found passages on water nymphs, Jenny Greenteeth, and Will-o'-the-Wisps, but so far nothing helpful. Something itched in the back of her mind as though she had forgotten some vital detail. And then she saw it:

Rusalka.

Her great-grandfather's journal had mentioned it, said that his secret lover told him stories of them.

In Slavic folklore, the Rusalka—also known as the vodyanitsa, kupalka, shutovka, lostotukha, and the mavka—are water spirits confined to a specific body of water, which they must be touching at all times. Originally morally neutral, the stories evolved until they fell into the archetype of wronged women turned temptress. Rusalki became the unquiet souls of women who either took their own lives or were murdered by their partners or their family. Her anger lasts beyond the veil of death, which is where the archetype of the temptress comes in. She lures in her victims, typically men, and drowns them. Sometimes, the stories say that, like the modern conception of the siren, she takes on the form they find most pleasing. Others claim that she is not a shapeshifter and simply irresistible for any unwary men unlucky enough to cross her path. The best way to appease her and put her soul to rest is to bring her murderer to her so that she might enact her own form of justice.

On a personal note, there is a family story of a similar vein. My father used to warn me away from the lake beside my childhood home, saying that there was a monster who appeared pulchritudinous at first glance but would drown me if given half the chance. He refused to elaborate on it, and later, my mother explained that the lake used to be a spot for dumping toxic waste and was currently a nesting ground for cottonmouth snakes, making it unsafe to swim in. My father assumed that the ghost story would be more understandable to me as a child than poison. Still, this story sparked my fascination with the supernatural and the mythological.

Her father knew about the lady in the lake. Sure, he thought it was just a story Bert made up, but he had made the connection decades ago. She leapt to her feet, all thoughts of Eliza behind her. So far, it fit her and Morgan's experiences, but she wanted more confirmation. And she knew just where to find it.

"Morgan!" she yelled, jumping to her feet.

Morgan emerged from behind the bookshelf. "What is it?"

"You wanna take a trip to the historical society with me?"

...

Michael Harris, the president of the Cherub Cove Historical Society, looked up when a very harried Rhea ran in followed trailed by a pensive Morgan. She approached the front desk and asked, "Do you have any records of drownings on the Ballard property?"

He blinked in confusion, obviously not expecting the question. "Yes, I—I believe so. We keep an archive of all our newspapers, and in a quiet town like this, any drowning on your property would make the front page."

"I'm not so sure about that," Morgan mumbled.

Rhea leaned in close, muttering in her ear, "Good point. Gramps and Grams would want to keep any negative press quiet." She turned back to him. "What about police records?"

"If the case is no longer active, then yes." He studied the two girls. "What's all this about?"

"A little project I'm working on. Can I see those reports? Or, actually, can I see any missing person's report from the Ballard House and in the general area?" She knew how she must have looked to him. After their previous awkward interaction where she was a bit rude to him, for the prodigal daughter of the Ballard family to show up in an almost manic state must have been bizarre. Perhaps more surprising to her, though, was that she didn't care. Bert and Astrid weren't around to get angry at her for 'making a scene' and Morgan was just as eager to see if her theory panned out.

He beckoned them into the basement archives. The room was old and had a musty odor. The warm, soft light cast everything in an eerie glow. He stopped them by a bookshelf. "These are the police records for any investigation that isn't ongoing for the last hundred years or so. They're all copies, but we would prefer it if you kept them in good condition. I'll be upstairs." He lingered, staring at them as though debating if he should ask more questions.

"Thank you, Mr. Harris," she replied with a genuine smile as she resisted the urge to tear into the records. As soon as he was gone, she grabbed the most recent box. "Okay, so what we're looking for is the suspicious death of a young woman and drowned men. How about I start with the most recent and you can start with the oldest and we'll meet in the middle?"

Morgan shrugged. "Sounds good."

She began digging through the recent pile, pulling out any that referenced drowning and the Ballard house. Bert's death was the most recent, followed by Joshua West's. There were a few John Does and missing male hikers that were last seen in the area. The first drowned woman she came across, though, was her mother. It had been clipped to her father's report and tucked away near the end of the box. She stared at the bloated and soaked faces of her parents, nausea growing in her stomach as she read the coroner's report. Her father's death had been ruled an accidental drowning, but her mother's toxicology report made her grow cold. They had found something that had later been blacked out with sharpie as though trying to cover it up. Her cause of death was ruled undetermined, but when she held the paper up to the light, she could just make out the indents of the pen on paper. Eventually, she parsed out *Cicuta Douglasii*—water hemlock.

The paper wrinkled with the strength of her grip as her entire body turned to ice. She wanted to throw up the few bites of sandwich and coffee she'd eaten that day.

Her mother had been poisoned. And she helped kill her.

CHAPTER TWENTY-TWO

Grandma Astrid had a bouquet of pretty, white flowers arranged in a Ming vase on a high table near the foyer. When six-year-old Rhea arrived at the Ballard House with her parents, she had reached for them at the table, trying to see if they smelled as pretty as they looked. Her grandmother smacked her hand away. "Don't touch those. They're special."

"They look like the ones by the lake," she said.

Grandma Astrid gave her a rare smile. "You're right. And just like the lake, you're not to go near them either. Now, let's go find your father. I think he's in the library." She took Rhea's hand and led her away.

They were only supposed to stay for two weeks, but she didn't think they would last that long. The passing days were marked by a growing tension in the household so obvious that even the six-year-old girl noticed the strange behavior of the adults around her. Her grandparents never acknowledged her mother, and her father had the same look in his eye that he would get when he caught her disobeying him. Her mother cried when she thought Rhea was asleep. At first, the mansion made her feel like a lost princess returned to her home, but as the week wore on, she felt more like a princess locked away in a castle guarded by a dragon.

That Friday, Grandma Astrid decided that she and Rhea would bake carrot cupcakes. Those were her least favorite kind because carrots had no business being in a dessert, but Mom told her that she should try to get to know her grandparents even though they were mean to her.

The classical music playing on the radio carried through the kitchen while the warm June breeze ruffled Rhea's hair as she shredded carrots. Because her Grandma Astrid could read the measuring cups and instructions better than she did, Rhea had been tasked with turning three carrots into a pile of orange confetti. By the time she was done, Grandma Astrid had the batter ready. She added it to the mix, stirred thoroughly, and then poured it into a muffin tin. Before she put them in the oven, though, she took a brown and gnarled root from a red bag in the refrigerator, shredded some, and added it and green food dye to one of the cupcakes.

"What are you doing?" she asked, peering curiously at the green cupcake.

"I have sore joints. Arthritis, you know," Grandma Astrid explained with tight smile as she washed her hands, "That root helps get rid of pain. I dyed the cupcake green, so I'd know it was mine." She dried her hands on her apron and picked up a pack of powdered sugar. "Now, let's make the frosting."

Rhea hadn't thought much of that moment. The next day, both her parents were dead and questions about her grandmother's story took a back seat to overwhelming grief. Her mother wanted to go out on the rowboat with her father. Now that Rhea thought about it, before her mother went rowing, Astrid insisted she try a cupcake. Rhea had encouraged her too because she was proud of their accomplishment. Looking back in the haze of childhood memory, she couldn't recall if the cupcake was the usual brown or if it was green.

"Rhea?" Morgan asked, snapping her back to the present. "What's wrong?"

She scrubbed at her face, realizing that tears streamed down it. At this point, what wasn't wrong? She was an accomplice to her mother's murder and consequently, her father's drowning, likely at the hands of a century old water ghost exacting vengeance on her family for her unjust death. Wordlessly, she handed the report to Morgan, who held it to the light. "It's water hemlock," she explained, her voice barely above a whisper. "Every part of it is poisonous, but it tastes like a normal carrot. The day before her death, Astrid and I made carrot cupcakes."

Morgan had a look of naked horror on her face, and she braced herself. She'd killed her own mother. Nausea churned in her stomach and bile rose in the back of her rapidly constricting throat. She was a monster. Morgan had every right to run away and never look back. "Oh, Rhea, come here," she said, wrapping her arms around her and following her to the floor as her shaking knees gave out.

A part of her wanted to push Morgan away. She didn't deserve her compassion or her pity. It would be better for everyone if she fired her and Andy with a generous severance package and then burned the Ballard House to the ground and salted the earth. Maybe give herself to the Rusalka as penance for her family's sins. The more selfish part of her relished in the comfort as Morgan rocked her gently and whispered over and over, "It's okay. You're okay. You did nothing wrong."

They didn't move until the motion sensor turned the lights out. When they separated, she straightened up, drying her eyes and pushing away the overwhelming disgust for herself. "Did you find anything?" she asked, praying that Morgan would drop the fact that she'd been sobbing in her arms moments ago.

Morgan gave her a look of concern before turning her attention back to the filing cabinets. "Uh, maybe, yeah." She pulled out coroner's report yellowed with age. "This is for a servant named Aniela Dach who worked for your family at the turn of the century. They'd ruled it an accidental drowning, but maybe it wasn't so accidental."

"My great grandfather mentioned an AD in his journal," she said, hating how thick her voice sounded. "I don't think that's a coincidence."

"You think it's her?"

"Yeah, and I might have a way to prove it."

...

"Hey Andy?" she called out as she burst through the door. No response.

Morgan pulled out her phone and called him, putting it on speaker. The phone buzzed for three agonizing rings before it picked up. "City morgue. You kill 'em, we chill 'em," he said from the other end.

Rhea let out a tension she didn't realize she'd been carrying. Morgan, too, relaxed and said with a laugh, "You're actually not that far off. How'd you like to help us solve a century's old murder?"

"Sure. Let me just finish up here at the boathouse. I've been assessing the damage, thinking that I'd make it my summer project to fix up this old thing. I know you said something about snakes, but I don't see any sign of them."

Morgan blanched and Rhea took the phone, saying, "Andy, we kinda need your help now. Please."

"If you say so, boss. I'll be right there." He hung up and they rushed to the portrait room, watching anxiously for him to appear. Morgan's restless pacing only abated when he sauntered into view. Unsure of what else to do, Rhea put her arm around her shoulders. Morgan tensed for a moment in surprise before relaxing and leaning into her touch.

"He's okay," she murmured.

Morgan nodded into her shoulder and straightened. "The journal is in the office, right?"

"I'll meet you in the kitchen." She'd stuck them both in the safe, figuring that it would be harder for a ghost to manipulate than a loose book or two, should one of them decide to take them. They were right where she left them, and she breathed a small sigh of relief as she hurried to Morgan and Andy in the kitchen.

Andy leaned against the counter while Morgan sat in a chair anxiously tapping her fingers against her thighs. His friendly smile turned concerned when he saw her face, so she must have looked terrible. Almost like she found out she killed her mother the same day she met with the girl who shattered her heart. *Heh.* "You okay there, Rhea?"

"No, but what else is new?" she replied with a false cheeriness, "You mentioned that you used to send your cousins messages in invisible ink, right? How do you make it visible again?"

"Well, we used grape juice or heat to reveal the message. Mom used to get mad at us for stealing her hair dryer to read our notes."

"I'll be right back," Morgan said, disappearing behind the pantry where staircase to the former servants' quarters was hidden.

They stood in silence, Rhea clutching the journal like the lifeline it was. It held a truth that had been long suffocated by her family, and maybe, she could end a cycle of suffering by airing it out for the world to see.

"Seriously, Rhea, you look like you haven't slept in a week," Andy said, breaking the silence and making her jump, "I know we don't know each other well, but Morgan's been acting weird too and I'm worried. What's going on with you two?"

She let out a bitter laugh. "It's hard to explain to someone who doesn't believe in ghosts."

He moved to stand next to her. "Try to tell me anyway. I can't promise I'll believe it, but there's clearly something weird happening."

"Why do you refuse to believe in the supernatural?" Rhea asked.

Andy sighed, his tool belt clinking as he leaned against the wall. "Isn't that kind of like asking me why I don't believe in Santa Claus or the tooth fairy?"

"No," Rhea said. "It really isn't. This house...it's not just stone and wood. There's something wrong with it. Like a sickness." She paused. That wasn't the right word. "No, not a sickness. It's poison. A poisonous family built a poisonous house, and now it poisons all those who live inside it."

"The only poison in this house—aside from the carbon monoxide leaks and the radon that I fixed—is the Schell's Green wallpaper in the Green Guestroom. That was made with arsenic, so I closed off that room years ago." He gestured with a paint spattered arm in the general direction of that guestroom.

"Andy, I'm being serious."

"I am too." Andy took a seat at the kitchen counter. "Have I gotten creeped out in this old house before? Sure. Have I seen things out of the corner of my eye and had the feeling of being watched? Absolutely. Does that prove the existence of ghosts? Definitely not. All those things have scientific explanations. For example, do you know what infrasound is?"

Rhea crossed her arms. "Yeah, it's sound at a frequency that we can't hear but messes with our mind. And yeah, a lot of hauntings are probably just infrasound, but can a sound frequency physically drag me into the tower room and lock the door?"

He blinked. "What?"

"Do you really think I would have willingly gone into the place where they held me captive for months?"

"But those diaries..."

"Whatever is in the house wanted me to read them. Andy, there's a very good reason why Morgan doesn't want you spending time in the boathouse by the lake. There's something out there that's dangerous. It's killed before, and will probably—"

"Got it," Morgan said, bursting in with a singsong voice. "Let's see what your great grandfather had going on."

She plugged in her hair dryer and set it to high while Rhea held the empty pages underneath. Soon, words began to form on the pages like magic. Tom Ballard wrote only on one side of the paper, probably because of the limitations of his invisible ink, but even a hundred years later, it was still readable.

10/10/20

Apologies for not having written, but life has been too boring to put to paper for the last few months. AD left near the end of July with glowing references to avoid scandal, but not much has been made of our indiscretion since then. At least, not until today when AD boldly knocked on the front door and demanded I speak to her.

It seemed that her job fired her when she began to show because she "lacked virtue." Because I am the father of her child, she wants me to support her. Mother and Father say that if I marry her, I'll be disowned, but if she goes to the press claiming to carry an illegitimate Ballard, it will bring scandal upon us all. There is one solution that I dare not entertain out of fear for my immortal soul, but it may be a necessary measure.

Minnie has become adept at botany over the years and says that water hemlock grows beside the lake. Perhaps I can solve our problem quietly.

There comes a time in every man's life where he must commit a necessary evil for the sake of the greater good of his family. Last night was that time. Minnie was all too happy to show me where to find the water hemlock, and only asked that I document the results of giving the carrot-like tubers to AD. She may be only a woman, but she frightens me. Her mind is like a man's while her wiles remain as feminine as any other woman's. A deadly combination, especially with for her strange fascination with poisons.

I told AD to meet me by the willow near where the white flowers bloom under the pretense that I planned to run away with her. Along with a full bag, I carried with me some leftover soup. AD looked thin and hungry—probably hadn't eaten in days, poor thing. She was none the wiser as she devoured her meal. The effects of the poison began within minutes of her swallowing the final morsal. We were walking along the lake's edge to the forest on the other side of the property when she doubled over in pain.

"Tom," she said, eyes wide with fear, "I think something's wrong." She fell to her knees and vomited the contents of her stomach. Once she'd finished retching, she looked up at me, wiping the vomit from her lips with a shaking hand. "You..." she began but cut herself off with a cry that sent her curling in on herself.

"I'm sorry, Aniela," I said, "There was no other way."

Her eyes rolled back in her head as she began to convulse. I couldn't let the mother of my child die in such agony, so I did the merciful thing. I dragged her to the lake's edge and pushed her in.

The cold water must have revived her somewhat because she grabbed my leg with a surprising strength. "I will not rest until the last Ballard walks willingly into the lake with me."

I'm ashamed to say I panicked. Kicking her hand away, I held her underneath the water until bubbles stopped rising to the surface. Terrible deed done, I returned to my room to relate this confession in invisible ink. May God have mercy on my soul.

11/2/25

Father is dead. Drowned in the lake. They say it was an accident, but I know it was Aniela sent to punish me. The funeral is tomorrow, and Mother is in such a state that I fear she may do something drastic.

CHAPTER TWENTY-THREE

Andy let out a deep breath. "Jesus. That's fucked up."

Rhea let out a half-hysterical laugh. "You don't say. I knew it would be bad but—" Unable to finish the sentence, she set the book aside. "God, this explains so much."

"What do we do now?" Morgan asked, her face pale, "because we all heard that curse and there's no way in hell you're going to let her drown you."

Rhea wasn't ready to think about that fun little aspect of Aniela's death. "I think we have some very public donations to make to the Historical society tomorrow. Today has been so shit that all I wanna do is forget. So, wine anyone? Or maybe something harder. Bert had some fine aged whiskey somewhere that he'd been saving for a special occasion. Too late for that, Grandpa."

"Rhea, I don't think that's—" Andy began, but she cut him off.

"Healthy? Oh, I know it's not, but who cares?" Her laugh was nigh hysterical and verging on tearful. "Eliza probably hates me, I helped kill my mom, my great grandpa killed a woman and now her ghost drowns people in the lake. Oh, and the house is also haunted by my grandma and the ghost that tricked me into almost killing myself. So of all the poisonings going on, I think a little self-inflicted alcohol poisoning is the least of my worries."

Andy looked imploringly to Morgan, which made her laugh even harder. Right, she forgot about the crush on her employee because she was just *that* desperate and lonely. Her whole family was poison, and both her employees would be better off with a fresh start somewhere else, far away from murderous ghosts and evil old money. Far away from her and her poisoned inheritance.

"Rhea," Morgan said softly, reaching out.

She stepped out of reach. "It's not safe here for either of you. Morgan, I'll book you a hotel room. Andy, it's probably best if you steer clear for a while. I'll still pay you, of course, but—"

"Wait," Morgan said, "What about you?"

She blinked. Right. It was probably a bad idea to stay for a moment longer in this cursed home. "Oh, I, uh, I guess I'll get a hotel room too. I don't think Aniela can hurt me, but I probably should've left days ago."

"You two really think this place is haunted," Andy marveled.

"We don't think," Morgan retorted, her voice growing louder as she ranted. "We know. We've seen them, felt them, watched them hurt people and lived with the knowledge that we won't be believed. That at best, they'll think you're crazy and at worst, that you're a murderer."

Rhea put an arm around Morgan's shoulder as she sniffled. "I think the only way you'd believe us is if you saw for yourself, but that'll just get you killed. So please, just believe us."

Andy showed his palms in placating defeat. "I'm sorry. I may not believe in ghosts, but I believe that you experienced something you can't explain, and I don't think you're crazy or stupid."

"Then whatever you do, stay away from the lake," Rhea said, "I don't care if it's overgrown or covered in trash, just don't go near it."

He nodded. "I won't."

She let go of Morgan, pulling out her phone. "I'll make the call. Morgan, you can go ahead and grab your stuff, and Andy, I think it's best if you took some paid time off. All I ask is that you take my grandfather's journal with you for safekeeping. I want it as far away as possible from the spirits that don't want it to get out. I'll call the press and collect it in the morning to make a big show of donating it to the historical society. Maybe telling the world the truth will free her soul without me having to die."

"It's worth a shot," Morgan said, "I'll get my things."

Rhea was about to go up and get her things when she felt Andy's hand on her arm. His fingers were rough and calloused from years of hard work. When she met his gaze, he was uncharacteristically serious. "Rhea, if you and Morgan need anything, I'm just a phone call away." He nodded to the sticky note hanging on the wall by the phone. "I'll even put aside my skepticism and grab a proton pack if you need to call the Ghostbusters."

Rhea chuckled and patted his hand. "Thank you. Really. You're a good friend, Andy."

He gave her a little mock bow. "I live to serve."

As Rhea packed her bag, she remembered the other journal. Minerva Ballard had her own secrets. Maybe her journal would reveal them. Before she could think better of it, she shoved the second journal into her bag alongside Otso before joining Morgan at the threshold. She wasn't leaving him behind again.

The Inn by the Sea was a quaint little hotel, the kind with bellhops and cubby holes for non-electronic room keys. It stood on a bluff overlooking the waves crashing against jagged rocks. An older man sat at reception—one she'd seen at the funeral but didn't know. He gave them both a smile as they approached. "Miss Ballard and Miss Reyes, I presume."

She gave a wan smile in return, much too exhausted to muster more than that. "Thank you for giving us rooms on such short notice."

"Of course," he said, turning and grabbing two room keys from two different cubby holes. "They're right across the hall from each other."

"Across the hall?" Morgan asked.

"I thought you might want your own space," Rhea replied, taking her set of keys, "Let's order pizza and get drunk off the minibar. My treat."

"Enjoy your stay," he said, eyeing Morgan with a look of disdain that filled Rhea with a seething anger. But what was she going to do? Yell at a man doing his job because he gave the girl she liked the hairy eyeball? Ridiculous.

In case it was the homophobia instead of the town's ridiculous belief that Morgan was a murderer, she shot him a suggestive wink, daring him to rise to the bait, and said, "We will."

...

Her grandparents rarely ordered pizza. When you have a personal chef, eating mediocre delivery is more trouble than it's worth. The pizza Morgan ordered from Tony's New York Pizza, though, was heavenly, especially when paired with the minibar vodka. It almost made up for the reproduction of her great-great-grandparents' portrait hanging on the wall. The concierge probably picked that room for her, so she'd feel more welcome, but it took all her mental strength not to tear it from the wall and rip it to shreds with her bare hands.

"Tell me honestly," Rhea slurred, leaning against the bed, "doesn't the place creep you out? Like the long dead people glaring at us in the ballroom, the ghosts, my grandparents..."

Morgan sat next to her, face red from imbibing in a nip of hotel rum. "Oh absolutely. No offense, but you seem like one of the only non-spoiled apples in the bunch."

"No, you're right. I come from a long line of thieves, cheats, and murderers. But we're rich, so it's just the cost of success." She took another bite of pizza before continuing. "The Puritans in the portrait room are Fly-Fornication Ballard and his wife, Placidia. They stole this land from the Wampanoag tribe who relied on the lake's fish and fresh water. When they tried to use it, my great times whatever grandparents shot at them."

"No," Morgan exclaimed, "Those are not real names."

"Hand to god, they're real. Puritans had some weird names. I guess my family has always been cruel to children. Joshua and Charity Ballard, for example. Never really got over the irony of her name. We got rich off of their factories and use of child labor. When word got out about the working conditions, they crushed every attempt to unionize."

"Wow," Morgan said, "I mean they can't be all bad. What about the family in the portrait room that looks like they just stepped off the set of *Leave it to Beaver*?"

"My great grandparents. Tom and Mary Ballard. We just read his diary. A few years after that painting was done, my great-grandmother suffered a mental breakdown of some kind and rather than treat it, my great-grandpa had her lobotomized. Grandpa Bert was thirteen at the time. When he was fifteen, his father drowned himself and Mary in the lake. Grandpa Bert liked to tell me this story to show how manly he was. He never shed a tear for his parents."

"Jesus," Morgan breathed.

She let out a bitter laugh. "Well, at least we know our rusalka got revenge on both the man that killed her and his father. From what I read, that should've appeased her, but apparently, she wants all of us dead. Not that I blame her. Welcome to the Ballard family. Screwing over any and everyone since the dawn of time. You know, I bet that when we were cavemen, we stole from our own tribe."

"Well, what about your parents?" Morgan asked, setting down her slice and shifting so that they almost touched.

Rhea thought for a moment. Nothing sprang to mind. Though her memories were hazy, she couldn't think of anything. She couldn't even recall a time that they spanked her or even yelled. "My grandparents called my mom a gold digger who filled my dad with hippie communist notions of peace and love. They said it was her fault I was too soft."

"But?"

Rhea sighed. "Do you know why *One Hundred Years of Solitude* is my favorite book?"

Morgan tilted her head, seemingly surprised at the sudden change in subject. "No? Why?"

"At the end of the book, there are only a couple people left in this once prosperous town, and two of the main family, the Buendía's. The previous generations had two major tendencies: incest and using the same names over and over. The last two Buendía's, Aureliano Babilonia and Amaranta Ursula fall in love, not realizing that she is his aunt. They thought that they were going to break the family pattern to a point where they were even going to use a new name for their future child. But the child is born with a pig's tail from the incest, fulfilling a fear that's been around since the first generation and they name him Aureliano. She dies in childbirth, the child dies of neglect, and he dies when the village is destroyed."

Morgan didn't look any less confused. "I'm not sure I follow."

Rhea sat up too fast, her head spinning. A waterfall of tears threatened to spill from her eyes. "*We* are the Buendías. My parents thought they were breaking old patterns, but they came back to this place, this home that was born rotten and they left their child to…to…"

"To die?" Morgan sat up too and placed a hand on Rhea's arm.

"It feels like that sometimes," Rhea said, her vision blurring. "My family is poison. We've never been on the right side of history. All we did was exploit others to get where we are. Honestly, I'm glad I'm the last of us. When I finally die, the Ballard name dies with me."

"You don't think you can break the cycle?"

Rhea gave a half-hearted shrug. "Maybe. I'm going to try. But when the rot is in the roots, how can anything grow."

"You're not rotten," Morgan said, getting on her knees and swaying slightly, bracing herself on Rhea's shoulders. She burned at the points of contact. "You know what you are? I think you're just like Buttons."

Rhea blinked. "Buttons?"

Morgan pulled out her phone to show a picture of a scraggly, old, orange cat sitting imperiously on a couch. He seemed to be missing an eye and a front tooth. "When I was ten, my mom found an alley cat living behind our house. I was scared of the way he hissed and swatted, but Mom fed him and let him come to her. Eventually, she caught him and took him to a vet. He was chipped and neutered, but his family had abandoned him. The vet offered to take him to a shelter, but Mom insisted on bringing him home. For months, he hid under the bed, and for years, he only came to her. One day, though, he got out. We wandered the neighborhood calling for him. My neighbors had these big, aggressive German Shepherds. One got loose charged me, and from out of nowhere there was like, this blur of orange. Buttons decided to come out of hiding and attack this animal three times his size to protect me. I grabbed him and brought him home before he or the dog could get hurt. You know what my mom said to me when I brought him home safe and told her what happened?"

"What?" Rhea asked.

"That the cat who hisses the loudest needs the most patience and kindness. When I first saw you, I thought of Buttons."

It wasn't exactly the most flattering comparison, but Rhea supposed it was apt. She always felt a kinship with the alley cats that lurked around her apartment, even leaving out cans of food for them when she could afford it.

Rhea chuckled. "You think I'm a cat?"

"No," Morgan said, languidly shaking her head. "I think you're a good person, and it seems like your parents were good like you. Too good to be placed among your other ancestors." She flipped off the painting. "Take that, assholes."

Rhea giggled and joined her with a double bird. "Fuck you."

They both devolved into giggles. Morgan sighed contentedly. "See? Already breaking the cycle. You're good, Rhea."

She shook her head. "No, you're a good person, Morgan. Too good for this place, for these people who didn't lift a finger to help you but still call you a murderer for something you didn't do. How are you so good?"

With a sigh, Morgan flopped beside her. "I'm glad Joshua's dead. And I hate that I'm glad. I didn't kill him, but I might as well have. So, I'm not good."

"Bullshit," Rhea said. "He would have killed you that night. And no one in this town would have cared because he was rich and handsome, and his mother is president of the yacht club. So, after you were dead, he probably would have fixated on another girl, and eventually killed her too, and no one would care because no one ever cares." Rhea took her

243

hand, intertwining their fingers. "I'm glad you lived, and he died. I only wish I could have killed him myself. Just like I'm glad my grandparents are dead." She laughed. "There. I said it. I'm glad they're dead. They did nothing but make my life miserable." She flipped the portrait off again, Morgan following soon after with a giggle.

"I am too," Morgan said with a sigh. "After everything you've told me, my only regret is that I didn't give them a taste of their own medicine. Water hemlock stew. Death Cap mushroom soup."

"Hell, if you'd seasoned Bert's chicken, that probably would've been enough to kill him," Rhea added.

Morgan nodded sagely. "Spicy chicken to kill Bert and a bodice ripper to kill Astrid."

"It's the perfect crime." Even as she laughed, Rhea's heart squeezed. All her life, she'd kept quiet about what they did to her, terrified that if she told anyone, they would say she was crazy, that she deserved all of it. And here was Morgan telling her that none of that was true. "Is it pathetic to say that was the nicest thing anyone has ever said to me?"

"Only if you don't think I'm pathetic for feeling the same way." She hugged her knees to her chest. "Andy treats me fine, and my family believes that I didn't kill him, but he won't believe the truth of what happened, and my family is weird about the whole openly bisexual thing. I spent years in that awful house with those awful people, terrified to venture into town because every time I did, someone would call me a murderer. I only just started doing my own shopping again rather than sending Andy out with a thorough list of ingredients. But meeting you felt like a fresh start. You didn't know me, and when people started calling me a killer, you defended me. No one aside from Andy and my family had done that in a very long time. You've always believed me."

"And you believe me." She sniffled, wiping her eyes. "Sorry. I'm a sad drunk, I guess. And I'm so tired. I'm calling it a night. Thank you for the—" She paused. Morgan had done so much more than just provide her with pizza and company. Through all of this she had been the one thing keeping her sane, an anchor on a roiling sea. "—Just thanks. For everything." She hoped Morgan understood.

She seemed to because she got to her feet and, barely swaying, helped Rhea to hers. She'd always been a lightweight, and the vodka had gone straight to her head. Dreading the hangover in the morning, she escorted Morgan to her door. "Goodnight, Rhea. Sleep well."

She squeezed Morgan's shoulder. "You too. Goodnight, and if you need anything, just let me know."

Morgan hesitated for a moment before pressing a kiss to Rhea's lips. Kissing her felt different from kissing Eliza. With her ex, her lips would always tingle with excitement, but with Morgan, they seemed to burn with want. She had wanted to deepen the kiss, to pull Morgan against her and lose hours just exploring every inch of her. But the kiss was over before she even realized what was happening, and Morgan disappeared through the door.

Rhea dazedly sat on the bed. It had to be a fluke, probably brought on by stress and alcohol. Tomorrow, Morgan will wake up and regret kissing her boss. Rhea was a shambling pile of red flags and intimacy issues. Someday, once she's had extensive therapy and no longer employs Morgan, then maybe...

She flopped backwards with a groan.

Upside down, she spotted her backpack, with Otso and the journal sitting out.

Right.

That.

She sat up and skimmed through the various sections on plants and their uses. This journal was newer than Tom Ballard's and seemed to end halfway through. Good thing the room came with a hair dryer.

6/23/25

I suppose I should be grateful that Mother and Father will at least allow me to write in this journal, but the invisible ink seems a bit absurd, like I am some kind of spy. I suppose that they don't want to risk a scandal even if someone discovered my journal. It feels rather excessive, as I will likely be dead by the time anyone reads this. Consider this my confession, I suppose.

I am in the tower.

I have been in the tower for two weeks, six days, and twelve hours if I am reading the sun correctly. Time slips by in here, like water through my fingers. It's enough to drive the strongest soul mad. And I am madder than most souls already.

All my life, there has been this hunger inside of me, a need to inflict pain. At first, I sated it with knowledge. I took an interest in plants and their impact on the living for both good or ill. I thought, perhaps, I could become a doctor, but apparently, that is not a position befitting a woman of my standing. When knowledge could no longer fill the yawning hole within me, I turned to experimentation, studying the anatomy of small animals and how various natural poisons affect them. I was most fascinated by the Water Hemlock growing by the side of the lake. I wanted desperately to see how it affects humans but could not find a test subject until my idiot brother's indiscretions created the need to rid ourselves of an unfortunate problem.

The night he promised to run away with her, I prepared the stew and followed him to the lake, keeping my distance so he would be none the wiser. I truly did not care if he caught me. All I wanted was to see how Aniela Dach reacted to the poison. So, of course, he had to spoil that for me too. He pushed his harlot into the lake and held her under until the water stopped bubbling.

Even after all these years, I am still galled by it. Some people have no scientific curiosity.

So, naturally, I had to try again. I went into the city because that is where you can find the truly desperate and alone. There was a woman on the street begging for work, and I had the perfect job for her. I verified that she was alone, an Irish immigrant who no one would notice if she went missing, and booked us a room in a cheap hotel. Under the guise of questioning her for a job interview, I slipped some of the hemlock into her tea and watched as she succumbed to the poison. It was fascinating.

She was the first of many over the years, as I experimented with different plants and dosages. No one was the wiser. After all, these were poor girls of ill repute. They never even made the papers. But Mother and Father suspected. They never accused me outright, oh no, but they began to complain about my spending: money on shopping trips to the city and time with my precious plants. All this foolishness when I should be spending my time finding a husband. Time and money. As if time spent in scientific endeavors is time wasted. Perhaps I was hasty with my threat when they gave me the ultimatum to find a husband or be cut off. But what else could I do? Marriage is a prison which 248ouldd sooner die than willingly enter.

I hear Mother approaching with dinner. Nothing like bread and gruel to make me repent of my threat to expose this family's sins.

6/25/25

I witnessed something fascinating by the lake today. One of our repairmen, Joe Something-Or-Other, was out by the boathouse assessing damage from the latest storm when a woman's head emerged from the water. Even after all these years, I still would recognize that red hair anywhere. I never believed in my parents' God or in the afterlife, but now, I have been gifted with proof because it was the woman my brother murdered who emerged from the lake to stand atop the water. She was resplendent in the afternoon light, nothing like the bloated corpse we'd fished out of the water five years ago. And Joe was mesmerized. I watched him walk into her arms and sink below the depths. He did not resurface.

I remember hearing her cry out something before Tom pushed her under the water—not the exact words but certainly was a curse. She would haunt us until the last in the family willingly walked into the water with her. Fascinating.

7/10/25

I had hoped that Mother and Father would let me out in time for Tom's wedding, but they seem to be stubbornly set on keeping me up here. The only reason I know today's date is that it had been set before I was locked away.

The ceremony was held outside, and I watched it from my room in the tower. Aniela Dach watched it too, her head just barely poking above the water. No one else seemed to notice her. I imagine that she was seething enough to make the water around her boil as she witnessed my brother's nuptials.

11/1/25?

Aniela has taken Father. Last night, he was strolling the grounds when she emerged from the water. Like Joe the repairman, he walked into her open arms and let her drag him below. Tom is in Europe for his honeymoon. I expect that Mother has already informed him of our father's death, or will do so shortly.

11/19/25?

Mother is dead. Not by Dach's hand. Likely by her own or from the stress of planning a funeral and settling your husband's affairs while your son is an ocean away. She was never particularly strong. I heard the commotion from below and watched as the local undertaker took a smoke break in the back.

But this puts me in an unexpected predicament. Only Mother and Father have been bringing me my food, and as far as I know, none of the servants know where I am. I have running water, so I will not die of thirst, but I fear that, unless Tom gets here soon, I will die of hunger.

11/20/25?

Mother is still here. I woke last night to her standing over me, her face ashen and twisted with anger and grief. And then she spoke, her voice hoarse as though from disuse. "I should have smothered you in your crib."

"And I should have killed you escaping the womb," I retorted, sitting up. Mother never loved me. I accepted that. After all, the feeling was mutual.. "What are you doing here?"

"I cannot move on. Your father calls to me from the lake, and I cannot reach him, but I also cannot leave. You have robbed me and your father of heaven, so I will walk these halls and ensure that your life is hell."

I doubted she would have ended up in heaven regardless of the curse, but this revelation raised concerns for my own immortal soul. If there truly is an afterlife where sinners are punished and saints are rewarded, then I am likely hell bound. Still, I didn't want to show mother that she'd rattled me, so I glared at her with my head held high. "Do your worst."

11/22/25?

Hungry. I am so hungry. All I can think about is eating, of escaping this place and heading to the kitchen to fill my belly until bursting. Water can only stave off that empty feeling for so long, and my clothes already feel looser. I've tried knocking on the door and screaming for help, but no one hears me. Or if they do, they don't respond.

Mother watches from the corner, laughing at my suffering.

I pray that Tom returns soon. If he doesn't let me go, he will at least feed me, and that's all I need. Anything to sate this hunger before I devour myself.

11/27/25?

He's back. I can hear the commotion as servants bustle to get him settled. I've screamed until my voice gave out and banged against the walls and floors until I was too weak to stand. Still, he has not come for me. Isn't he wondering where I am? Why hasn't he searched for the source of the cacophony?

Tom, if you find me, I will never call you an idiot again. Just find me. Please.

12/1/25

Too weak to scream, to make noise. Can barely write. Mother won't stop laughing at me, and now I find myself laughing too. I will die up here and join her soon enough.

Rhea didn't expect to find herself pitying the Smiling Lady, but here she was. The woman was evil, an admitted serial killer, but she knew the mortal terror of being forgotten and left to starve. No one deserved that. If Rhea hadn't escaped, this would have been her dying alone and forgotten. How long did it take for them to find the body? Was it when the odor became too much? Was it when she was already half-mummified? Or was it decades later, and this was the catalyst for Tom and Mary Ballard's murder-suicide?

With a groan, she put the diary back in her bag and laid back, falling asleep the moment her head hit her pillow. Tomorrow. She would deal with the implications of this nightmare tomorrow. Now that she was away from the oppressive atmosphere of the house, she hoped that her sleep would be restful for once.

CHAPTER TWENTY-FOUR

She woke on her agonized feet, staring down the great oak doors of the Ballard House. Her blood ran cold as her heart raced, and panic sapped all the liquid from her mouth. How? How did she get here? Pain shot through her as she took a step forward, and with a gasp she looked down at her dirty pajamas and bloody, bare, blistered feet. She had somehow walked home. Aside from the chapel incident the night before, she'd never had a history of sleepwalking, and certainly never sleepwalked miles. Though summer was on the horizon, the nights were still chilly, and she shivered. Her feet were too damaged to walk back to the hotel, which meant that, as much as she hated it, she had to go inside alone.

With a dry swallow, she raised a shaking hand and opened the door, venturing in as pain shot up her feet with every step. The first aid kit was in the kitchen along with a wall phone that she prayed was still connected. A silence had settled over the Ballard House like a snowfall. Even her breaths and footsteps were muted as she limped through the moonlit house.

She flicked on the kitchen lights, flinching as the sudden brightness caused a flare in her budding hangover headache. With a low groan, she sat up on the counter and washed her feet in soap and hot water before grabbing the disinfectant and bandages. She hissed at the sting of the disinfectant and quickly wrapped her feet. Next step: phone. Her first instinct was to call Morgan, but she was probably still too drunk to drive. So, Andy.

He picked up on the third ring, and said in a voice muzzy with sleep, "Hello?"

"Hey, Andy, sorry to wake you, but I'm kind of stuck at the Ballard House."

The bed creaked as he shifted, likely sitting up. "I thought you were staying at a hotel," he said, more alert. "What happened?"

"I honestly don't know. I fell asleep in the hotel but woke up here. Would you believe it was some kind of ghostly possession?"

Andy laughed, much darker and more bitter than his usual jovial chuckle. "Come on, you don't really believe that, do you?"

She blinked. "I'm sorry, what?"

"A ghost is possessing you? Really? You know why you're here. You belong in the house. It's your birthright and as much a part of you as you are of it," he said, his voice cold and flat. "Rhea, you can pretend otherwise, run away and change your name, but the family's poison taken root in you, growing deep like a willow tree. It's only a matter of time before it spreads to me, Eliza, or Morgan just like it did to your mother."

"You're not Andy," she said, surprised at how her steady her voice was despite the shaking of her hand holding the phone.

"Does it matter? I'm just a friend giving you some advice. Everyone around you will suffer and die. Might as well put yourself out of their misery right here."

She laughed. "Really? That's the pitch?" The call abruptly cut off and the lights flickered off. She grabbed a candle and a lighter. "How about I put you out of my misery?" She lit the candle and left the phone hanging by its cord as she stalked to the portrait room. First, she took down her parents' portrait and set it outside for safekeeping. Then, the fun would begin.

"Astrid," she called out, taking down the portrait of her grandparents, "I know you're there." She held the lighter to the canvas. "I'm burning the family legacy, starting with the woman vile enough to trick me into murdering my own mother."

The flames caught quickly, and then she moved onto the next two. Tom and Mary, looking wholesome in their fifties style suits and dresses, and then Joshua and Charity, a portrait of gilded age opulence. Joshua Ballard looked stately next to his wife in a bright, poison apple green dress and both held precious jewels and Fabergé eggs. As she flicked on the lighter for another generation, a force pushed her down, sending her sprawling. Ice cold hands grabbed her ankles and dragged her out of the ballroom, up two flights of stairs and into the tower room. With her whole body feeling like a bruise and her vision swimming before her, she just barely made out two pairs of feet staring before her before she knew nothing.

After three and a half months of imprisonment, Rhea knew she had to escape while she still had the strength, or she'd be trapped forever. She briefly considered faking an illness, but if they wouldn't even let her out to shower, they'd probably let any illness she'd suffer just take her. In theory, she could try to overpower them. She was, after all, young and had been building some muscle with the exercises she did to entertain herself. But Grandpa Bert was much stronger than he looked and was a crack shot. Even if she overpowered her grandmother, he'd probably hear and show up with a gun. Besides, she didn't want a direct confrontation. Not really. Some nights, as she laid awake staring up at the ceiling, she truly hated them with such a passion that she thought she might spontaneously combust. But despite everything, she didn't want to hurt them, and especially didn't want to kill them. They were the only family she had left. They took her in, fed her, clothed her, raised her. It was sick and awful the way they treated her, but she felt equally nauseous at the idea of hurting them.

Rhea grew up on stories of princesses trapped in towers, and though her hair was too short for her to climb down like Rapunzel, there were alternate means of rappelling down prison walls. She would run away to Eliza, and they'd get their happily ever after.

But the idea of leaving everything she'd ever known terrified her. She'd barely left the estate, let alone Cherub's Cove. How would she and Eliza survive on their own? She'd barely finished high school and wasn't going to college anytime soon, so job prospects were scarce. She had no place to go, no food, no extra clothes outside of the emergency bag hidden by the mausoleum. Would she be trading a lonely death by imprisonment to starvation in the streets? At least in the attic, she had food and warmth. But nothing else. Leaving was a risk, but she had a chance out there, something she didn't have if she stayed.

She waited two weeks, until the moon was full so she'd be able to see better in her escape, and smashed the bottom of the window using the heavy leatherbound Bible. This was the critical point in her escape. They definitely heard the glass break and would be up soon to see what happened, so she had to tie her bedsheet sheet around the frame quickly, heedless of the jagged glass slicing into her. Footsteps began approaching as she swung her legs over the sill. She scrambled into her descent, her muscles burning as she inched her way down. She knew it was too short, that she would have to jump the last two stories and pray she didn't break her legs.

"Rhiannon!" she heard her grandmother yell as she reached the end of her rope. Rhea closed her eyes, said a prayer to herself, and let go.

She landed hard on her ankle but rolled with the momentum so it wouldn't shatter. She laid for a moment, catching her breath. They were coming, though, she knew, so she forced herself to stand, biting her lip against the agony in her ankle as she limped to the lake. Her plan was to cut through it and to the national park side of the woods where she could hide as they searched for her.

"Rhiannon," Grandpa Bert yelled. He was holding one of his rifles. "Rhiannon, get back here now!"

"No, no, no," she gasped, forcing herself to move faster. He wouldn't shoot her, would he? No, he wasn't crazy enough to shoot his own granddaughter. A bullet whizzed past at thigh level. *At least he's not aiming to kill,* she thought wildly to herself. She was close enough to just dive into the lake just as another bullet whizzed past.

The ice-cold water was a shock to her system. It took her breath away, and within seconds, her teeth were chattering.

"Rhiannon, I don't wanna hurt you, but I will if I have to," he said, aiming his gun at the lake. He fired a warning shot.

Suddenly, a hand wrapped around her wrist and dragged her under. She fought against whatever had her as her lungs burned, but its hold was too strong, and the cold water slowed her movements. She was going to die. So close to freedom only to die at the hand of something she couldn't see. Panicking, she tried to draw a breath, only to inhale water.

And just as suddenly as it grabbed her, the thing let go. Breaching the water, she took a sputtering breath, coughing up the water in her lungs. She dragged herself onto the lakeshore and, curling into a ball, struggled to take stock of where she was. The lights of the house reflected on the other side of the lake. She was on the park side of the property. Whatever grabbed her dragged her away from her grandparents, and, for that, she was grateful. But she had to get moving if she didn't want to die of hypothermia.

While her grandfather trudged through the woods calling for her, she quietly doubled back to the mausoleum for her emergency bag. Bag in hand, she limped in the direction of Eliza's house.

CHAPTER TWENTY-FIVE

Rhea woke up coughing. While the flames had not yet spread upstairs, the smoke sent her lungs raging.

"Sleeping beauty's awake," the Smiling Lady said.

"A shame," came Astrid's voice, "I'd hoped it would be painless for her."

"Come on, when have you ever cared if I was in pain?" Rhea retorted between coughs as she forced herself to sit up. "What do you want from me?"

"Not much. Just your life." The Smiling Lady, now Minnie, leapt off the windowsill where she'd been sitting, "I wasted mine up in this very room. When I realized that the woman I helped kill somehow became like Charybdis sucking in every soul on the property, I knew the secret to an afterlife free from hell would be in the end of the Ballard family line. That's you, Annie."

Rhea gritted her teeth at the old nickname and turned to Astrid floating beside the ancient mattress. She looked exactly like how Rhea remembered her—a severe face and long, silver hair tied up in a bun. "So what, you let me die here so you get stuck in the burned-out shell of this place for all eternity?"

Astrid tilted her head, flashing a condescending smile. "Everything ends and something new will grow in its place. I want to be around to see it."

"You're scared of what comes next, aren't you? For all your piety, you know you're unforgivable."

"She got you there," Minnie said before peering out the window. "Oh the handsome repairman's here. Looks like he's calling 911. He's pretty close to the lake."

"Andy." Rhea staggered to her feet and stared out the window. He must've gotten her call after all. Andy was on the phone, probably calling the fire department, when Aniela emerged from the water wearing Rhea's face. He visibly sagged with relief. With a growing nausea, she broke the window with her elbow and yelled, "Andy!"

He looked up from the phone and saw her. But he was too close to the water. She watched in horror as Aniela grabbed him and dragged him under. With a cry, she forced the window open further and then glanced around the room for something she could use to climb down or break her fall. Her eyes settled on the mattress in the corner.

"I'm ending this now," she said, picking it up. The mattress was ancient and worn, more of a futon than anything, so she folded it in half and sent it, and some of the straggling glass out the window.

Astrid arched an eyebrow. "Honestly, Rhiannon, what makes you think we'll let you leave here alive?"

"Well, I guess you'll have to kill me. But you've never been one to get your own hands dirty." She stuck her leg through the broken window, biting her lips as the remaining shards of glass sliced into her thighs. "Halfway there," she muttered, taking a break as she straddled the window. The roar of the fire drew ever closer, and the heat scorched her. Her throat was sandpaper dry, and she struggled to breathe without coughing. Gathering her strength, she swung up her other leg up so that she was sitting on the sill. The broken glass raked along the back of her legs, forcing a whimper from her throat. She closed her eyes. "Okay, moment of truth. Just tuck and roll."

But then something jerked her backwards onto the floor. The agony buzzed through her bleeding skin. She screamed as her legs were shredded, her blood pasting her pajama pants to the back of her thighs. Minerva stood over her with a shard of glass in her hand.

"Throat or wrists?" she asked, raising her eyebrows as though actually expecting Rhea to answer. "Which would look more like a suicide?"

Rhea was running out of time. Andy had probably run out of air by now, if he wasn't unconscious already. If she was lucky, she might find and revive him in time, but she had to get out of the tower first.

Minnie brought down the glass, aiming to stab her in the throat. But Rhea brought up a hand, letting the shard pierce her palm instead. The pain didn't register at first, but as she pulled it free, the wound burned like frostbite. This time, she didn't hesitate, and with something between a scream and a battle cry, she leapt out the window.

For a moment, she twisted weightless in the air. Then, she landed hard on the mattress, something snapping in her ankle and sending shockwaves of pain up and down her leg. The cool night air was a welcome shock to her system as she laid on the ground, gasping for breath. Beside her, the heat from the Ballard House was a blazing inferno. She thought vaguely of the valuables, of centuries of history going up in flame. Good. Her family's ill-gotten pride and joy deserved to burn. But there was also her father's textbooks. It was the last she had of him.

And poor Andy was at the bottom of the lake. He was her friend, and, like everyone else she cared about, she only brought about his suffering. The grief made her want to curl up into herself. But there was still a chance. A chance to pull him out, do CPR, and bring him back. Maybe Aniela would give him back to her in exchange for her own life.

Then, she heard it, so softly that it was almost drowned out by the roar of the flames, her mother singing:

"Meet me by the willow
Where the elder flowers bloom
And the soft grass is your pillow
And the night will be our tomb."

Without realizing it, she sang along,

"Please, my love, don't tarry.
For in the light of day
My fiancé I must marry
But for tonight we'll stay

Underneath the willow.
I beg, my love, be true
For in the light of moon glow,
It's only me and you."

She forced herself to stand, gritting her teeth as every part of her lit up in agony. Her broken ankle nearly gave out on her, but she steadied herself on the wall. Through the smoky haze, she could see her sitting under the willow, her feet still in the water. Aniela Dach and Faith Dominguez, two mothers intertwined in spirit until they became one. A mother's love and instinct to protect and the rage at their unjust deaths all twisted and confused until it was impossible to tell where one began and the other ended. If she could do nothing else to atone for her family's sins, she could at least free them and the souls they took.

She made her slow, painful way to the Rusalka under the willow. When she looked at her, there was no anger in the Rusalka's eyes. She looked at her like the prodigal son returned. Rhea held onto the willow tree, clinging to it to take the weight off her broken ankle.

"Is Andy gone?" she asked, staring into the dark water. In the moon's pale reflection, it seemed to swirl with faces: Tom Ballard, her father, Bert, Joshua West, and so many other young men that she didn't recognize. Were their souls all trapped with her below the water? For a moment, Andy's face appeared, and then it was just ripples on the lake.

"He's with the rest," the Rusalka replied. "I am sorry. I do not know why I must do what I do."

Rhea's breath came out in a stutter. Andy was gone. But her choice was made. He would be the last of her family's victims. "What do you remember about who you were before?" she asked.

Aniela tilted her head. "I remember...working for a handsome man with kind eyes, carrying his child—" Her eyes flashed in anger. "How he abandoned me to die at the hands of his family." She blinked in confusion. "But that isn't quite right. I also remember having a child, a little girl sweeter than sugar—you, I think—and the handsome man being my equal. That he was with me when I grew ill on that boat and died in the waters trying to save me. And I remember the song I sang to the little girl to help her fall asleep. How can that be? How have I lived both lives? Which of my memories are real?"

Rhea's eyes brimmed with tears. She wrapped her arms around Aniela's shoulders. "You were once only Aniela Dach, a maid for the Ballard family who fell in love with their son. He lied to you, pretended to want to run away with you, and poisoned you. And as you died, you cursed us with the promise that you wouldn't rest until the last Ballard followed you into the lake. When my mother died, the circumstances were similar enough that you became confused and somehow became one, believing that I was your daughter. But I'm not. Not really. I'm the last Ballard, and I'm here to atone for my family's sins."

Aniela cupped Rhea's cheek. "You've done nothing wrong. I know what they did to you. I watched your fear of them grow until it consumed you. You're as much a victim as I am."

"Everything my ancestors did, they did in the name of legacy, so their descendants could live in luxury. I wouldn't have wanted them to, but they did it in my name nonetheless." She closed her eyes, letting the tears fall freely. God, poor Morgan. She hadn't known her for long, but they'd grown close and losing her and her best friend in one night would be hell. A part of her hoped she'd be forgiven eventually. She had no one else to mourn her. It would be no great loss. Her life in exchange for the lives of anyone else who might be pulled under by Aniela. She got to her feet, Aniela following as she stood on the water. "I'm ready. I'm ready for this stupid house to burn to the ground and this stupid family line to end. I want to do the only good thing anyone in my family has done and help you rest."

Aniela wiped away a tear on Rhea's cheek and pressed a kiss to her sooty forehead. "Perhaps we both can rest."

"Absolutely not," Astrid said, yanking Rhea back away from her and throwing her to the ground. The old woman's spirit straddled her, wrapping her cold, bony hands around Rhea's throat. "I should have done this the moment I saw you sinning with that girl."

With a cry, Aniela tried to grab Rhea, but she couldn't leave the water, and they were beyond her reach.

"Go to hell," Rhea gasped as she rolled, pulling them both into the water and into Aniela's waiting arms.

This time, the cold was a balm, numbing her and taking her breath away. The moment she plunged in, Astrid let go. This was the Rusalka's domain and her grandmother had no power here. Aniela held her close as she forced them both deeper. At first, Rhea felt at peace, but, as her lungs began to burn, animal panic kicked in. She fought against Aniela, her movements clumsy and numb, too weak to fight against her supernatural strength. The water was pitch black, and her inability to see made her struggle harder. All the air left her lungs, and she tried to inhale, only taking water, making her panic further. She knew taking Aniela's hand meant her death, but only in those final moments could she bring herself to fear it. *I'm sorry, Morgan. I'm sorry, Eliza. God, I'm so sorry, Andy. Please don't hate me for this.* She took in one more inhale of water and then felt nothing.

She floated in a black void, but it no longer inspired terror. There was no more need for air in her lungs or a heart to beat in her chest. It was quiet, peaceful, like waking with the sunrise.

And then a violent yank backwards from her chest. She was in the void again. Yank. Her heart thudded in her chest. Yank. Her lungs burned. Coughing, she rolled over and expelled the water in her lungs. There were voices above her, and hands grabbing at her, and a familiar face framed by dark moonlight.

Morgan smiled, relieved, as tears streamed down her cheeks.

Then Rhea felt nothing for a long time.

CHAPTER TWENTY-SIX

She woke in an unfamiliar room with a strange kind of numbness spreading throughout her body. She could feel the tubes and wires she was hooked up to. One was in her nose, and a gentle breeze flowed from it. Beside her was a steady beeping. She wiggled her fingers on her right hand, and then her left. Then, her toes, only to find her left foot was mostly immobilized by something hard. Every inhale felt strange, like the time she'd had walking pneumonia as a teenager. She forced her gummy eyes open. The light in the room was dim, lit mostly by the various monitors she was hooked up to. A hospital room.

Oh, she thought giddily, *I'm not dead.* Turning her head, she realized she wasn't alone in the room. That was odd. She'd only been hospitalized once, when she ate the water hemlock, and no one sat at her bedside then. CPS had put her grandparents under investigation for what looked to them like a suicide attempt. So, she spent those two weeks alone. Shaking her head, she banished the thought of them, and all once complicated feelings. They took everything from her. They didn't need to take up more space in her mind.

The figure in the chair stirred and sat up abruptly. "Rhea?" Morgan asked, "Are you awake?"

Morgan stayed for her. She didn't have to, but she did. Tears prickled in Rhea's eyes and rolled down her cheeks. Seeing this, Morgan rushed over to her. "Are you in pain? Do you want me to call the nurse? I should probably call the nurse to check on you, anyway." She pressed the call button.

Within a minute a nurse came in and picked up a clipboard. "Hi there, Miss Ballard."

Rhea winced at that. The name sounded wrong. "Actually," she croaked, every word grating her sore throat, "I prefer if you call me Miss Dominguez."

The nurse looked confused but nodded. "I'll add that to your chart." She wrote something on the clipboard and then scanned the rest of it, raising her eyebrows. "You went through a lot last night," she said. "A house fire and near drowning. You're very lucky Miss Dominguez. It says here that you coded for a bit. If this young lady hadn't pulled you out and performed CPR until the paramedics arrived, you probably wouldn't be here."

"Oh," Rhea croaked.

"Are you in any pain at the moment?"

Rhea waved her hand in a so-so gesture and said, "I could use some water."

"Alright, I'll get that for you. Be right back," the nurse said.

Morgan looked at her quizzically. "Dominguez?"

"Mother's maiden name," Rhea said, closing her eyes. Despite being conscious for only a few minutes, she was already tired. "I want to have a fresh start, but I need to tell you—"

"Not yet," Morgan said, tears sparkling as she took Rhea's free hand, "We're gonna talk about what happened when you feel better but just rest for now."

Rhea nodded, already drifting off.

When she woke again, it was dark, but Morgan still hadn't left her side. As soon as she saw her, Morgan sat at attention. "Hey."

"Hey," Rhea repeated. She braced herself. Morgan had a right to know about Andy, even if it meant that she'd hate her for taking away her best friend. "Morgan, you should know..."

"That Andy's dead," she said, tears once again forming in her red rimmed eyes. It looked as though she'd been crying on and off for hours. "I know. After you called him, he called me and told me you were somehow back at the house. I-I tried to get there but I was too late for him. I found him floating in the water." She swallowed. "And I was almost too late for you too. The Rusalka did it, didn't she?"

She nodded. "It's my fault." She explained everything that happened that night, her voice catching when she described watching him be taken by Aniela. By the end, both were sobbing, Rhea holding her broken ribs as each sob sent another shooting pain down her side. Good. She deserved it for all the hurt she'd caused.

Eventually, the tears petered out into silence. Morgan, who was sitting stiffly on the hospital chair and hadn't spoken since Rhea finished telling her story. Rhea felt a familiar anxiety rising in her chest. "I'll cover the cost of his funeral and keep paying your salary until you find a new job. I-I understand if you never want to see me again. Are you okay? I mean obviously not, but—"

"I'm fine," she replied in a tone that meant she was not fine.

Rhea wanted to curl in on herself, but remembering her ribs, thought better of it. "You're mad."

"No. Yes. I don't know." She let out a frustrated groan before getting to her feet.

"Then what is it?" Even without curling in on herself, she felt small as Morgan paced the room.

Morgan stopped suddenly and turned to face her. "Are you suicidal?"

Rhea blinked. "What?"

"You went into the water willingly, knowing that she would kill you."

This was why she was mad? Rhea let out a surprised chuckle and crossed her arms. "Yeah, I did. To break a century old curse."

"You didn't try to find another way first?" she asked, clenching and unclenching her fists.

"What was I supposed to do?"

"Literally anything else."

This was the one good thing Rhea had ever done. Why couldn't Morgan see that? "Gee, I'm sorry for putting a murderous ghost to rest and trying to atone for the suffering my family has caused. My bad. Next death curse, I'll try something else."

Morgan threw her head back with a wordless frustrated sound. "I can't believe you."

"What? That I actually did something good for once? It wasn't like anyone would miss me for long. It wouldn't have been a great loss anyway."

Morgan looked at her as though she'd been struck. "You really think no one would miss you?"

Rhea sighed. "I mean, yeah. I don't have any family and since it's my fault Andy's gone, I don't have any friends either. So, yeah, not a great loss."

Morgan let out something between a laugh and a sob. "Do you really think so little of yourself? Or of me? Did you seriously think that I would blame you?"

"I'm realistic," Rhea retorted. "If you'd never met me, he'd still be here. If I'd just jumped into the lake when we read how to break the curse..."

"God," Morgan said softly, "Rhea, that's—"

"Okay," Rhea said, interrupting, "I knew what I was doing, even with the smoke inhalation and the shock. It was simple math. My worthless life in exchange for all the— mmpf!" She was abruptly cut off by Morgan's lips on hers. They were soft and tasted like hospital coffee. She hadn't let herself think about that night in the hotel hallway. Everything after had happened so fast that she didn't get the chance.

But now, Rhea kissed her back, delighting in something she hadn't dared to dream of. It was as electric as her idle daydreams. Morgan shifted so that she was practically straddling her without putting weight on her injuries.

"It's not true," Morgan said, pulling back and resting her forehead on Rhea's. "You're worthy, just by being you."

Tears welled up in her eyes. Morgan reached up and wiped them away. "I wish I saw in me what you think you see."

Morgan shifted again, sitting beside her and wrapping her arms around Rhea. "Okay, here's what I see. You're handsome, clever, brave, kind, and stronger than any other person I know. You literally died to save my best friend's soul. It's an honor to know you and would be a great loss to lose you."

Rhea sniffled. "If you say so."

Morgan pressed a kiss to the top of her head. "I know so. And I'll keep telling you until you believe me."

Rhea steeled herself, suddenly overwhelmed by the warm arms wrapped gently around her, enveloping her in a comfort she hadn't felt in years.

The next day, Rhea woke to Eliza hovering in the doorway. She had her arms wrapped around her chest as though trying to self soothe. God, Rhea was way too tired for this.

"You can come in," she said.

Eliza gasped and rushed to her side. "God, Rhea. Did-did you do this because of me?"

The laugh that burst from her lips rattled her aching ribs. The failed lunch date with Eliza felt like centuries ago. "God, no. This is all family bullshit."

"Oh." Eliza almost sounded disappointed that this wasn't some kind of elaborate suicide attempt.

No, no, that wasn't fair. She was here visiting Rhea, after all. And unless she wanted to try talking Rhea into an IVF treatment or two while in the hospital, Eliza was here to be a good friend.

Eliza took a seat in Morgan's spot at her bedside. The latter must have stepped out into the cafeteria for some lunch. "I'm sorry," she said, not meeting Rhea's eyes. "About what I said at the café and everything else. Can we try again?"

"In what way?" she asked.

"In whatever way you want." Eliza took her hand. "I never stopped loving you." Her voice was whisper soft, forcing Rhea to strain to hear. Those were the words she always dreamed of hearing but never expected Eliza to say. If she'd said it a week ago, Rhea would have been elated, but now, she felt only sick.

"Eliza, you're married."

"I don't love him. Never have." Her eyes went glassy with unshed tears. "I tried. For years, I tried. But now, you're here. This could be our chance." Her smile was tremulous and full of fragile hope.

"You would leave your husband to be with me?" Rhea asked, unable to keep the wonder from her voice. She would never agree, not now that she had Morgan, but the idea of someone willing to blow up their lives for her was a novelty.

Eliza's smile became forced. "Well, no, but we can still be together. Just like when we were kids."

"You mean I'd be your secret." Rhea deflated. Of course. She pulled her hand away from Eliza's grip.

A look of hurt crossed her face before she smiled again. "And you would be mine."

"Aren't you tired of secrets?" Rhea sighed. "Aren't you tired of hiding and pretending you're normal and respectable and trying to be everything the world wants you to be without ever getting to just be yourself?"

"Rhea, I can't just give up everything," Eliza said, pulling further back.

"And I'm not going to ask you to." Rhea sighed. "The answer is no; I don't want to be your secret lover or your surrogate or have any part in your desperate attempts to look like you're perfect. All you're doing in making yourself miserable."

"You just don't know what it was like! Mom and Dad threatened to send me to conversion therapy if I didn't find a man to be with. Right now, they're helping pay for our house. If they find out, I'll lose everything."

Rhea's bitter laugh made everything ache. "Are you really going to say that to me with a straight face, Eliza?"

Before Eliza could respond, Morgan entered with a box of pizza. "Hey, I know the food here is awful, so I—oh." She froze when she spotted Eliza sitting beside Rhea. "I'll come back another time."

"Thank you," Eliza said at the same time Rhea replied with, "Don't."

She shot Eliza a pointed look. "She was just leaving."

Another hurt look crossed her ex's face, but she nodded. "Okay. If that's what you want."

"It is." Rhea forced a smile. "I did appreciate the visit, though. Really. I hope you do find happiness, Eliza."

"Just not with you," she muttered.

"No," Rhea said, reaching for Morgan. She took her girlfriend's hand. "Not with me."

...

The next people to visit her were the mayor and a reporter three days later. By then, she was about to be discharged but staying one final night for observation. He'd given her a head's up, which meant that Morgan could run to Andy's apartment and grab Tom Ballard's journal. She had already collected Minnie's from Rhea's hotel room.

When he entered, he immediately crossed to shake the hand without the IV drip. "Miss Ballard, I'm so sorry for the loss of the family estate. It's such a tragedy. I can't imagine someone wanting to set fire to the place."

"Well, you didn't grow up there," she replied, and Morgan held back a snicker, "but that's not why you're here. Not really. You're here because I have something of historical significance to donate to the city." Morgan passed her Tom and Minnie Ballard's journals, and she opened them to the pages written in invisible ink. "This is a confession to the murder of Aniela Dach, a pregnant maid, written by my own great-grandfather. And this is an account of my great-great aunt confessing to multiple murders before starving to death while locked in the tower room of the Ballard House"

The reporter's eyes widened, and he scribbled down notes while Mayor Parker examined the books with a frown.

"I'm donating it to the historical society, but I also want to make a public announcement about it...and to proclaim the innocence of Andy Higgins. I know that you want to pin the blame for the fire on him. He was my friend and took pride in his work at the house. His name will not be tarnished."

"Well then, who did set the fire?" the reporter asked. "There weren't any accelerants on the scene, and the police couldn't figure out the cause."

"It was an accident," Rhea said, "I knocked over a candle when the power went out. Didn't realize until the blaze was out of control."

He scribbled in his notebook. "But what about your room at the Inn by the Sea? You and Miss Reyes both checked in that night."

Damn. He got her there. She chewed her lip before giving him one of Astrid's patented sneers. "Do you really think I'd create an alibi for paying someone to burn down my ancestral home only to take the blame for it?"

"No offense, Miss Ballard," Mayor Parker interjected, "but your story doesn't add up."

"It's Dominguez," she snapped before taking a slow breath, "I honestly don't remember much from that night. I think I got drunk in the hotel room and decided that I needed to organize Bert's office. You know how drunk people are. We make bad decisions like walking a couple miles barefoot to organize a family estate. Now, I'm getting tired, and I think I want to rest a bit. You can hold onto the journals for your article. Just be sure it gets to the historical society."

The reporter took the journals, and both thanked her for her time. "You think that was a good idea?" Morgan asked.

"If I had good ideas, do you think I'd be lying in a hospital bed?" She sighed. "I'm just glad it's almost done, and we can move on."

Morgan sat beside her on the bed. "Where do you wanna go after this?"

Rhea smiled. "Anywhere, as long as it's with you."

EPILOGUE

Two Years Later

Rhea Dominguez stood in front of the blackened rubble that marked where the Ballard House had once been. She once thought that godforsaken place would outlast her and every other Ballard until the heat death of the universe. But its worst secrets were unearthed and cleansed by the fire.

Staring at the remains of the once proud manor, she was reminded of the story her father liked to tell about the Phoenix. How it would die in flame only to be reborn from the ashes. She had no interest in rebuilding here, the monument to her family's ill-gotten glory. In fact, this was her last look before signing the land back to the Wampanoag people. It was never really hers to begin with. She could visit the family plot whenever she wanted, though she probably wouldn't come often. Just Mother's Day and Father's Day, and her parents' birthdays. They planned to turn it into a community center, which seemed like a much better use of the land than a stuffy old mansion.

She sat under the willow, taking in the gentle lapping of the waves and the cool autumnal breeze and running her thumb along the grooves of the *agimat* that Morgan's mother gave her. Softly, she closed her eyes and began to sing,

> *"Meet me by the willow*
> *Where the elder flowers bloom*
> *And the soft grass is your pillow*
> *And the night will be our tomb.*
>
> *Please, my love, don't tarry.*
> *For in the light of day*
> *My fiancé I must marry*
> *But for tonight we'll stay*
>
> *Underneath the willow.*
> *I beg, my love, be true*
> *For in the light of moon glow,*
> *It's only me and you."*

When she opened them again, she half expected to see a red-haired woman with the face of her mother by the side of the lake, but there was only the water and the blue sky. "I know you've moved on," she said to the lake, "Mom, Dad, Andy, Aniela, but if you can hear me, I want you to know I'm okay. Well, more than okay. I'm better than I've been since...ever. And I'm ready to let go completely. No more ghosts. No more bad memories. But before I go, I want to show you something." She pulled a small black box from her purse and opened it, revealing a small ring. "We decided to propose to each other. I know she has one just like this in her sock drawer, but I'm gonna beat her to it." Closing the box, she stuck it back in her purse.

Just then, her phone buzzed. Seeing it was Morgan, she picked up.

"Hey, where are you?" Morgan asked. She could hear the din of their restaurant, A Touch of Manila, in the background.

"Just finishing up at the old Bastards House," Rhea replied with a chuckle. "Aren't you supposed to be working?"

"I'm allowed to take a break. And as owner of this establishment—"

"Co-owner," Rhea interjected, lying down on her stomach and staring at her reflection in the water. It was strange. She wasn't used to looking this happy.

"Okay sugar mommy," Morgan said, and Rhea could practically hear the eyeroll over the phone.

She made an exaggerated gagging noise, "Ugh, don't call me that."

"What else would I call you? Buying the restaurant for me is a total sugar mommy move."

Rhea chuckled to herself, skimming her fingers along the water. "How about business partners? You're the face and the talent, I'm the finances." She rolled onto her back and stared up at the gently swaying branches. "Besides, all that critical acclaim and those lunch and dinner rushes are because of you."

"Thank you madame number cruncher. Speaking of numbers, have you paid spring tuition yet? That social work degree isn't gonna pay for itself."

"Yes, mom, I paid it yesterday," she said with exaggerated annoyance. As much as she loved running the business side of A Touch of Manila, she wanted to do something more, something that helped people. So, she decided to become a social worker, hoping to use her experiences to help queer kids who are now where she had been. One day, she planned to set up her own foundation, building halfway houses and shelters throughout the city. For now, though, she was busy balancing the restaurant with her schoolwork.

"And don't forget your next therapy session is tomorrow at 3:00."

Rhea chuckled. "Was there a reason you called other than to remind me of things I already knew about?"

Morgan's voice softened. "I'm just checking in. It can't be easy, being back there. I wanted to see if you were okay."

Rhea smiled and twiddled a blade of dying of grass in her fingers. "I'm okay. More okay than I thought I'd be."

"If you need me, you know where to find me," Morgan said, "Love you."

"Love you too. Bye." She hung up the phone and sighed. Turning to the lake, she said, "You don't have to worry about me either. She takes good care of me."

With a grunt, she stood up and took one last look at the willow. It might have been her imagination, but she swore the wind picked up slightly there, the branches swaying back and forth as though waving goodbye. With one last look at the burnt-out rubble, she got in her car and drove out the front gate.

As she drove off, she thought again of the phoenix. She used to think of herself as the last Ballard, the final remnant of a dying line that deserved to go extinct. But that night in the lake, she had been reborn into something different.

Rhiannon Ballard, the terrified, lonely girl was dead and buried.

Long live Rhea Dominguez.

ACKNOWLEDGEMENTS

The people who have helped me along the way have been too numerous to count, but I'll do my best to remember you all. First, I would like to thank my editor, Brooke Reyes, the CEO of Miravalle books, Roger Gonzales, and the entire wonderful team for putting this together. Thank you for believing in the book and helping me tell Rhea's story.

As an eternal teacher's pet, I want to say thank you to the many teachers who encouraged my writing over the years, especially my first-grade teacher, Mrs. Sampson, and my high school creative writing teacher, Mrs. Hailey. Thank you, Mrs. Sampson, for seeing talent in me that no one else saw and working with me to bring it out. Thank you, Mrs. Hailey, for creating the kind of supportive and creative environment that allows writers to grow. And finally, I'd like to thank my thesis advisor, Professor William Orem. Second drafts are always the hardest for me, but you truly helped me get through it and made The Last Ballard so much better.

I'd also like to thank the Instagram writing community. You all have been so wonderfully supportive and kind.

Finally, I'd like to thank my friends and family for their support. I especially want to thank my ancestors for not being the Ballard's. I'm so glad you were not as terrible as you could have been. I'd like to thank my sisters for their love, and last but definitely not least, my parents. Thank you for believing in me and supporting me as the artsy weirdo in the family. I can only hope I've done you all proud.

ALSO BY KAY HANIFEN

TILL THE YULE LOG BURNS OUT

*No rest ye frightened gentlemen
Full of horror and dismay...*

When the St. Wenceslas Episcopal Church choir bus gets trapped in a snowdrift on the way to a Christmas Eve competition, the eleven members find their way to an inn run by the mysterious Innkeeper. Though disappointed that they won't get to the competition, they decide to make the best of it by opening their Secret Santa gifts.

But the gifts they open are not the original presents they bought for each other. Every one links back to a dark secret in their past, one that they are compelled to share: stories of Christmas monsters, cursed objects, and vengeful spirits. Featuring stories by David Washburn, Nick Aucoin, Julia C. Lewis, Nikki Kossaris, Zach Swasta, Loki Dewitt, Greta T. Bates, M. Rook Grimsley and a wraparound and story by Kay Hanifen, these travelers will tell their tales Till the Yule Log Burns Out.

Scan to Learn More

ABOUT THE AUTHOR

Kay Hanifen was born on a Friday the 13th and once lived for three months in a haunted castle. So, obviously, she had to become a horror writer. Her work has appeared in over fifty anthologies and magazines. Her first anthology as an editor, *Till the Yule Log Burns Out*, was published in 2024. ***The Last Ballard*** is her debut novel.

When she's not consuming pop culture with the voraciousness of a vampire at a 24-hour blood bank, you can usually find her with her black cats or at:

@katharinehanifen (Instagram)
@TheUnicornComi1 (Twitter/X)
Kayhanifenauthor.wordpress.com

www.ingramcontent.com/pod-product-compliance
Lightning Source LLC
Chambersburg PA
CBHW050027120726
47903CB00006B/1938